Marriage is a Shore Thing

LAURA LANGA

BY LAURA LANGA

WILKS BEACH
Holiday Tides

En Route to Romance

Seas the Dating Coach

Marriage is a Shore Thing

LOVE TUCSON
Haley and the Yeti

Date the Alphabet

An Unexpected Roomie

MEDICAL ROMANCE
My Heart Before You

A Guarded Heart

Between Our Hearts

For Geneva, for letting me borrow her name

And for *anyone* who feels the need to keep their guard up. I hope you know how incredibly **strong** you are. But I also hope that someday, you'll meet the right kind of person who shows you it's okay to let your inner sweetness shine.

ONE

Geneva

One thing everyone should understand is that your brain is a dirty, rotten liar. That devious, spongy organ likes to come up with creative scenarios to weasel you out of whatever you're trying to accomplish. Every athlete knows this. Your brain will scream like a toddler being buckled into a car seat to stop you from running, swimming, what have you.

I know better.

That's why I'm ignoring the story my brain is trying to sell me right now. Sure, it might *seem* like the women I came with have abandoned me, but that's complete bull. By all accounts, Vivian, Brynn, and Cade don't seem like the kind to drop me at this swanky resort bar and never look back. Particularly Vivian, who organized this trip to Vegas with the help of her billionaire boyfriend. She doesn't seem to have a vindictive bone in her body.

A niggling voice whispers, *But you've been fooled before. You know how ruthless women can be.*

Ignoring that thought, I gather counterevidence. Evidence number one: Vivian texted the group twenty minutes ago, stating that she's spending time with her boyfriend, Finn, and she'll meet us at the room later. Though 'room' is an understatement since our penthouse suite is larger than most houses, Vivian letting me know where she'll be isn't the action of someone trying to leave you behind.

Evidence number two: On the empty stool beside me sits Cade's woven crossbody purse. She wouldn't have left that behind if she planned on never coming back.

Before Cade left, I think she said something about checking on Brynn, who'd been playing a slot machine.

I'm pretty sure, anyway.

I hadn't exactly been paying attention. The post-fight interview between heavyweights Simmons and Bellinger had been on the screen above the bartenders at the same time. I'd missed most of the match because this had been Vivian's night—starting off with a Raven Sacaria concert, followed by a lavish dessert tasting with a celebrity chef, and ending at this bar in the center of the casino.

Normally, I'd be worried about Cade and Brynn's safety. That'd been the reason I agreed to come on this trip in the first place. Three small-town women alone in Vegas for the first time?

Yeah. Not on my watch.

Brynn is sharp and observant, and Vivian finally started throwing punches correctly at the boxing classes I teach at my gym, but neither of them had ever traveled outside Wilks Beach. Vegas is teeming with people, some of them undeniably shady. But the second our private plane touched down, Mateo, our trip coordinator, put my mind at ease. He's bubbly and has all the connections, but he's undoubtedly doubling as security—something I doubt the other three women even registered.

Since he's also absent from the casino's noisy gaming floor, that means he's with Brynn and Cade.

Good. I can take care of myself.

I've been doing it for years.

My index finger taps the side of my phone, debating if I should reach out. I've only responded to a few of the—frankly, gratuitous—texts about this trip. But in the twenty long minutes I've waited for Cade and Brynn to return, I've fended off three pick-up attempts, downed a glass of ice water, and cursed myself for joining in the last round of vodka shots on an empty stomach. Though the other ladies enjoyed the dessert tasting, the last thing I ate was a spinach-and-salmon salad before the concert.

"Just text them," I mutter to myself.

An anxious tendril collects at the nape of my neck. *What if they don't text back? What if they meant to leave me just like everyone else?*

My fingers flip my phone, slamming it down so hard the square jars of sliced lemons and limes rattle.

"Easy now. You'll crack the screen." The southern-accented sentence comes from the man beside me. Ever since I got here, I've ignored how it feels like I'm perched next to an electric fence instead of a broad set of shoulders.

To his credit, he's ignored me as well.

Briefly, my mind wanders, wondering if he noticed that I had the seat directly in front of him at the concert—though, no one sat during the two-hour performance from one of the most iconic women in music. What surprised me was that this man sang along to nearly every song, the soulful twang of his deep voice intermixing with that of the headliner.

"If you don't take a breath soon, you'll asphyxiate and ruin everyone's fun."

He takes a sip from his fruity cocktail—a yellow concoction in a hurricane glass topped with whipped cream, a pineapple slice, and a curly straw. The frivolity of his drink makes me loosen the grip on my phone, not realizing I'd been strangling it.

"You don't look like you're having fun," I say, crossing my arms.

I steal a glance to my right, clocking a sharp jawline. I've long since noticed the basics about him—strong build, blond hair, wrinkled dress shirt, hunched posture. He looks like a man down on his luck. An ache settles over my ribs before I remind myself that I don't care. Maybe he's done it to himself by blowing a month's salary at the blackjack table.

When he leans back to meet my gaze, a shock runs down my spine. The sensation is a near replica of the two times it happened before. The second time was just minutes ago when we made the same comment about the boxers finishing out the last round of their famed match. The first time had been when I'd glanced over my shoulder after hearing him singing at the concert.

What I hadn't noticed before is that his eyes are the oddest shade of gray—like overcast skies clouding the ocean. And in the brighter light of the bar, the dark hollows beneath his eyes are obvious.

He hasn't just had a bad night. He's had a bad week. A bad month?

I know that kind of exhaustion. The kind that sifts into your bones, making you feel like nothing will ever be normal again.

"I'm having a blast." The corner of his mouth smirks unconvincingly around blond stubble. "No need to worry about me."

"I wasn't."

The words come out before I can temper them, but it's as reflexive as breathing, having my guard up. Keeping everyone at arm's length with biting remarks and disinterested glares is a well-worn pattern.

No one can hurt you if you push them away first.

He dips his head with a breathy exhale that could almost be a chuckle, his straight hair falling over his eyes. It's a touch too long, like he's in between haircuts. Is that by choice or because basic self-care has fallen by the wayside?

As his focus returns to his drink, slowly drawing overlapping triangles in the glass's condensation, tension settles just behind my breastbone. I open my mouth to apologize, but before I can say anything, my phone rings. My instinct is to ignore it and smooth things over with this stranger—I *don't* want to leave him worse off than he already is—but it could be Cade or Brynn.

"Hey," Brynn says when I pick up her call. "I just wanted to check in. Cade said that you wanted to be left alone because you were hitting things off with the guy from the bar, but—" Her sentence cuts off when I snort.

The corner of the man's mouth quirks, genuine this time, and I feel my own lips twitch in response.

"You never said that, did you?" A groan comes over the line. "Cade! We can't just leave Geneva with a stranger in Vegas. That's dangerous."

"But he could be her soulmate! Sometimes fate needs a push," Cade's voice calls from a distance, over what sounds like water splashing in the background. She's probably in the hot tub on the terrace of our exorbitant penthouse suite.

Brynn mutters unintelligibly, obviously annoyed.

And I should feel the same. I should be completely ticked that Cade decided to play matchmaker, but the relief over not being intentionally abandoned overpowers everything else.

"Oh!" Cade calls out. "I think I left my purse behind. There are breath mints and a tiny can of pepper spray inside—just in case things go *really well* or *really badly*. Not that you'd need the pepper spray, you majestic goddess of fierceness!"

An unexpected peal of laughter rips from my belly. Normally, I'd restrain it, maintain my aloof, unapproachable persona, but I'm too tired from this whirlwind of a day. It's hard to imagine that I awoke in my seaside cottage this morning, the ever-present sound of waves gentle against my bedroom window.

"I'm sending Mateo," Brynn tells me, her tone brisk.

"Don't bother." My eyes scan the event information on the TV screen above the bartenders. "I'm going to make another stop before I head back."

"You sure?"

I smile to myself. Brynn is nearly as protective as I am.

"Yes. I'll call if I need anything," I say before hanging up.

Mateo made us store his number in our phones when we stepped off the tarmac earlier, and it's not like being alone in a large city is foreign to me. It'll be easy enough to wrangle my way into the boxing afterparty that was just advertised. And I'd bet—I flick a furtive glance to the man to my right—based on how engrossed he'd been in the match, I'm guessing being in the same room as the new heavyweight champion would be an improvement over sitting alone at this bar.

"I think it's pretty obvious you're in the middle of a tough break." I keep my gaze trained forward, setting my phone face down on the bar and flicking a polished fingernail toward his cocktail. "Only bachelorette parties and people running on fumes order that yellow monstrosity."

When I'm met with silence, I glance right.

His lips lift a fraction more, a dimple poking out. "That right?"

A sweep of heat rushes from my cheeks down my neck, but I keep my expression even, almost bored. My naturally tanned skin doesn't give away a blush, so I keep my movements calculated, raising one shoulder.

"Why else would you drink it?"

His gaze slips to my mouth, just briefly. "Maybe I like sweet things?"

I don't get a chance to respond because two inebriated men push into Cade's and Vivian's open seats. The one closest to me uses his meaty hand to slap Cade's purse onto the bartop. Before I can even protest, the second man lurches to the side, completely missing his stool and toppling onto his friend. The man nearest me flicks his arm out like a whip crack to regain his balance. My forearm comes up to block the impact, but I'm spun away from the two newcomers as a crash resonates through the bar area.

Instinct takes over. All I feel is hot, unyielding hands on my waist and the rapid pulsing of my heartbeat in my ears. Every cell in my body screams for me to defend myself. My hips angle away from the body behind me at the same time my elbow comes back for a punishing blow. I pivot, preparing for another strike, when reality slips in.

I just hit the man I'd been talking to.

"Sorry," I blurt, placing my hands on his hunched-over shoulders as he wheezes. "I didn't think. I just reac—"

"It's alright." His eyes meet mine as he lets out a pained grunt. "I startled you."

A strangled sound escapes me. I was hoping to make this man's night better, not worse.

"Is everything okay here?"

Three black-suited security members surround us. Two of them pick up the drunken men and escort them away while one remains beside us.

"Everything's fine," I answer, still surveying the man I hit as his breathing evens out.

"I wasn't talking to you," the behemoth of a security agent tells me.

Oh. That's fair.

The man chuckles, low and deep, and I'm overwhelmed with a sudden longing to see him laugh—to know how his eyes would curl with mirth, to see his mouth fully relaxed. Then he stands upright, taking my hands with him. I should let go, step back, but my fingers stubbornly remain on his firm shoulders.

"I'm fine. Thanks for checking," he tells the security agent while keeping his gaze zeroed in on me.

He's only a few inches taller than me with my heels on, making his lips distractingly close to mine. I bite the inside of my cheek to banish the wild thought.

The agent murmurs something into the microphone clipped to his lapel before striding away.

"I'm Evander, by the way. Everyone calls me Van—in case you write the names of your victims in a log somewhere." A playful twinkle settles over his mesmerizing eyes.

I release a controlled exhale. "I'm sorry again."

"It's okay." A half-smile settles over his mouth. "I'm sure we'll laugh about this someday."

An unfamiliar yet soothing sensation slips over my muscles. They should be tensing, moving away from this man, but I feel almost pliant in his reassuring presence.

"Ma'am?"

I welcome the bartender's interruption, using it to break contact and regain my composure. I've never had it slip so quickly, but there's something disarming about Van's dimpled grin.

She hands me Cade's beer-sodden purse and my smashed phone before sliding over a thick stack of bar napkins. "They went over the edge. Sorry."

"It's okay," I mutter, checking the contents of Cade's unzipped purse to see if her phone needs to be dried like mine.

Besides the aforementioned breath mints and pepper spray, the only other things inside are three lipsticks, a New Orleans fabric patch, and a tiny rubber duck. My ID, credit card, and room key are in a secret pocket of my scoop-neck black mini lounge dress, so Cade probably has her essentials in the pockets of her sparkly jumpsuit.

My shoulders settle before I assess my phone. The screen isn't just cracked; it's annihilated. It blinks helplessly at my attempts to get it to function. I sigh, using the napkins on Cade's small purse before drying my phone.

"You can use my phone if you need to," Van tells me.

Under normal circumstances, this would be where I'd turn, march back to the expensive suite, and put an end to this long day.

But I made a decision before everything went sideways, and I *always* follow through on my commitments.

Straightening my spine, I face Van. "Since I made your night worse, I can get you into Bellinger's afterparty to make amends."

Van just stares, amused.

"However"—I pause, my jaw hardening—"you need to understand that nothing is going to happen here." My index finger flicks between us. "After an hour, we'll go our separate ways. That's it. The end."

He runs a hand through his hair as a shadow passes over his face. "I'm honestly in no state for..."

His words trail off in an exhausted exhale, leaving a painful twist in my belly.

"I'd just be grateful for a bit of company." Van tugs his lips up, the effort to appear normal as obvious as a neon sign in the dark. "Are you a boxer?"

"I teach it, but I don't enter the ring," I say, grateful for the subject change. I excel at getting people into fighting shape, at helping them understand their full physical potential. Navigating amorphous emotional situations...isn't my strong suit. "Are you?"

"No." Van rubs his jaw with another slight chuckle. "But my buddy in med school boxed. He turned me into a fan."

My face remains expressionless as I absorb this information. It explains why Van was as engrossed in the heavyweight match as I was before my friends took off. With the casual drop of "med school," I can assume he's a doctor, making him less capable of standing by when someone needs help. That is, if he's even telling the truth. In my experience, men rarely do.

Van's smile grows genuine at my silence, and the relief at seeing it has no right being this dizzying.

"Am I allowed to ask the name of my benevolent hostess?"

"Geneva."

The way Van processes this information, as if he's tucking it into his chest pocket for safekeeping, makes my skin tingle. Maybe I *should* go straight back to the room. That vodka seems to have done a number on my common sense.

Instead, I turn and stride deeper into the casino. "Keep up, Van."

"Yes, ma'am." His quick response is cheeky—almost flirty—sending goosebumps down my arms.

I exhale slowly, disregarding the sensation.

We'll have just one hour together, then go our separate ways, and then I'll never see Van again.

What's the worst that can happen?

TWO

Van

One month later

I stare at the front door to the quaint two-story cottage for longer than advisable. It's just...stalling feels...necessary. So that's how I notice that while the rest of the homes on this residential street are painted peach, yellow, or seaside blue, Geneva's house is a drab beige. How there's neither a welcome mat nor a cheery ocean-inspired wreath.

"Come on, man. Buck up."

It's not the first pep talk I've had with myself. The thing is, I doubt Geneva will be excited about the life-changing news I'm bringing with me, especially since it'd been her idea not to exchange contact information after our evening in Vegas.

The late-August sun beats on my neck as I knock, a sheen of perspiration dampening my skin. When there's no answer, I glance at the car in the gravel driveway, boxing equipment strewn over the backseat. That's one of the things I remember about that night: Geneva's love for teaching others the sport she'd picked up a few years ago.

The truth is, I remember a lot about that night.

Maybe Geneva has been playing those memories on repeat as well.

After another round of loud knocking with no response, I move to check the backyard. Before I can get close to the high garden gate, a scratchy voice stops me.

"What are you doing?" an elderly woman asks as she crosses the street. She's wearing a pantsuit with a jacket buttoned to the neck in frank defiance to the stifling heat and humidity.

I smile, grateful to be able to ask one of Geneva's neighbors where I might find her. I jog to meet the woman since she's using a cane to walk.

"Hello, ma'am. Do you know where I could find Geneva?"

"Who wants to know?"

It's only now that I realize this woman isn't squinting in the bright sunshine. Her face is pinched in distrust.

"Evander Young, ma'am, but everyone calls me Van." I extend my hand.

Her tattooed brows raise, glancing at my outstretched hand like it's a warm tuna sandwich from a gas station. "Like a minivan?"

I force a chuckle. "Something like that."

Her cane comes down hard on the asphalt. "State your business."

"I...uh..."

I'm used to curveballs—you have to be when working in the ER—but I don't think telling a stranger the truth before I get a chance to speak to Geneva is the best idea.

"Just what we need—another floundering mainlander who doesn't know what he wants," the woman mutters, rolling her eyes.

Main—what?

"I need to speak to Geneva," I say.

"Obviously, cowboy, but *why?*"

I'm two seconds from telling her, as politely as I can, that it's none of her business, when another woman appears in the doorway of the house across the street. She's holding two glasses of lemonade, her long white braid draping down the front of her yellow sundress.

"I leave you alone for one minute," she calls into the street with an amused smile.

The woman in front of me makes a buzzing sound with her lips, waving a hand at her friend. "Don't interrupt me in the middle of an interrogation."

"Is that what this is?" My eyebrows lift.

"Naturally."

Her tilted chin and defiant nature remind me of the woman I'm here to meet, and I can't help the smile blooming over my lips.

Maybe wariness is filtered into the drinking water of this small beach town.

"You know," I begin, "I was here to see Geneva, but now I'm thinking I'd rather get to know you."

I send her a genuine smile. Usually, when I ask nicely, even the most obstinate patient will agree to a necessary CT scan or to stop throwing medical supplies at the nurses. But the gesture backfires—spectacularly. The woman laughs right in my face, starting with an amused cackle that escalates until she's leaning hard onto her cane as if needing it to support her weight.

"Ignore her," the woman in the sundress tells me, coming to her friend's side. "How can we help you?"

"We? Don't rope me into this."

"I'm Wendy, and this ball of sunshine is Carol." Her hand is warm and soft as we shake. "Geneva is probably in her backyard with her chickens."

I shouldn't be delighted by this piece of information, but my cheek quirks even higher. For as much as Geneva projects a tough exterior, she'd been undeniably nurturing when we'd happened upon a woman who'd been crying barefoot in the hall of the casino.

It'd been just after we left the boxing afterparty and were supposed to go our separate ways. I'd offered the woman my shoes and to escort her to her hotel three blocks away, but Geneva marched up to the front desk and demanded a pair of en suite sandals since the woman's feet were considerably smaller than mine. After we'd safely returned the woman to her room and her friends, Geneva asked if I wanted a drink.

And then, I had to keep the shock out of my smile when Geneva extended that second hour to three, and then four, nearly pushing daylight.

"Earth to Tex." Carol snaps her fingers at me.

"Van," I correct.

"Whatever. I can assure you that whatever snake oil you're selling, Geneva doesn't want any. She's even tougher than I am."

But that's just it. I've seen Geneva soft.

It'd been after hearing the sound of her bright laughter as I grimaced while drinking whiskey neat. Well after we began the game of *truth or dare* that ended up being all dares. It'd been after too much whiskey and at the beginning of that very last dare when I heard Geneva's voice soften.

"I can't get married." Geneva's muscles tense in response to my dare.

"It won't be real." I chuckle at the absurdity of marrying a stranger. "We won't sign the marriage certificate afterward. I just love the idea of Elvis performing a wedding ceremony."

"But I'm not supposed to get married."

"Why not?"

Her jaw clenches as she shakes her head.

"I know it's never going to happen, because we're going our separate ways after this, but if I had the chance to chip away at that armor and really know you, I'd want to marry you in a minute," I tell her, more than a little drunk but the words still feeling right in my chest.

"You'd regret it."

Though her sentence is a challenge, her tone softens into a surrendering murmur. My fingers graze the back of her hand, and her posture relaxes even more.

I lean closer, my gaze never leaving hers. "No, darlin'. I don't think I would."

A sharp voice snaps me back to the hot street. "Is this man bothering you, Carol?"

I flip around too quickly, and there she is.

Geneva.

My wife.

The sight of her unexpectedly knocks the wind out of me. Her hair is pulled into a ponytail, and an oversized tee nearly eclipses her tiny shorts. Her arms are deceptively loose at her sides, but I know she could strike quicker than a viper. It takes my cloudy brain a few seconds to process the graphic on her shirt—a hissing opossum baring its teeth below the words *First of all, I'm a delight.*

My head shakes with a growing grin when Geneva's expression gives nothing away. She simply stares me down—fierce and breathtaking at the same time.

Absolutely freaking perfect.

I roll my shoulders back, preparing. As an emergency physician, I've had to tell countless families the hardest news they'll ever hear. I can tell Geneva that we're accidentally married.

Because the signatures we laughingly scribbled at the *beginning* of the ceremony weren't just for the bill. We'd unknowingly signed a digital wedding certificate—brand new to the Chapel of Endless Love and very much legally binding.

"Hey, darlin'." A smile quirks the corner of my mouth. "We need to talk."

THREE

Geneva

I try—and fail—to mitigate the effect Van's smile has on my heart rate. But while that foolish organ is skipping like a gleeful teen, my brain is collected enough to know we can't have this conversation here. Carol Cook, the resident queen of gossip, is visiting my neighbor, Wendy. Though Van's presence at my house will be all over town before nightfall, the other part of this equation *needs* to remain buried—forever.

"Come inside," I say, turning around.

I don't look back. I don't allow myself to dwell on how Van looks impossibly good in his white shirt and shorts, his hair cut and cleanly shaven. The fact that he seems to be doing better soothes the ache I've had ever since I learned *why* he looked disheveled in Vegas.

It'd been so hard not to call him after finding out. At random intervals, I'd open the private investigator's report to stare at his phone number. Once or twice, I even typed it into my phone, only to come to my senses and delete it. Even now, I want to ask if he's okay, but that's not the reason why Van is here—which, honestly, is good. Having me in his life would only complicate things for him, and that's the last thing he needs right now.

I tighten my muscles, preparing to take this blow like the many I've weathered before.

"Let's get this over with," I say when Van closes the front door. It's been broken for a year now, so it takes him two tries to set it correctly into its hinges. "Where are the papers?"

"What papers?" he asks with a slight quirk of his brow.

Heat splinters over my collarbones when I catch a whiff of his distracting cologne—a warm, woodsy scent with a crisp apple top note. Leave it to Van to wear a cologne that's masculine with a hint of sweetness.

I clench my fingers to regain control.

Attraction is physiological, I remind myself. *Just like being afraid when you see a snake. It means nothing.*

Van's gaze flicks to my fists before returning to my face. "What papers, Gen?"

I usually bristle when people truncate my name. No one calls me anything but Geneva. I also detest pet names, *especially* given by men. But just like when Van calls me *darlin'*, I don't correct him.

"The divorce papers."

A soft, "*Ah,*" escapes his distractingly full lips. "You already know."

I say nothing.

"What was the plan? To stay married forever?"

"Since I never planned on getting married, it was a nonissue for me." I lift my chin. "You'd come with divorce papers in hand whenever you found someone you wanted to be with."

Van rubs his eyebrow. "I…"

He sets his hands on his hips with an exhale, staring at the scuffed hardwood floor for a few beats. My chest seizes. I want to apologize, to tell him I'm so sorry he's dealing with this legal snafu on top of everything, to relent—just this once—but habit is a powerful thing, and my self-preservation instincts are even stronger.

"Okay, I'm going to lay it all on the line. I recently—" Van's hard swallow as he struggles to get the words out feels like a knockout punch. "I recently lost my sister. We were incredibly close and—"

"I know," I interrupt, my lungs impossibly tight. I don't mean to cut Van off, but I don't want him to have to detail something that's so painful. "I'm sorry."

"How would you know?"

A flush of embarrassment rushes from my ears to my scalp, but after realizing I accidentally married a stranger, my actions weren't only practical, they were necessary. If my past has taught me one thing, it's never to trust a man's word.

"I had my PI do a full profile on you once I saw the public record."

Van blinks, his mouth half open. I know from experience he's not easily stunned. Van rolled with every curveball I threw him in Vegas, that irresistible smile never wavering.

"*My PI* implies you have a private investigator on retainer."

"I do."

He nods to himself, muttering, "This is going to be harder than I thought."

My thoughts fire off automatically.

I tried to warn you. You don't want any part of this. It's too much trouble.

I'm *too much trouble.*

"Let me tell you how this went from my perspective. I went to Vegas to see my sister's favorite singer because we planned that trip together, and if it'd been reversed, Taylor would have gone in my memory. Afterward, I ended up on an unexpected adventure with the most intriguing woman. It resulted in us getting *fake married* and then amicably parting ways."

Van's gaze is steady on mine, and I struggle not to fidget.

"Then a week ago, I was in the shower, and a wild thought occurred to me. One quick search of the public record and, yep, I'm hitched. Then it was a mad rush of coordinating a leave of absence from my job and finalizing plans to drive to Wilks Beach to tell you in person because that seemed like the decent thing to do."

My shoulders inch upward, my skin growing hot.

"Because though it's obvious that none of this matters to you," he says, his cheekbones flushing, "I actually care about the sanctity of marriage. I promised my sister that if I ever got married, I'd do the hard work and stick it out. I wouldn't pull a disappearing act like my father did when my mom was pregnant with me, forcing my sister to raise me since Mama had to work three jobs to support us. And since I've never, not once in my life, gone back on a promise to Taylor, I sure as heck don't plan to now."

His chest heaves, and all my muscles twitch in response. I want to pull him into my arms more than I want to maintain my permanent distance, but for the first time since we've met, Van is irritated with me. The best thing now would be to lean into that, to push him away just like I've done with everyone else.

"How long would you need to stay married to keep your promise?" I can tell I've stunned him again, and honestly, I didn't see myself asking that question. "Under different circumstances, I'm sure you'd agree that it doesn't make sense for our futures to be entwined from a technicality we had no knowledge of. But to keep your word to your sister, to say you tried, how long would you need to stay?"

Van's investigative report came back squeaky clean. Twenty-seven. Decent credit score. Brilliant student—graduating from college and medical school early. Emergency physician with outstanding patient satisfaction scores. Communally liked. Very close to his mother and late sister. Volunteers in his nonexistent spare time. No criminal record—not even a speeding ticket. If I was forced to be legally bound to someone for a short period of time, Van seems like the best option.

A few seconds pass as Van surveys me, and my core tightens out of habit.

"One year."

A choking sound escapes me.

"What? No! One month."

Van crosses his arms, and I try not to get distracted by the flex of his toned forearms. "Six months."

I mirror his posture. "Six weeks—not a second longer."

Van steps right into my space, his face inches from mine, but I stand my ground.

"Do you have any idea how breathtaking you are when you're like this? Fighting me?"

A halting inhale pulls silently into my lungs, but I maintain my facade and say nothing.

"Everything is easy for me. You probably saw that in your report, but *you*, Gen... You are..."

His sentence drops off when he tucks his bottom lip between his teeth, and I have to pinch the underside of my arm to keep myself from doing something reckless.

"Four months," Van says, his tone firm.

"Three."

"Perfect." That mystifying smile lifts his cheeks. "That's what I wanted from the beginning."

My teeth grind as I barely restrain a growl.

His head shakes slightly, his grin growing. "This is going to be fun."

Then Van is moving toward the door with a determined stride.

"What are you doing?" I get to the door before he does, putting my back against it.

Van's eyes twinkle with delight. "Moving in, darlin'. What's it look like?"

"Not with Carol across the street, you're not."

His head tilts slightly. "I know you're not afraid of that sweet old lady."

"I'm not." My answer is too rushed, impulsive. Nothing like how I'd normally speak—calm, calculated, or not at all.

"If you say so."

That smirk. That darned smirk.

"We need to establish ground rules," I tell him, chin lifting.

"Let's hear them."

"There will be no *marriage* part to this marriage." Van and I might have gotten accidentally married in Vegas, but we hadn't even completed the ceremony with a kiss. There'd been a tense moment, a swaying of noses too close, shuddered breaths mixing, but nothing official.

"You're going to sleep over there." I point to the couch in the adjacent living room. "We'll keep our own schedules and lives. I'm just helping you keep a promise. I'm not signing up to be a spouse." My mind whirls, thinking of all that would entail, before I reel it back in. "And we're not telling the town the truth. We can say that—"

Van sucks in a breath through his teeth. "That's where I have to stop you. I don't lie."

"Never?"

"Nope. Chalk it up to having a deadbeat dad, but I don't. Not even white lies. If you have spinach in your teeth, I'll tell you. If you're worried about how a dress looks and want an honest answer, I'm your man." His gaze unconsciously slips down my frame before he focuses on my face again. "I won't budge on that."

I mentally recalibrate. It won't be the first time the town knew about my dirty laundry. Fortunately, most of them are terrified of me, so I never hear wind of it.

"Fine."

"As far as the rest of it, I'm not here to force you into a relationship you don't want, but I'd like us to at least be friends. We enjoyed spending time together in Vegas, didn't we?"

We had. Spending time with him had been more fun than I'd ever expected.

Van waits, his brows expectant.

I simply stare, not giving him the answer he wants. If anything, this delights Van more than my agreement would have.

"If you'll excuse me." He tugs on the door handle again. "I don't want my guitar to warp in the heat."

"You play guitar?"

My question makes the dimple in Van's cheek pop. "That didn't show up in your report?"

"It mostly focused on whether or not you had a criminal record," I tell him with an unimpressed glare.

Truly, I've always wished I could play an instrument. My mom had been disappointed that so many of the other girls in the beauty pageant circuit had been artistic while I'd been as creative as a cinderblock. Fortunately, I'd always enjoyed helping others, so my community work for local women's shelters satisfied my hobbies requirement.

It's something I still do today, though no one—not even my half-brother, Noah—knows I drive to the mainland to teach women self-defense and job interview strategies twice a week.

After another amused look from Van, I move out of the way.

Once he's on the other side of the closed door, reality slaps my cheekbone. I've already accepted the news that I'd unknowingly married a stranger, but now that man will be occupying space not only in my mind but my house for the next three months.

I spin, looking out the window to find Van beside his white truck parked near the beach access at the end of the short neighborhood road. His easy smile graces his mouth as he chats with Carol. She glances toward my cottage, a wolfish grin on her wrinkled face. Van follows her gaze, waving at me and then blowing a kiss my way.

I let a growl rip free as my fingers fist.

This is what I get for letting my feelings take control. I should have listened to that protective voice in my mind that'd warned me not to extend our time together weeks ago. I should have insisted Van leave the second he arrived today. I should've kept myself more guarded against his effect on me, but Van's effervescence is as addicting as exercise-induced endorphins.

Because as Van slings two duffel bags and a guitar case across his back, the sensation sprinting through my bloodstream isn't dread. It's wishful, foolish anticipation. And I know from experience what happens when I get my hopes up.

So as Van moves toward the house, I tug on my shoes, slip out the back door, and head toward my gym.

FOUR

Van

"It's real quaint, Mama. You'd love it." I try to smile, though my stomach feels like it's digesting itself.

This is why I don't lie. This awful, nauseating sensation makes me want to heave up the gas station breakfast burrito I ate en route. But as much as I needed to be here, keeping my promise to Taylor, I also didn't want to break Mama's heart when losing her daughter already smashed it to smithereens.

So I'm lying. Just this once.

Just this one lie to keep my mother from worrying about me when she's still grieving. Taylor's unexpected death four months ago has already pushed back Mama's wedding to her long-time boyfriend,

Mark. I don't need her to be anxious about her son spontaneously marrying a stranger.

We've all been reeling, trying to make sense of life without my sister. Mama had holed herself away, barely leaving the house, and I'd thrown myself into extra shifts at the hospital. The idea of me taking personal leave in this coastal Virginian town after working myself to the bone is something Mama can digest.

"And who are you staying with again?" she asks.

I switch hands on my phone since my nervous palms are sweaty. Of course, the ninety-degree temperature doesn't help. There's no sign of the ever-present ocean breeze I'd noticed on the weather app when I looked up Wilks Beach.

"My friend, Gen. She's got a cottage steps from the beach. And the neighbors are really nice."

This isn't another lie, because even Carol softened a bit after I told her about my background. It's not the first time that I'd mentioned being a doctor and someone's behavior toward me completely changed. Often, it's positive, but sometimes people will whip out a festering wound or questionable mole in public places. I once picked a woman up for a date, and her roommate unzipped his pants to ask if he had a hernia seconds after shaking my hand.

Carol didn't ask for medical advice, just remarked that having an emergency physician in town could be helpful before giving me an unimpressed glare, efficiently undermining her words. Wendy pinched her arm, reminding Carol that they were supposed to be more open-minded about 'mainlanders.' When I asked what that meant, Wendy explained that Wilks Beach locals have a long history of being leery of outsiders, but they're trying to be more accepting after a newcomer ended up being the perfect match for the town sweetheart.

"That sounds wonderful, but..."

"I know, Mama. I miss you already." I left yesterday morning, deciding to split the ten-hour drive into two days. Though I've vacationed with friends—camping mostly—I've never lived in a different city. "This is just something—"

"You have to do. I know. I can tell when my baby can't set something down. You've been like that ever since you were little." There's a smile in my mother's voice. "If you need this break by the sea, then you should take it. Nashville Medical Center will be happy to have you back once you're rested."

Though the lie eats a hole through my intestines, I distract us both by describing Wilks Beach. Since Gen had been nowhere to be found when I came back inside the house earlier, I set my bags beside the couch and decided to explore my new neighborhood. A single two-lane road runs the length of the beach, short residential streets with single-family homes jutting off it. When I walked south, I found a condo tower and a nice city park with a playground that dead-ended into an inlet.

Two younger men—Cliff and Leo—were fishing off the jetty in blatant disregard to the signs warning them not to. They didn't mind answering my questions about the area, explaining that the wide inlet next to us separated Wilks Beach from North Carolina's

Outer Banks, and that a large, inaccessible wildlife preserve borders the northern edge of town. With the Atlantic Ocean stretching to the east and Back Bay to the west, most locals called Wilks Beach an island, though it's technically a peninsula.

"Sounds kind of romantic, how remote it is," my mom muses after I tell her the town is an hour from the next closest city, Virginia Beach. "Maybe Mark and I should honeymoon there instead. It'd probably be cheaper and a lot easier to get to."

They'd initially had plans to honeymoon in Hawaii—a once-in-a-lifetime trip for the both of them. Fortunately, Mark had been able to recoup ninety percent of their money after Mama wanted to postpone everything.

"I can testify to the beach's quality," I say, walking along the wet, packed sand. "Golden sand for as far as the eye can see."

After talking to Cliff and Leo, I wandered past the lifeguard towers and beach crowded with families, continuing northward. I only made it a hundred feet before the lack of breeze forced me to take off my shirt and tuck it into the back of my shorts.

"I'm happy you're doing this," Mama tells me. "Taylor—" My heart seizes when her voice cracks. "Taylor was always getting after you to take more time for yourself."

My feet stop, the remnants of a wave almost touching my shoes. "She was."

Was. I hate that word. For that matter, I hate the past tense. I hate that, a few months ago, my sister was alive and well, and now, she's gone, and I'm wandering up an—albeit stunning—beach, questioning my sanity *while lying* to Mama.

A part of me knows I should have come with divorce papers, like Geneva expected. Asking to stay with her is sheer lunacy, but something won't let me simply walk away. I know that three months of sleeping on Geneva's couch doesn't make a marriage, but I can't bring myself to apathetically scrawl another signature to make this go away. I don't believe in fate, but even I can't deny that bone-deep sensation that I'm supposed to be here.

At least for a little while.

"Well...I should be..."

"Okay, Mama," I say, recognizing the well-worn pattern.

Taylor would always talk to me about anything, but Mama doesn't like getting into tough, emotional conversations. When our calls get to this point, she makes an excuse to hang up. Mama often cautioned me about wearing my heart on my sleeve, but my sister always said it was her favorite attribute of mine.

"Being open-hearted isn't a flaw, Van. It's your biggest strength."

That was why I chose to become a doctor and work in the ER. I've always wanted to help others, and being in the emergency department allows me to be the first person they see when their life is going off the rails. Sure, there's the added bonus of each shift being unique, since you never know what'll walk through the doors, but providing my patients with much-needed compassion during their scariest moments...that fulfills me.

Mama and I exchange *I love yous* before I tuck my phone into my pocket, staring out over the ocean. I'd never seen it in person before. My upbringing, education, and professional life have always existed within Nashville city limits. I should be awestruck, or at the very least enjoying a sense of tranquility, but it feels like someone took a cheese grater to my heart. My head tilts back as I close my eyes against the bright-blue sky, dragging in a deep breath.

Sometimes, this is all I can manage—breathing.

Because I can't deal with the hole in my chest. As much as my extroverted soul will talk to anyone about anything, I've only ever confided in *one person* when things got really tough, and now...she's gone.

The sudden breeze caressing my face is so tender my eyes water as they spring open. Air swirls around my arms, between my fingers, and around my ankles. A staggered inhale slips between my lips as goosebumps dot my skin, but the breeze doesn't cease. If anything, it increases, gently ruffling the umbrellas of beachgoers, sending the flags of the oceanfront houses snapping.

"I miss you too."

My head snaps around, looking for the source of my sister's voice, but then my forehead wrinkles as I shake my head. Paracusia. That's the medical term for auditory hallucination.

Nothing can bring my sister back.

Abruptly, the wind picks up, whipping towels from the sand and thudding louder than my jackknifing pulse. I cover my ears with my palms, closing my eyes against the spray of sand pelting my legs, my chest, my cheeks. As suddenly as it came, the gale abates, almost as if we were in a momentary dust storm.

Beachgoers scramble to right pop-up tents, spread towels, and shake sand out of beach bags. In the remaining quiet, the lulling, rhythmic sound of the water washes over me. Gleeful children giggle as they rush to play in the waves. The briny tang of sea air mixes with the scent of sunscreen. Sunlight sparkles over everything, turning the sea into thousands of liquid diamonds.

I wait for a buoyed sensation to ribbon through my ribs, to finally feel at peace, but...nothing. There's nothing but the ever-present ache in my chest. The urge to do something—*anything*—to distract myself is oppressive.

I think of the last time I felt a reprieve from this agony, and a pair of narrowed brown eyes flash before my vision. Being with Geneva in Vegas had been the only time I felt alive—like my old self—since losing Taylor. Even as that thought fills my mind, I know it's too much pressure to put on one person, especially someone I'm just getting to know. But I don't know another way to deal with the incessant emptiness. Working until I could barely stand these last few months hasn't helped.

"Alright." I clap my hands together, distracting myself. "Time to find the missus."

Geneva wasn't the only one who did a little cyber-snooping after discovering our situation. Once I had her full name, I did a simple search, finding years of beauty pageant photos and videos before reading a few articles about her converting an old auto repair store into a no-contact boxing gym. But unlike Geneva, I don't know anything about her personal relationships beyond the fact that she celebrated her thirtieth birthday shortly before we wed.

I continue northward, stopping to read the signs posted on the fence separating the beach from the sea turtle hatching ground beyond. Then I weave past the library, the market Cliff said he was the assistant manager of, a tailor shop, a coffee shop, a water tower, and the fire station until I end in front of The Garage Gym.

It's an older cinderblock building with two automotive garage doors. There is a glass front door, and what used to be a waiting area now holds a water cooler and shelves of boxing equipment. Several punching bags hang from the ceiling, and there's a separate section for free weights, a squat rack, and medicine balls. The exterior is painted white with a dark-gray awning that matches the color of the floors and the words written on the far wall.

Rule number one: Check your ego at the door.

Heavy-metal music pours out of the half-opened garage door as Geneva lays into a punching bag like it personally offended her mother. Since she's facing away, I take a moment to decide my next move. One thing's for sure: I don't want to startle her like I did in Vegas. I'd had a bruise for several days after taking an elbow to the solar plexus.

I stoop under the garage door, making a wide circle around the bag Geneva is punching with wrapped hands. You'd think that would hurt, not using gloves, but she doesn't even grimace. She's also discarded her oversized shirt, exercising in only a longline sports bra and snug athletic shorts. It's not until I'm closer that I notice Geneva has her eyes closed, placing targeted hits from memory. I wait for her to sense that she's not alone, but she continues, a little wrinkle between her dark brows as she shuffles her feet between punches.

A helpless sigh slips from my lips.

There's *nothing* sexier than a strong woman.

I clear my throat, but the sound barely registers over Metallica's screaming guitars. My hands settle on my hips as I consider the least lethal way to let Geneva know I'm on the other side of her punching bag. Then her eyes pop open, and she misses her next punch, grazing the bag. Her mouth falls open with a startled sound as her momentum carries her straight into my bare chest.

FIVE

Geneva

My fingers splay open to brace my fall. One hand lands on Van's firm pectoral muscle, and the other rakes down his unnecessarily defined abs. How does Van even look like this? He's supposed to be an overworked doctor without a gym membership. Sean, my private investigator, mentioned that Van ran a few mornings a week, but that doesn't explain the definition my fingertips are currently experiencing.

"Whoa there." Van's arms come around my body, pulling me upward. It's probably in an attempt to steady me, but the action brings me flush against him.

A shuddered breath fills my lungs when our eyes meet. I feel his responding inhale, how his heart sprints beneath my palm.

"I...um..." Van says, blinking.

Inarticulate isn't a word I'd use to describe Van. During our time in Vegas, and even earlier this morning, he always had a quick quip for whatever I threw at him.

But I guess I never *threw myself* at him before.

"Hi?" My voice is too soft, too breathy, and Van's responsive grin is entirely too sweet.

I get lost in it for a minute—the feel of him, his easy smile, and the crisp apple top note of his cologne. The fact that Van's expression isn't one of flirtatious triumph but unguarded sincerity allows my shoulders to settle.

But then...I register that the music has shifted. The Darkness's "I Believe in a Thing Called Love" has replaced Metallica, the title lyric screeching through the speakers at an ear-splitting decibel. I always keep the music loud enough to overpower my thoughts, but now I'd give anything to be able to voice-command my speaker off.

"What are you doing here?"

Van lets go of me easily when I break away to click off the music.

"I could ask you the same thing," he says, that smile slipping into flirty territory. "Are you avoiding me, dearest wife?"

Wife singes through my ribs, leaving a pinpoint hole in its wake, but I remain visually nonplussed.

"First of all, I'm not—"

"Technically, you are." There's no mistaking it this time. Van's smile has gone full dimple.

Since I apparently cannot control my ridiculous heart's response to an insignificant facial indent, I grapple for something I can control.

"If we're going to repeat this conversation, you could at least put your shirt on."

"You first." Van winks, and I am *not* a fan of my stomach's swoopy response.

I toss an annoyed grunt his way as I crouch to pick up my tee. My hair gets ruffled as I hastily pull it over my head, but I don't care. Folding my arms, I eye him expectantly. Van chuckles softly and then proceeds to pull his shirt on at the speed of a geriatric turtle. Seriously. I've seen clock hands move faster.

"I envy the people who don't know you."

My tone comes out with icy perfection, but Van just laughs, fixing his rumpled sleeve.

"Is that the best you can do?" A challenging eyebrow quirk accompanies his question.

I roll my eyes, moving toward the free weights to reorganize them. No matter how many times I tell my boxers to put them back in their labeled places, someone always mixes them up. Noah, my half-brother who attends class when he's not working shifts at the fire station, probably does it on purpose just to irritate me.

"I'm not bored enough to talk to you right now. Why don't you scoot on home?"

It's only after I've said the well-worn dismissal that I remember that Van's home is also mine for the time being. My stomach does another flip, but this one leaves nausea in its place.

"You know, you're cute when you're trying to scare me away. It's adorable, really. But in all seriousness, I thought we could run through a few practicalities."

I glance over my shoulder to scowl at him, but then my heart rate ratchets for an entirely different reason. Joanna is speed-walking across Sand Bend Road—a woman on a mission. Van catches the change in my expression and glances behind him.

"Who's that?"

"No— No time—"

Joanna bends under the half-closed garage and practically runs me over, surrounding me in a death-grip hug. As always, she smells delectably of cinnamon and vanilla.

"I came as soon as I heard the news. Congratulations!" She leans back slightly, squeezing my shoulders. "I should be furious I wasn't invited to your wedding, but Carol said it was a spur-of-the-moment elopement after a year of dating long distance. You didn't want to share your news with anyone until your new hubby finished out his work commitments and could move here."

I glance at Van for clarification, but his brow furrows.

Darned Wilks Beach rumor mill.

This isn't the first time misinformation has been spread around town. But that's fine. I'll clear everything up right now, and in three months' time, it'll be like this never happened. Van will go back to his life. I'll go back to mine. The end.

Joanna moves her hands from my shoulders to frame my face, her eyes misting. "I had no idea. I mean, how could I? You always keep so much to yourself."

"I'm sorry," I croak. Someone has my windpipe in a chokehold.

"No, no. This is good. *So good.* Can't you see how good this is? And it's just like when you decided to stay in Wilks Beach or open your gym. Everything was completely finalized before you said a word." A soft laugh bubbles free. "You're always six steps ahead of the rest of us."

A noncommittal sound eeks from my throat before Joanna continues.

"I'm just so happy." Her lips drop in contradiction to her words. "I worry about you all the time. You and Noah. With everything that dirtbag—" Joanna cuts herself off. "With everything that happened to us, I figured we were all broken. You. Noah. Me. Shattered beyond repair."

Joanna hiccups, blinking back tears, and two sensations sprint in opposite directions. My sternum breaks open, watching the woman who's been my surrogate mother for the past five years trying not to cry, and my skin itches to be anywhere other than here, discussing the subject I hate most—feelings.

"But you're so much stronger than the rest of us." Her wobbly lips tip up. "Just don't tell Noah I said that," she adds with a watery chuckle.

"I'm absolutely telling Noah," I answer automatically before taking a deep breath to tell Joanna the truth.

She might not like the idea that Van's and my marriage is the result of a mistake, but she'll understand Van's reasoning to stay. Joanna has always been tenderhearted. She'll likely try to adopt him too. At the very least, she'll offer to be his Wilks Beach guide during his temporary stay. Then I'll reassure her that I'm fine—and that Noah is too. Honestly, we're both better off than we've been in a long, long time.

"I'd been having a rough few months—a rough year, really—and you being happily married is..." Joanna runs her hands over her flushed face. "To find out that you found someone, found love...it's just what I needed. I had no idea how much I needed this until I heard the news."

A squeaky sound comes out of my open mouth as my gaze shifts to Van, Joanna following my eyeline.

"Oh, gracious. I'm being so rude. Hi!" She crosses to him, enveloping Van in a fierce hug. "I'm Joanna."

"Nice to meet you," Van says warmly, his questioning gaze on me.

"*Go along with it,*" I mouth, frantically gesturing between the two of us.

His eyes widen with alarm.

"*Please,*" I mouth.

Van's straight blond hair shifts over his forehead as he shakes his head.

Not beyond begging, I clutch my hands in front of my chest. This time, my *"Please"* is a hushed whisper. Van's gaze darts from my joined fingers, to my face, to my surrogate mother still clinging to him.

"Fine," he mouths back.

My relieved exhale is noisy, drawing Joanna's attention.

"Did you say something, Geneva?" Her chin-length curly hair bounces around her round face as she lets go of Van.

"No." I slide my wrapped hands into a crossed-arm position. It feels awkward, though I often stand this way.

"Okay." When a genuine smile lifts Joanna's lips, the tension in my spine eases. "Well, I'm off to finalize things with Clara for the party tonight."

"What kind of party?" Van asks after a beat.

"Yours, of course. To celebrate your nuptials. The whole town is coming out." She beams, more radiant than I've seen her in a long while. "Seven o'clock at Bayside Table."

Van barely breathes as Joanna squeezes his fingers on her way out.

She pauses before slipping under the garage door. "Just so, *so* happy."

We both watch, stunned, until Joanna is beyond the view of the windowed garage doors.

"Gen, I can't—"

"Let me think," I cut him off, beginning to pace.

I bite my thumbnail, my brain more fried than a phone left in the August sun. Dozens of options present themselves and are swiftly dismissed. The only thing I know for sure is that I can't let Joanna down—not after everything she's done for me. Almost instantly, the memories of how I ended up in Wilks Beach, of how Joanna selflessly took me in, overwhelm me. I press my lashes closed to push the thoughts away just as another idea pops into my mind.

"We'll get divorced." I stop pacing to face Van. "I mean, we were going to get divorced anyway, but we'll divorce publicly. A messy, ugly divorce after three months. You can do something horrendous and—"

"Why am I the one to do something horrendous?" Van's hands settle on his hips.

I snort. "It's usually the man who screws things up."

"Not this man."

"What does it even matter? You won't be here anymore. Who cares if people from a tiny town think you're the villain?"

Van steps closer, his jaw tight. "I care."

Warning flashes in my mind, but the words rush out anyway. "You can't be perfect all the time, Van. You're going to mess up eventually. And you know what happens then? No one's going to want you around."

His gaze softens as he closes the distance between us. Adrenaline surges through my body, sending a tingling rush pricking my exposed skin. I should've shifted back into stony silence and not given this man an inch, but something about Van makes the truth fall out of my usually clamped mouth. And because of that, he's learned more about me in two non-consecutive days than anyone on this island has learned in five years.

"I'd ask who hurt you, but I'm guessing from what your mom said, it was your dad." Van tucks a wayward strand of hair behind my ear. "I'm sorry. I know from experience how much that stings."

His touch is so lovely that moisture gathers at the bridge of my nose. I'm instantly angry at myself for reacting this way when I should be shoving him away.

"She's not my mom." I spit the words like a petulant child, not like the composed thirty-year-old I am.

Joanna is Noah's mom, though he and I share a father—something we hadn't known until five years ago.

I wait for surprise to resonate over Van's mystifying gray eyes, but he softly nods his head. "Yes, she is, darlin'. Someone who cares about you like that is family. Maybe not by blood but family nonetheless."

It's all I can do to lift my chin and keep my breathing even, to not spill the stupid tears threatening to make a fool out of me. The corner of Van's mouth lifts slightly, the soft affection in his gaze making everything harder.

"This is what we're going to do," he says, stepping back so I can finally release my tight muscles.

"We'll head home, get cleaned up, and prepare for tonight. If people think we've been dating for a year, they're going to have questions. Since you're the strong, silent type, you can grunt and scowl at everyone while I talk," Van says, sending me an endearing grin. "I'll take care of everything, keep the lying to a minimum so I don't get heartburn, and afterward, we'll stay out of the limelight. Deal?"

I nod, finally loosening my fisted fingers.

"Don't worry, Gen." Van gives me that dimpled smile. "I've got you."

As I lock up my gym and numbly follow Van back to my house, my mind whirls. But I'm not thinking about how my life is spinning out of control or what a circus tonight will be. A single thought repeats itself, insistent as a drumbeat, as we trudge through the afternoon heat.

Only my husband calls me Gen.

SIX

Van

"**D**on't you own something other than black?" I ask while sitting on Geneva's bed.

She glares at me through the mirror of the ensuite bathroom, applying lipstick. It's maddening, that bright-red color—nothing like I've seen her wear before. Geneva's dress, however, is very similar to the one she wore in Vegas—tight and black. Her entire wardrobe seems to revolve around various shades of pitch darkness.

"It matches the color of my heart," she quips, capping the lipstick and tucking it into the side of her dress's bodice.

I glance away, certain that my ears are turning pink.

That's another reason I don't lie. Both Mama and Taylor could always tell if I was fibbing—my ears gave me away.

49

I keep talking to distract myself, moving to thumb through her open closet. "You could pepper in a bit of color. Perhaps a muddy brown or morose burgundy?"

When Geneva doesn't answer, I look over my shoulder to find her leaning against the door jamb to the bathroom, arms crossed and frowning.

My little storm cloud.

"If you really wanted to shock people, you could add in yellow or chartreuse," I say, needling her.

Geneva marches over, shutting the slotted closet doors and nearly taking off my finger. "I'm already shocking the town with your existence."

We spent the afternoon learning about each other in preparation for tonight. Or rather, Geneva tossed my file at me, asked for me to point out inaccuracies—which creepily, there were none—and I pulled teeth, gathering barely enough information about her to satisfy the impending crowd. Geneva's rationale was that no one in Wilks Beach knows much about her, so me knowing details was irrelevant.

I did discover that she's originally from Philadelphia, she has a degree in business administration, and the rough details of her philandering father. Geneva admitted with an unconvincing shrug that everyone in town knew the basics, and therefore, so should I. Every cell itched to hold her, but since Geneva's body language gave off *touch me and die* vibes, I maintained my distance and made us a late lunch instead.

It'd also been necessary to subdue my impulse to ask follow-up questions, knowing there's so much more to that story. Following that instinct usually proves right in my medical practice. When I get a hunch to order a seemingly unnecessary CT scan or an extra lab test, I usually find a disorder that, if left to fester, would have created problems later on. I want to understand Geneva on a cellular level, but I know earning her trust will be a slow-going endeavor.

I cock my head, waving my hand in a small circle. "Would putting me down help dispel some of this black-cat energy before we're supposed to be social?"

"You smell like a bag of wet grandmas," Geneva tells me with a straight face.

The laugh bursting from my belly causes the corner of her lip to quiver. It's a beautiful sight until she forces it down.

"That's a good one. Hit me again."

This time, she doesn't restrain her smirk, and I freaking love it.

"Talking to you is as riveting as reading a car manual."

I splay my hand over my chest like I've suffered a bullet wound. "Stop. I can't take it."

Geneva leans in, a delightfully wicked gleam in her eye. "I love how you walk around with the confidence of a tall man."

"Hey now." I pull my shoulders back, rising to my full height. "Those are fightin' words."

"Don't I know it," she says, bouncing her eyebrows at me before striding out of the room.

I chase after her, grinning like a lunatic, down the stairs and toward the door to her backyard. Once we're both outside, Geneva engages the smart lock, waiting until it's done whirring to double-check it's secure.

"Should I know the code to that?"

She's halfway through rolling her eyes before she exhales sharply. "Probably. It's 0270."

I nod. "Your birthday backward."

Geneva is wearing dark sunglasses over her eyes, but her lips part in surprise.

I tap the side of my temple with my index finger. "Brilliant mind, remember? I believe that was the exact phrasing in the report."

She snorts, striding through the dirt yard in pencil-thin heels without a hint of a wobble. "Be good, ladies," she tells the closed chicken coop before opening the gate to the street.

Before we got dressed, Geneva ensured that her chickens were safely tucked away for the evening. It'd been sweet, watching her softly chat to each one while giving them kitchen scraps and changing out their water.

"What are their names again?" I ask, jogging after her.

I remember exactly, but I want Geneva to tell me again.

"Prunella, Stella, and Hank."

"And Hank is a hen."

It'd been mistaken gender identity when Geneva had rescued the chicks two years ago. She'd been on a beach run and seen the three chicks struggling to stay afloat in the surf. After getting them safely home, Geneva had searched the internet for how to sex chicks, only getting two thirds of it correct.

Geneva exhales noisily. "Yes."

"Who lays eggs?"

She stops in her tracks, wheeling on me. "Are you going to be like this all night?"

"Most definitely." I can't help the enormous smile overtaking my face.

I'm rewarded with a growl but decide to refrain from poking at her for the rest of the short walk to Bayside Table.

From my excursion earlier today, I discovered that Bayside Table is the only restaurant and bar in town. It seems more than enough, though, with its large outdoor entertainment space—a grassy area that stretches beyond an open-air bar and dance floor situated beside the restaurant. The waterfront restaurant has large glass windows facing the bay and a dock holding six boat slips for patrons to arrive by sea. It seems, though, most Wilks Beach residents arrive like us, on foot.

I follow Geneva to the outdoor space where picnic tables and Adirondack chairs are interspaced with a giant Connect Four, oversized Jenga, and several cornhole setups. String lights frame the grassy area, adding an ethereal glow to the sun setting across Back Bay. A handmade *Congrats, Newlyweds* banner stretches across the covered bar area already teeming with locals.

"Are you ready for this?" I mutter out of the side of my mouth.

Geneva looks ready. She looks like she could take on a gang of ninjas without wrinkling her dress.

"Not even a little," she murmurs, spine perfectly straight, chin poised.

"Hey." I step in front of her, loosely framing her arms and cheering internally when she doesn't shrug off my touch. "Let's just stick to the basics. The more honest we are, the easier this will be."

Geneva rolls her lips, the slightest hint of uncertainty tracing her brow. "Thank you for going along with this. I know you didn't want to, and—"

"It's okay." I ignore how she shivers slightly when my thumb slides over her bare shoulder. "Joanna seems like a wonderful woman. I understand why you'd want to protect her feelings."

"Just for a little while."

A small smile lifts my mouth. "Just for a little while."

That's the last moment we're alone. Initially, Joanna steers us around the grassy space, making introductions. I quickly learn that Geneva had been in Vegas with Vivian, a local dress tailor, and her twin sister, Brynn, who owns Seabreeze Beans—Wilks Beach's only coffee shop. Cade, a beachside masseuse, went along too, while Summer, a pediatrician, missed the trip to attend a medical conference.

Geneva stays nearly silent as I chat up every person who congratulates us. Geneva doesn't remove her sunglasses, hiding her eyes as the sky blurs from orange to purple to deep blue.

"This explains everything," Cade, a pink-haired woman who just introduced her boyfriend, William, tells me. "We could all feel that connection between the two of you in Vegas, and now it makes perfect sense. You already knew each other!"

"I missed out on *so much* by not going to Vegas," Summer mutters to her boyfriend, Nick.

Cade brightens. "We'll have to do it again! Maybe make it a yearly girls' trip."

They erupt into animated chatter over the suggestion, but Geneva doesn't move an inch. Her rigid muscles will need an Epsom salt bath after how tight she's kept her posture tonight.

"The two of you being married is so crazy," Vivian says, leaning onto the arm of her boyfriend, Finn. "But, like, a good crazy. We should do a double date sometime."

I'm about to say that would be wonderful when a man in firefighter blues marches toward us, and impossibly, Geneva's posture stiffens even more. Brynn, who's said nothing other than to introduce herself, stops eyeing me dubiously and excuses herself.

The man's gaze follows Brynn—disappointment dotting his brow—before zeroing in on me, his jaw tight. My shoulders slide back automatically as I quickly scan the area around us. There are too many people surrounding us, but perhaps I can convince him to speak to me near the water's edge. Though we usually have uniformed officers in the ER to help us if a patient or family member becomes aggressive, I often need to diffuse things before they can get into the room.

"Noah!" Joanna trots over, the silver bangles around her wrist tinkling with the movement. "Meet your new brother-in-law, Van. Sorry he's late," she tells me. "They were out on a call. Nothing dangerous, I hope?"

"Just a medical call in Pungo," Noah answers, crushing my outstretched hand.

I give him a fierce handshake, but his hard expression doesn't drop. His arms fold over his chest, mirroring Geneva's favorite posture, but Noah's features are a duplication of Joanna's. They've got the same curly brown hair, blue eyes, and freckles.

Joanna lays a hand on her son's arm. "Isn't this wonderful? Our little family is expanding."

"Stupendous," he says, glaring at me.

The following silence is as stagnant as mosquito-egg-infested swamp water. Everyone but Joanna drops away with murmured excuses.

"Van is an ER doctor," Geneva blurts, speaking sentences for the first time since we arrived. "I bet the two of you could trade stories for hours. Right, Sugarpieface?" Her brown eyes nervously slip to Joanna before returning to mine, pleading.

Sugarpieface? I nearly choke on the chuckle trying to break free.

"Always happy to talk shop," I say, turning toward Noah with an affable smile.

"That's actually perfect." Joanna grins at me before focusing on Geneva. "Camille wanted to chat with you about organizing a mom-and-me boxing class for middle and high school girls and their mothers."

When Geneva hesitates, I lean close to whisper. "I'll be fine."

I give her my biggest smile as Joanna tugs her away.

"Alright, I think we both know you're lying," Noah says once we're alone. "There's no way you're married, so why don't you just tell me the truth. I'm going to find out anyway."

"We are married."

"Sure. And I'm a merman—just look at my shiny scales."

I sigh internally, taking another tactic. "This sure makes your mom happy."

Noah's gaze slips over the distance, finding Joanna with an eclectically dressed woman of the same age. Geneva removes her sunglasses, some of the tension in her frame softening while speaking to the wildly gesticulating woman. When the corner of her mouth quirks, a helpless exhale leaves my lips.

"Oh crap. You really like her. I thought this was some sort of insurance scheme or something."

Geneva is smart and strong-willed, unexpectedly funny, and undeniably gorgeous. I liked her when I first met her in Vegas, and that feeling hasn't diminished since.

"It's complicated, but it's not insurance fraud," I say, not taking my eyes off Geneva.

Her head turns toward me in halting degrees, almost as if she's fighting herself. When our gazes catch, an electrical spike shoots through my bloodstream. I should be used to the sensation by now, but man, it sucks the air from my lungs every time.

"This is weird," Noah says, dragging my attention back to the conversation.

"You don't know the half of it."

"No. Look." Noah points above my head, and I glance up to see a cluster of fireflies.

My brow furrows. "Lightning bugs? What's weird about that?"

"No. They're— Maybe you can't see it from your angle." Noah pulls out his phone and quickly snaps a picture of me before showing me his screen. "They don't usually do that for mainlanders."

"What in the—" I lean forward, seeing how the fireflies hover above me in a heart outline. "That's—" I glance up at the flitting insects. "Are they still doing it?"

"Yeah." He laughs, running his hand through his hair. "Honestly, you don't need the lightning bugs broadcasting your emotions when they're written all over your face."

I should probably protect my pride here, but I've never bought into that macho nonsense. Another byproduct of being raised by strong-willed women is that I'm not afraid of talking about my feelings. After having to lie through my teeth all night, it's refreshing to be given the opportunity to tell the truth. I open my mouth, but Geneva swatting violently above my head surprises me.

"This crazy island." The words are hissed through clenched teeth. "Like tonight wasn't enough of a spectacle."

"Come on," Noah goads. "Aren't newlyweds supposed to be surrounded by cosmic signs of love?"

"That's it. We're going home." Geneva grabs my hand and starts to drag me toward the road.

"Hey," I start at the same time Noah says, "You can't leave. You're the guests of honor."

"Tell everyone the guests of honor needed to get to bed." Her steps falter slightly when she realizes the alternative meaning to that sentence.

"But you still haven't told me what's going on," Noah says, voice low. "You've sworn off men, Geneva. I know this can't be something you planned."

She groans, looking skyward. "Fine. Come over tomorrow, and I'll explain everything. Just don't mention anything to your mom."

Noah hesitates a breath. "Okay."

Once we're a few blocks down the road, I ask, "Are you going to explain the light show?"

"Stupid island magic."

I didn't think it was possible for Geneva's scowl to deepen.

"Island what? I'm going to need more details."

"Not tonight, you don't."

Her jaw is so rigid I worry about her dental work, but her steady grip on my fingers hasn't decreased. I wonder if she's even aware of it. So instead of poking, instead of trying to lighten the situation with a joke, I stay silent and let my gorgeous wife hold my hand and lead me home.

SEVEN

Geneva

The sound of a deep voice yanks me from sleep, instantly putting me on alert. I jump out of bed, grabbing the baseball bat I keep tucked behind my bedroom door. It's only when I'm on the landing that my sleepy brain registers Noah's voice. It sounds like he's downstairs, clanging around in the kitchen. Relief shifts to annoyance in an instant, and I reach up to pull the heatless curlers out of my hair before I confront him. My half-brother likes to poke at my "primping habits" even though his skin could really benefit from a ten-step routine.

"So, boom, she just elbows this guy, making it look all nonchalant." Noah's voice climbs artificially high in a—frankly, offensive—imitation of me. I don't even have that high of a vocal tone for a woman. "Oh, I'm sorry. I didn't realize you were there."

Then I hear a sound that stops me in my tracks—Van's laugh. In my sleepy state, I'd forgotten that he's here.

Sleeping on my couch.

For the next *three months.*

When he chuckles again, a fizzy sensation slips to my toes. I'll never admit how much time I've spent contemplating what it is about Van's laugh that sends energy teeming through my body. The sound is deliciously low and velvety, but it also tumbles free easily, in an almost unbothered way. Like his natural state is bright smiles and effortless laughter. He definitely charmed everyone at the party last night without even trying. There's something that's so...*annoyingly genuine* about him.

"She did the same thing to me when we first met," Van says. "I was trying to keep her from getting clobbered by two drunks, and she elbowed me right in the solar plexus."

There's not a smidgen of irritation in Van's voice. If anything, there's a touch of pride. I shift my shoulders to dissipate the bloom of warmth slipping down my spine, frustrated with myself.

"That's Geneva in a nutshell—punch first, investigate later. But honestly"—by the way Noah says that one word, I can tell he's going to get all mushy—"you'll never meet a more loyal, protecti—"

"Why on earth are you two making so much noise this early?" I interrupt, stepping barefoot into the kitchen.

They're huddled around my ancient coffee maker, early morning light bending around them in an almost cheerful way—like it, too, wants in on the gossip. Noah is still wearing his uniform. I guess he decided to pop by after his 24-hour shift ended. Van has on blue scrub pants and a threadbare t-shirt, rumpled from sleep. Can't a doctor afford something that doesn't have tiny, distracting holes across the collarbones?

Though...I suppose it could be worse. He could be shirtless. The memory of what it felt like being pressed against his sun-warmed skin inundates me before I can force it away.

Van's smile vanishes as he looks at Noah. "You said she was an early riser."

My half-brother brings his mug to his wicked lips. "Sorry, man. This was too good of an opportunity to pass up. I mess with my sister any chance I can get."

"Half-sister," I amend, needing to gain some ground.

Noah rolls his eyes so dramatically he might as well be on a reality TV show. "Will you cut that out? We're siblings, plain and simple."

I make an irritated sound in my throat but don't argue. That is, until I see the empty container on the counter between them.

"And you ate all my pineapple?"

"Not all of it. There's one piece left." Noah picks up the remaining piece, extending it toward me only to pop it in his mouth.

My hands fist as I bare my teeth. It is *way* too early for his nonsense.

"It's okay. I'll get more pineapple at the market when it opens," Van offers.

"Dotty's doesn't carry pineapple, except for the one she orders and sets aside for Geneva each week," Noah says, eyes trained on me.

He's clearly trying to punish me for blindsiding him with Van's existence yesterday. Well, join the club, buddy. I'm thrown off kilter as well.

"That's fine," Van says, his gaze bouncing between the two of us like a referee wondering if a brawl will break out. "I'll drive into town and get one."

"You'll drive to the mainland," Noah corrects, breaking our stare-down to direct his attention at Van. "If you're going to be an official islander, you'll need to use our lingo. That is, if this marriage isn't a complete sham."

I sigh, pushing between them to fill a mug with coffee. I'm halfway through when Van murmurs in my ear, nearly causing me to drop the glass carafe.

"Do you mind if I explain?"

I don't glance right, don't dare see the exact hue of gray his eyes are in the morning light. It's also too early for his silky voice, for his warm, steady presence.

I give my steaming mug a tight nod, letting my feet carry me to the far countertop as Van explains our situation. Noah tries to give me judgy looks but caves when Van explains his sister's sudden passing and Joanna's response to the news.

He runs a hand through his curls. "Okay. I get it. But if this is temporary, you can't get Mom's hopes up."

"I know," I say, leaning my hip on the counter and placing my foot on the inside of my other calf. "We'll need to let her down gently. I don't think anyone will expect us to be out and about much now that we're supposed to be newlyweds, and when we're around town later, we can project *trouble in paradise* vibes. Maybe a small argument here, distant body language there."

Noah guffaws. "Geneva, you didn't touch him once last night, and that was supposed to be a wedding celebration."

I release a slow exhale. "Everyone knows I'm not...expressive. I don't think it was strange."

"It *was* strange. In fact, the over/under at Seabreeze Beans this morning is that he won't last the month." Noah tilts his chin toward Van.

I bristle, though I should be ecstatic hearing this news. Everyone else in this town sees me as I truly am—an unlovable grump. Them betting against me makes rational sense. So why does it feel like something sharp is lodged in my throat?

"You went to the coffee shop before coming here? I suppose that brushoff last night wasn't satisfying enough?" I lift my eyebrows innocently as Noah visibly stiffens.

A small voice inside tells me to stop here, but my words are already locked and ready. So I do the only thing I can think of when I'm backed into a corner—I lash out.

"He's in love with the coffee shop's owner, Brynn, even though she wants nothing to do with him."

"At least I'm trying," he says, his hand unsteady as he picks up his mug for another gulp. "That's more than I can say about a certain someone who hides behind her fists."

"Okay." Van claps his hands, efficiently disrupting our death stares. "It feels like this went off the rails."

Noah smirks. "Bickering is pretty much our status quo. You'll get used to it."

"Maybe so, but this feels like more than bickering. I don't want either of you to say something you'd regret."

My stomach twists.

Too late.

"You're really this good of a guy all the time, aren't you?" My brother settles himself against the counter, crossing one black boot over the other. "That story about you delivering twins at a music festival only to turn around and help birth a baby goat wasn't a lie?"

Van chuckles. "No. That was just a very weird night—much like last night, if I'm being honest. What was the deal with those lightning bugs?"

"She didn't tell you." Noah shakes his head. "Figures. Geneva doesn't let herself believe in fluffy stuff, like the goodness of others, baby giggles, life-long friendships—"

"Enough," I bark.

I want to smack the look of victory off Noah's face.

"Basically, there are some strange occurrences that most locals attribute to magic—the library presenting you with a book you should read, or the items you need repositioning themselves in your house, or it'll rain everywhere except right around you. That kind of stuff."

"Huh." Van rubs his jaw. "So with the lightning bugs, that wasn't some fluke?"

I'll give it to Van, he takes things in stride. I nearly had a heart attack the first time fireflies flew in shape patterns around me.

"Nope."

"Alright." He takes another sip from his mug. "Unexpected wife. Magic island. Let's roll."

Noah's smile grows ridiculously large. "I officially like you. You can stay. I mean, we've got to figure out a way for you to leave peacefully so it doesn't ruin my mom, but in the meantime, you're my new best friend."

"You already have a new best friend. And he's a billionaire," I quip, just to keep the floor from slipping from beneath my feet.

"Wait. You're kidding." Van's eyes widen.

"Technically, but he's a down-to-earth guy. He's a librarian, if you can believe it. Oh, wait, you met him last night. Finn." Noah's expression brightens, which should be impossible since the two of them in one room are like twin suns. "We should all get together sometime."

"That'd be great."

"No!" My outburst sounds ridiculous even to me, but I've never lost so much ground so quickly. I can't have Van folding into the life I've carved out here. It's the only one that's ever felt genuinely mine. "He can't because we're supposed to be laying low, remember?"

Noah shrugs. "We can hang at my place. I live in the condo tower at the end of the— Dude, you play guitar?" When my easily distracted brother takes a step toward the living room, I catch him by the shoulders.

"Nope. None of this." I forcibly push Noah toward the back door—since no one ever uses my broken front door. "Besides, you need to head home and get some sleep. Have a nice day, and we'll see you never."

Noah chuckles, allowing me to lead him outside. "Love you too, Geneva."

I grunt in response as I close him on the other side of my gate. Then I take my first deep breath when I notice I'm alone in the backyard. Now that everything isn't spiraling out of control, I let my chickens out of their coop.

"Good morning, ladies." I give each of them an affectionate pat on the head, tucking Hank beneath my arm since she loves morning cuddles as much as I do.

When I turn around to get a scoop of their layer feed, Van is standing on my small deck, two steaming mugs in hand.

"I topped you off," he tells me, coming barefoot into the yard and extending my mug.

It's only then that I notice he doesn't have coffee in his.

"What are you drinking?"

"Hot chocolate."

As much as I don't want to, I set Hank down to accept my mug. "I don't have any hot chocolate."

A soft-pink color sweeps across his cheekbones until it stains his ears. "I always carry instant packets with me since I don't drink coffee."

My heart does an involuntary pinch. How dare this man be this sweetly wholesome.

"What are you going to do with yourself while you stay here?" I ask, busying myself with scattering feed. "We can't be in each other's space all day, every day."

"Technically, I've only been in your space less than twenty-four hours."

"And it's already too much," I fire back.

"You know..." Van's introspective tone makes me glance over my shoulder. "You get this little divot between your brows when you think you've gone too far."

I should maintain my unflappable composure. After all, I just gained the upper hand, but my mouth drops open, stunned. How is it possible for Van to pick up on these little tells in such a short period of time?

"But to answer your question," he continues, oblivious to the exposed sensation slipping over my skin. "I'm not sure. I've been working non-stop since before I can remember. I'd like to get the full beach experience for a few days. Then I'll probably volunteer at the free care clinic Noah told me about on the outskirts of Virginia Beach."

That could work. With him being gone during the day and me teaching classes at night, we could harmoniously co-exist. And hopefully, that'll decrease the moments of sweet domesticity, like the one we're experiencing now. Moments like this are dangerous. I know better than most that they're fleeting. The second you get comfortable and expect someone to be there every day, they vanish.

"I'd also like to help around here—in lieu of rent since I'm still paying for my place in Nashville. I could fix the front door. Paint the siding." He puts one hand on his hip, surveying my bare-bones backyard. "Put some clover down for the girls. That's supposed to be better for chickens than grass. I looked it up last night when I couldn't sleep."

I try not to let that last thoughtful suggestion arrow through my heart. Van is just looking for ways to do his fair share. I'd do the same thing in his position.

"That would work," I say, picking up Hank again.

We'll keep things friendly and platonic. And eventually, I'll figure out some way to let Joanna down easy—since I don't want Van to be the villain of the story anymore. He doesn't deserve it.

Van smiles, a simple lift of his lips somehow brighter than the sunshine beaming down on us.

"I'll head to the mainland and get those supplies, then."

I watch him turn and climb the deck stairs, pressure building in my chest. It isn't until his hand is on the doorknob that my words burst free like steam from a hot kettle.

"I'll come with you."

EIGHT

Van

"I'm driving," Geneva tells me when she comes downstairs twenty minutes later.

I glance up from my phone and nearly swallow my tongue. Geneva's oversized gray tee partially tucked into snug black shorts is something I've seen before, but it's the first time she's kept her long hair down. Even in Vegas, she'd worn it in a sleek ponytail. Loose brunette curls tumble from beneath a Waves baseball hat, nearly touching her waist.

When Geneva looks at me expectantly, my brain struggles to come up with a response. I should make a joke that only she would buy a black version of the major league baseball team's blue-on-blue logo, but nothing comes out of my mouth. Geneva interprets my speechlessness as resistance, crossing her arms.

But before she can speak, I pop up from the couch. "Nice. I never get to be a passenger princess."

I'm rewarded with a bone-quaking scowl.

"You don't have to be so excited about everything." She tosses the comment over her shoulder, striding toward the back door.

"Does my natural exuberance for life irritate you, dear wife?" I ask once we're outside.

Geneva's sneakers stumble on the mold-stained walkway bending around the side of the house, and I bite the inside of my cheek to keep from chuckling. Once we're in her silver sedan, the console screen pops up with GPS presets. The first one is an acronym, but the second is a place called Hotties.

"Hotties? I had no idea you moonlight as a cocktail server at a biker bar," I say, touching the screen to initiate navigation.

"Don't—" Geneva reaches forward and cancels navigation. "And what if I was? Would you think less of me?"

"Not in the least," I say, settling into the seat. "Serving is hard, honest work."

She eyes me stonily before putting the car into reverse, throwing gravel as she pulls onto Sand Bend Road.

Silence slips between us as Geneva weaves through the farmland that separates the town from the larger city of Virginia Beach, where the home improvement stores are located. Rows and rows of soy-beans and corn stretch on either side of the two-lane road, butterflies flitting in the air. I'm smiling at a tiny yellow one arching over the tall stalks when Geneva's voice draws my attention.

"It's a restaurant."

"What is?"

"Hotties. They serve hot wings."

I tilt my head back with a groan. "That sounds *amazing*. I haven't had good wings in forever. Can we go after the hardware store?"

When I glance over, Geneva's gaze is fixated on my Adam's apple, and she nearly misses the next curve in the windy road. The lane-departure alert beeps as she rights the car.

"Um...sure," she says, punching her finger on the console screen so that heavy-metal music pulses through the speakers.

I glance out the window, smiling to myself. As much as Geneva might not want anything romantic to happen between us, she's undeniably attracted to me. And as a man living on crumbs and sleeping on the couch, I'll take it. I'm beginning to figure out that I'll take anything she'll give me.

An hour later, I utilize every opportunity to pester Geneva at the gigantic home improvement store. We select clover seed, a watering system, and hardware to fix her broken door before stopping in the paint department.

"I'm not painting my house pink," she tells me, assuming her favorite cross-armed position.

"Why not?" I ask, pulling down a variety of rose-colored swatches. "Wendy's house is a joyful peach, and with the yellow house beside yours, pink would be perfect."

Geneva doesn't dignify my comment with a response. She only reaches up to grab a gray color pallet.

I snatch it from her and hold it behind my back. "We can do better."

"There is no *we*," she says, reaching up to select another one.

I'm quicker, though, spreading my palm over the gray display area so she can't select another swatch.

Geneva glares. "Were you dropped on the head as a child?"

The corner of my mouth quirks. "This will be the color your house will be for at least five years, accounting for how the salt air takes a toll on paint. Really think about what you'd like."

"What if I like gray?"

I'm unprepared for the way her mouth softens, how her words are slightly uneven. I'd expected her to spar with me until the end of time. I'd been prepared to bring up the information I found online, but this question feels...earnest. When Geneva's gaze falls to her shoes, hiding her face beneath the bill of her hat, my chest caves in.

"Gray is—" I clear my throat of its grit and remove my hand from the display. "Gray can be nice."

Geneva selects four ashen swatches, surveying them with a rigid jaw. "It's a safe choice."

I want to press the issue. I want to push for why. Why doesn't she feel like she can have color in her life? Why is she limiting herself? Instead, I gesture toward the service counter.

"Why don't we get a few samples to try out?"

Back in the car, my stomach rumbles—loudly. It sounds like a thunderstorm is brewing inside me. Geneva takes one look at me and releases a long-suffering sigh.

"I'm fine," I preempt. "I can wait until we get home."

In all honesty, I'm starving. I shared a few bites of pineapple with Noah, but I'm used to a big breakfast. I didn't want to eat any more of Geneva's food without asking her, and when she came downstairs, we headed right out.

While I'd been waiting for her, I explored the downstairs. Besides the couch, there's a wall-mounted TV and...that's it. There are no wall hangings or curtains. Simple, functional blinds cover the windows, but they likely came with the house. Her dining room is empty. There's no table in the kitchen. Maybe she eats over the sink? I get the feeling that had I ventured upstairs, I'd have found it just as barren. Noah mentioned she bought the house four years ago, but it looks like she moved in yesterday.

"I'll order pickup." She slips her phone out of her sling bag and opens an app. "What sauces do you want?"

"For wings?" I sit up straighter. "Sweet chili and honey garlic please."

"Of course you only like the sugary flavors," she mutters while jabbing at the screen with punchy fingers.

I decide not to take the bait, too pumped that we're getting delicious, delicious wings. But the closer we get to the restaurant, the more Geneva's shoulders tighten.

"Why don't you stay in the car?" she says after she's pulled into a parking spot.

It's not a question. It's a command.

"I know you like to tease that I'm like a puppy, but I am not, in fact, a dog. Besides, I have to use the restroom." I open the passenger door before Geneva can protest, whistling to myself.

Geneva tucks her hat low over her eyes as we enter the restaurant, almost hiding behind me. It's a strange move from a woman who usually walks like she expects buildings to rearrange themselves out of her path.

Her fingers clutch my sleeve as she drags me past the cashiers. "Go use the bathroom. I'll grab the pick—"

"Geneva!" Two older men from the kitchen cheer when they look up from tossing wings in saucy bowls.

The teenage cashier pops an oversized gum bubble, glancing over. "Geneva's here?"

"Sweetheart, come tell Charlie that he can't mix lemon pepper and honey barbecue. It'll muddle both their flavors." A mustached man in his seventies comes out of the galley kitchen.

"Sweetheart?" I whisper, raising my eyebrows.

Geneva doesn't seem like the type to tolerate nicknames. I know I'm barely getting away with *darlin'*, chalking my tiny victory up to Southern charm.

Geneva ignores me, grabbing our sauce-stained to-go bag and looking like she's two seconds from sprinting toward the exit.

"Tell Eugene that I should be allowed more creative freedom. I'm not just the pretty face of this operation." The bald man preens, jutting out his white-bearded hairnet-covered chin.

Geneva hesitates, rolling her lips. "Eugene is right. Good to see everybody, but we're in a hurry."

"Geneva!" Another employee—a middle-aged woman with streaks of gray in her dark hair—walks in from a back room. "You're not usually here on the weekend."

"You're Norm," I say, a laugh bubbling free.

"Who's Norm?" She tugs on her brim again, even though the jig is well and thoroughly up.

"From *Cheers*. It's a sitcom from the 80s. Norm enters the bar, and everyone is excited to see him. Just like this." I gesture to the smiling staff.

Her eyes narrow. "Aren't you younger than me? How are you versed in 80s sitcoms?"

"It's a classic," I say, brushing off her comment about our ages. Though I'm only three years younger than Geneva, I don't need to give her any more reasons to push me away—not when everything about her is inconceivably intriguing. And now this...the supposed ice queen of Wilks Beach has a hot wing fan club. Who knew?

"Why don't you stay a bit?" the middle-aged woman says, wiping a table clean with a rag. "I just made tea. I'll get you a cup before I sweeten the rest of it. Would you like some, young man?"

I can practically feel Geneva's smug smile at the *young man* comment, but I keep my gaze on the woman in front of me, grinning. "I'll take it sweet if you don't mind, ma'am."

"Oh, don't you have the nicest accent."

"Thank you kindly," I say, dipping my head.

When the woman turns back toward the kitchen, Geneva sets the bag on the clean table and pinches the back of my arm—firmly but not to the point of true pain.

"Thank you kindly? Are you kidding me right now?" she hisses in a hushed whisper.

I lower my chin, my voice quiet. "Looks like some people appreciate my good manners."

"You are a menace wrapped in pretty packaging."

"That so?" A smirk tugs on my mouth, preparing to point out that she just called me pretty.

Her eyes flare—a warning and a dare at the same time—but then Geneva rises onto her tiptoes.

The higher-functioning part of my brain knows it's to gain an advantage—to make herself taller than she already is—but all I can think about is how that simple action shatters the distance between our lips. Then the world tilts sideways when Geneva has the same realization at the exact same time. Her fingers on my triceps shift to a possessive grip as her gaze dips to my mouth. My hand flexes at my side, unsure if I should palm the back of her head, tip up the brim of her hat, or slide my thumb over her jaw—perhaps all three.

A prickling sensation runs backward from my fingertips to my shoulders as I wait. Our short history has proven that she'll probably sneer, or poke fun at my manhood, or step back and ignore me altogether.

But then—unfathomably—Geneva leans in.

NINE

Geneva

A high-pitched ringing sound pierces the air of my favorite restaurant as loud as a fire alarm. I startle, knocking Van in the forehead with the brim of my hat, before staggering back. It takes two thudding heartbeats to realize that one: I'd been leaning toward Van—*to kiss him!* Two: the piercing sound is coming from the sling bag across my chest. And three: it's my ringtone for Joanna so that I never miss her call.

I turn away, my shaking fingers nearly fumbling the phone twice. "Hello?"

"Hi, Geneva. Are you still on the mainland?"

"Uh-huh."

The barely verbal answer is all I can manage, because my heartbeat is still in my ears.

I almost kissed Van.

The thought is a bomb blast and an admonishment wrapped into a shame sandwich. Despite my best defenses, Van's needling smile keeps messing with my well-layered armor. I have no idea why he can make me yield when I've successfully kept every man away since finding out what my father did.

It'd been the wakeup call I'd needed, because prior to that, I dated men who were unreliable, self-centered, commitment averse, and emotionally unavailable. That level of betrayal forced me to come to terms with an irrefutable fact: I inherited my mother's cruddy taste in men.

So as much as Van *seems* to be the exception to the rule, I need to remind myself that rules exist for a *reason*.

"Oh, shoot. I think the call must have dropped. Geneva?" Joanna's voice brings me back to the room.

"I'm here." I clear the sawdust from my throat.

"Noah mentioned you were going to the superstore."

I pull the phone away from my ear, putting the call on speaker and tabbing over to my notes app. Since all islanders have to travel two hours round trip for supplies not available at Dotty's small market, we usually share the burden. Joanna almost never leaves Wilks Beach since I'm on the mainland so often and buy her anything she needs.

"Yes. What do you need?"

My index finger is poised to type Joanna's request for bulk cereal, a tray pack of canned soup, or six tubes of toothpaste.

"I just wanted to remind you not to buy rings at the jewelry counter."

"Rings?" I ask, tension curling at the base of my skull. "Why would I need—"

Van's hand on my upper arm, flipping me toward him, nearly makes me lose my balance.

His eyes are the size of Joanna's cherished heirloom tea saucers.

"*I lied,*" he mouths to me.

"*Lied about what?*" I mouth back.

Van gives me an exhausted eye roll. "*Everything.*"

The otherwise sweet smell of wing sauce grows acrid in my nostrils. I want nothing more than to be outside—away from Van, away from this conversation, away from this careless mistake that's upending my organized life.

Joanna continues, oblivious to our silent conversation, "Van said you two were picking up temporary silicone rings tomorrow because you didn't like any of the ones in the jewelry store in Vegas. But—" It's the way Joanna's voice changes that tightens my grip on my phone. "It would really mean a lot to me if you could wear my grandmother's ring."

"You want me to what?" I nearly choke on the words.

"Don't worry. It wasn't *my* wedding ring," she explains, mistaking the reason for my shocked response. "It's not tainted like everything else was with…"

The sentence drops off. Joanna hasn't been able to say my father's name since she learned about his duplicitous lifestyle. To be fair, I haven't called him Dad since then either. On the rare occasion I have to refer to that treacherous jerk, I call him Henry.

"Nona wouldn't give it to him. I guess she had a sixth sense about him that I dumbly ignored. Since he couldn't give me the simple antique gold band inlaid with tiny diamonds that's been in my family for generations, he bought me an ostentatiously large diamond ring instead. Of course, I had no idea about any of this until much later."

"You want me to have your family's ring?" I try, but I can't hide the wobble in my words.

Van's thumb smooths back and forth on my upper arm. I hadn't realized he was still touching me.

"Of course, honey." Joanna's voice softens. "You're family."

I have never lost it in public. I've shed a fake, tasteful tear when accepting a beauty pageant crown onstage, but I have never allowed my true emotions to show in front of others. But right now, I want nothing more than to cry like a lost, fragile thing at Joanna's unwavering inclusion.

And I am not fragile.

Even before I took my life into my hands—or rather, my fists—I was taught not to break. Winners don't bend to the relentless pressure and catty underhanded jabs of the other contestants. They tilt their flawlessly contoured cheekbones to the light, set a dazzling smile on their whitened teeth, and never let the clawing remarks of the competition faze them.

When I open my mouth to answer, nothing comes out—only my lower lip shakes.

I bite it for its insolence, frustration teeming through my bloodstream.

Van steps forward, moving close enough that if I needed to, I could lean on his sturdy chest. I should push him away. I should push all of this away. I should tell Joanna that we are dirty rotten liars, but I don't want to break her heart when she just called me family.

Family.

That word had been problematic even before I learned about my father's second household. My whole life, my mother would get angry when I wasn't the perfect daughter. If I didn't smile big enough, or say the polished polite answer, or apply eyeliner flawlessly. Over and over, she blamed me for the amount of time my father traveled for work. Had I been a better daughter, he'd want to stick around more.

Looking back on it, only seeing him one week a month should have been a tip-off, but I knew kids whose parents deployed for months at a time. My father supported us financially, paying for our house and my schooling. He was just distant—emotionally and physically.

My mother kept saying that if I won Miss USA, my father would come home to stay. Even through attending college and moving out, I aimed to win every crown I could. But after graduating, the tension between my mother and me grew. I'd breathe a sigh of relief when she didn't call back or took two days to answer a text.

At that point, contact from my father had been sparse at best. I kept striving for Miss USA, but it became something I shared with my friends who were my roommates and fellow contestants. Not everyone had great parents, but at least I had a group of women I could trust.

Once I narrowly lost the Miss Pennsylvania title—therefore blowing my chances at Miss USA—my mother announced she was moving to Florida.

"I'm going to start over. You probably should too. We spent way too long waiting for that man to choose us."

I don't know what possessed me to have a private investigator look into my father, but I never expected that he'd have a whole separate family. And when I told my mother, looking for an ally for this massive betrayal, she told me she already knew—she'd known for years.

Just when I thought things couldn't get worse, my so-called friends informed me they wouldn't renew my lease. They didn't want my 'family drama' or my losing streak to infect their perfect lives. In their eyes, I was washed up and no longer of use.

I moved out immediately and checked into a hotel, more untethered and alone than ever. It'd been a lifetime of bad days in the span of a week. Before I understood what I was doing, I found myself on Joanna's doorstep in Wilks Beach, needing to notify her of my father's deceit.

When I'd told Joanna who I was, she pulled me straight from her welcome mat into a hug, telling me she'd found out two months ago but didn't know how to find my mother and me. It'd shocked me when she whispered wet apologies into my hair on my father's behalf. The moment Joanna asked how my mother was holding up, I crumbled and told her everything.

It'd been the one and only time my sparkling veneer shattered.

In the months afterward, I built a new life here. Joanna helped me find a rental, introduced me to the town and to the half-brother I'd never known existed. For her kindness, I'll always be grateful. But I had learned my lesson. No matter how kind the people of Wilks Beach seemed, I could never fully trust them. Over the years, I honed cold stares and snappy responses into a near-perfect defense mechanism.

Until I accidentally married a stranger and everything went sideways.

I sigh, my arms suddenly leaden. My phone dips until the edge of it rests on Van's collarbone.

"You might want to get silicone rings for when you're teaching or when you're at the beach, but wait to get something more permanent for Van. That way, his ring can match yours. When you get home, I'll give it to you. Well"—a little laugh bubbles over the line—"I'll give it to Van so he can give it to you."

Her voice is practically sparkling. For the ten millionth time since she mentioned it, I chastise myself for not seeing that Joanna's light had been dimming for months. I should have noticed. I should have *done something* about it.

"Oh, and while you're there, can you get me three containers of kitty litter for Princess and Demon?"

Van's eyebrows shoot up at the names of Joanna's cats, but I'm too mentally exhausted to glare back, to tease. His expression shifts, examining me—almost as if he has x-ray vision. That must be super handy for an emergency physician. I'm sure it saves on hospital charges when the doctor assessing you can see right through you. I turn my face away a second before a broad hand settles between my shoulder blades, rubbing in a slow, steady circle. My body sways even closer to him, like the traitor it is.

"Sure. Anything else?"

"No, that's it. Oh, and also, I want you two to come over for dinner. I didn't get the chance to hear the story of your wedding since it was so busy at the party."

A sinking sensation tugs low in my stomach. It feels like two rusted-out trucks are chained to my ankles, and someone just threw me off a pier.

"Sure," I manage. "We'd—"

"Joanna, hey. It's Van. You're on speaker. As much as I'd love to get to know you better, would it be okay if we moved dinner to later in the week? Maybe Friday?" The entire time he speaks, Van never takes his careful gaze off me. "I'll happily drop off the kitty litter later today, but we'd love some time together."

"Oh. Of course." Joanna's chuckle bursts through the line. "It's technically your honeymoon, after all."

"That it is, ma'am." It's baffling how Van is able to infuse bashful warmth into his words when a little knot is forming between his brows.

"Don't worry about the kitty litter. I can get it Friday."

"Much obliged, Joanna. See you then. Please be sure to let us know if we can bring anything."

After a short exchange of goodbyes, Van disconnects the call, because apparently my fingers don't work anymore. The din of the noisy restaurant is suddenly too loud. My pulse is too frantic in my ears. My entire existence zeros in on three distinct things: where Van's warm hand is still rubbing comforting circles on my back, the way his full lips look fundamentally wrong as he frowns, and how his gray eyes mirror the skies of an impending storm.

"Why'd you do that?" I ask, not pulling away. Why am I not pulling away?

The crease between his brows deepens like he's...worried? Why should Van care about me? We're essentially strangers. I'll admit that we're both attracted to each other, but that shouldn't mean...

"You..." Van pauses, almost like he's carefully considering his words. "You looked like you needed help."

It's the last hit, the one I can't come back from—him paying attention, him being there for me, him *wanting* to help me. The second I lean on someone is the moment I fall flat on my face.

"I didn't." Using the last of my self-respect, I grab the to-go bag and storm out the door.

TEN

Geneva

My hands squeeze and release the steering wheel as I drive to the superstore. *I should have said goodbye.* That's the thought that keeps circling my head like water down a drain. I should be focusing on keeping distance between Van and me, but all I can think about is how rude I was, leaving without Evelyn's tea or saying goodbye to everyone at the restaurant.

Van brought the cups to the car—one with my name written in swoopy handwriting. He likely made an excuse and smoothed over my abrupt departure, but that's not how I behave at Hotties.

It's the one place where I can be...me.

Kind of.

I'm not even sure who that is anymore.

It started off as an experiment. Because the stakes were low, I thought I'd try *not* walking through the world like a bulletproof tank. If I let my guard down and the three generations of family that ran the restaurant gave me the cold shoulder, I could always walk away. I'd never have to see any of them ever again, and I could easily pick a new place to grab food when I was on the mainland.

So I gave it a try. I wasn't the dazzling beauty queen full of the right answers. I wasn't the gruff boxing instructor who kept to herself. I was some melted version of the two of them.

I helped Raquel, Evelyn's daughter, pick out prom dresses because she'd said she liked my style. I usually came straight from volunteering at the women's shelter, wearing business clothes so the women I was teaching would see what's appropriate for interviews. When I overheard Eugene and Charlie arguing over who would win an upcoming boxing match, I chimed in. Now we talk about matches like dads at the bus stop recounting the previous night's NFL game.

I started to enjoy being there, loosening up each time. Eventually, I learned the story of the long-time best friends' dream of owning their own business and how everyone in Eugene's family worked there in some capacity. Charlie—a perpetual bachelor and flirt—ran a surprisingly effective social media campaign for someone in their seventies. His signature winking signoff even had its own hashtag—#winkysilverfoxhottie.

I still haven't figured out the exact middle ground between perfect and untouchable, but I desperately want to get it right. Especially now that after our impromptu trip to Vegas, Vivian, Brynn, Summer, and Cade expect a normal friendship from me—something I'm not sure I'm capable of anymore.

"There you go strangling things again." Van's tone is playful.

"This is all your fault," I snap and then immediately regret it. I'm being a jerk again, but all my wires are frazzled.

Out of the corner of my eye, I see him shift in his seat to face me, but I don't dare keep my eyes off the road. "What's my fault?"

"I was rude. I stormed out. I don't do that there. I'm—"

I abandon the sentence, realizing that it probably sounds like gibberish to Van. I'm always rude in front of him. It's my self-preservation bread and butter. They can't hurt you if they don't like you enough to stick around. But I can't explain that I'm *never* that way at Hotties.

"If you're worried if Evelyn was upset, she wasn't. I told her we were in a hurry. You said so yourself when we arrived."

"I'm not worried." The words come out with frosty precision, but Van lets out an unconvinced hum.

"What's going on, Gen?"

Only my husband calls me Gen.

I nearly snarl at my brain's annoying reminder. Why does it keep telling me that at the worst possible times?

"Pull over."

I've never heard Van be so direct, commanding. Is this his doctor voice? The one he uses to shout "Get me ten cc's of propofol!" or "Clear!" like they do on those medical shows.

He points to a small city park just ahead. "Pull over there."

"But—"

"Geneva Cecila Bradford, so help me—"

I cut off his impending tirade by jerking the car into the one of the slanted parking spots beside the fenced-off dog park.

Van makes an approving sound in his throat as I shift into park. Then he bolts from the car, jaw tight as he crosses in front. I have the fleeting thought to throw the car in reverse and leave him behind, but he left his door open.

I expect another command when my door is swung open, and this time, I'm prepared to fight. I really hate being told what to do. I spent way too much of my life following my mother's orders and haven't let anyone boss me around since I carved out my own life in Wilks Beach.

But Van's fingers smooth over my clenched ones, still strangling the steering wheel. "Let's just take a minute to eat. Nothing makes sense when you're hungry."

I don't move, not an inch. I'm pretty sure I don't breathe.

"Come on, darlin'."

It's the darlin' that gets me. Darn him and this effective Southern charm—though I'd *never* let Van have the satisfaction of knowing that.

My shoulders fall from my ears in helpless surrender as I shift to unbuckle my seatbelt. I hate this too—conceding—but Van's murmured words of encouragement as I pick up the to-go bag soften the blow. He stoops into the car to grab our teas and turn off the ignition. I hadn't even noticed I left it on. My brow furrows because I'm never anything if not meticulously careful about *everything*. But before I can question it further, a strong hand at the base of my spine leads me to a picnic table.

It's too hot for a midday picnic, but the table is shaded on one side by a mature magnolia. Van places my drink in the shade and silently portions out our food, setting my mango-habanero and atomic paper boxes in front of me. When he digs in, unabashedly enjoying his wings, I open my boxes. The delicious scent of spices tickles my nose, and my mouth waters. I guess I'm hungrier than I thought.

The wing sauce burns my tongue, and it's a welcome sensation—something expected, predictable. Because the last two days with Van are confusing. My brain shakes off its foggy state, reminding me I need to set strong boundaries with Van. The last thing I need is to open up to someone who's leaving in a few weeks.

"We have to stop doing this."

"Having wings?" Van asks, a smear of orange across his right cheek. It's dangerously close to slipping into the dimple that's winking at me.

I abandon my previous train of thought, tossing him a napkin. "You've got a little something." I point to my right cheek.

Instead of picking up the napkin, Van swipes his wing across his forehead, leaving a messy sauce trail. "Where?"

I blink, and it takes several seconds to recognize the sound coming from me as laughter. When my abs squeeze to the point of pain, I have to admit that I'm not just laughing, I'm cackling. Unattractive, noisy guffaws escape my body without respect for my mind's futile signals to stop. *It's not even that funny*, my brain protests. *A toddler can smear sauce on their face.* But controlling the chuckles tumbling from my body is a lost cause.

Van simply sets his chin on his palm, his smile soft. There's no way for him to know that I don't do this with anyone—not Noah, not Joanna, not my fledgling friends. Though, I guess Cade pulled a surprised laugh from me *once*, but that's because her chaos is—at times—genuinely entertaining.

When Van casually dots his nose with a wing, a mirthful snort shoots out of me.

"Knock it off," I say, appalled by the sound I just made.

Van gives me that dimpled smile. "I could play dumb here and say I don't know what you're talking about, but I think we both know I'm irresistible."

I groan. "There's nothing worse than a cocky man."

"I agree," Van says. "But I'm not being cocky. I'm being confi-dent—confident in my abilities to make even the surliest version of you smile." He pauses, his grin shifting into devious territory. "Or to convince you to like pink again."

Alarm bells ping in my skull, but I give him my best *You're insane* glare. I thought we dropped this topic when I walked out of the hardware store with two gray sample cans.

"I've never liked pink."

"Come now. We both know that's a lie." The way he leans back, blatant satisfaction rolling off his shoulders makes mine tense. "You weren't the only one that did a little internet sleuthing. Granted, mine wasn't as official as yours, but I have it on good authority that tween Gen often chose pink as her favorite dress color when competing. In one interview, you even called it your lucky color."

I should have thought of this. I should have accounted for the thousands of videos and photos of me from a lifetime of being in front of audiences.

"You," he says with the smugness of someone who solves the world's trickiest crimes, "like pink. You don't even have to admit it, because I already know." Van uses the edge of his last wing to tap against his temple, leaving even more sauce on his face.

I pick up the napkins and throw them at his chest. "Clean yourself up. You're a disgrace."

"Disgrace?" His eyebrows wrinkle adorably. "That's weak sauce. I know you can do better."

My head tilts with a small smirk. "I'll never forget the first time we met, but I'll keep trying."

"Not bad." His eyes practically twinkle.

Van leans over to steal a wing, but I tug my box away before his fingers dip into it. "You can't handle this heat."

All the jokey mischief drains from his face as he pins with me with a focused gaze. "How about you let me decide what I can handle?"

A shaky breath rattles free, but I keep my chin up, extending my wing box to him with a nonchalance I don't feel.

Everything is too intense as Van slowly brings the wing to his lips. The sunlight is too bright, somehow sharp as it cuts across his chiseled cheekbones. The children at the nearby park seem to screech instead of giggle. Each dog bark, passing car, and chirping bird grates on my nerves, because I know how this will go—how it's always gone.

Van takes a bite, and to his credit, he barely flinches as he chews. He's even able to grin a bit with a semi-convincing hum of approval.

His watering eyes give him away, though.

When an unintentional tear slides down his cheek, my hand fists under the table. "Just admit you don't like it. You like sweet and fun and easy, like everyone else."

His steady gaze never leaves mine as he takes another bite, chewing before answering. "I like sweet things and having fun, but..." The corner of his mouth quirks, almost imperceptibly. "I've never liked easy. Easy is boring. Anyone can do easy. I need"—that slight tug morphs into a wicked grin that I feel down to the soles of my feet—"I need a challenge."

We both know we're not talking about Scoville units anymore.

I'm the first to break eye contact, which I immediately regret. I should have fought harder, stayed strong, but I can't think straight when it's suddenly a thousand degrees out here. I need an ice bath, and a frontal lobotomy, and a slap in the face, because I believe Van.

Which is stupid.

Haven't I learned time and again that everyone lies—*especially* men.

"Let's finish up," Van says, licking sauce off his fingers even though his eyes continue crying on their own. "We've still got to get kitty litter, pineapple, and fake wedding rings."

My appetite vanishes at the reminder of buying rings, but Van keeps chatting like he's discussing the weather.

"I'd also like to take a dip in the ocean. I've never swam in it before. Can you believe that, before today, I'd never even seen it? What a sheltered bumpkin I am."

It's bait, but I don't take it. Words of caution about rip tides, undercurrents, and wave strength bounce around my mind instead. Also, sunscreen. Van's skin isn't as naturally tanned as mine. He looks like he could burn in ten minutes. In fact, he should be the one in the shade right now. I make a mental note to pick up three bottles of SPF 70 at the store.

Van uses the napkins to clean his face, tidily putting his box and the dirty napkins back in the to-go bag. "I'll start on chores a bit later so the house doesn't heat up while I fix the door. The seed would do better if I spread and water it this evening as well."

I don't say anything as I stand up with my half-eaten box of wings or when Van stops to pet a golden labrador and chat up his owner. I don't even snap at him as he hums a melody when I leave my playlist off once we're back on the road.

All I think about is that, when Van goes to the beach later, against my better judgment, I know I'll go with him.

ELEVEN

Van

"It's okay, mister. The mermaids ain't gonna get you today." A young girl with a tumble of blonde curls stops beside me.

I've been stalled on the damp, packed sand, transfixed by the dolphins swimming down the coast.

The corner of my mouth quirks as I glance down. The girl's focus isn't on me, though. It's out at sea, surveying the waves as she shades her eyes with purple-painted nails. She can't be more than eight—nine, tops.

"What do you mean the mermaids will get me?"

"If they're swimming, you have to stay outta the water." Her blue eyes meet mine, not a drop of mirth in them.

"Why?"

"Cuz they'll drag you to a watery death."

I want to snort a laugh at her deadpan delivery, but I manage to keep my expression even. "That's a little dark, isn't it?"

The girl settles her hands over the hips of her shiny, fish scale-patterned one piece, her eyes narrowing. "Not if it saves your life. You want to stay alive, don't ya?"

"Lily, quit bothering him." A woman who looks like the grown-up version of my quirky little companion jogs up to us, carrying a two-year-old boy.

"Sorry," she says with an exasperated chuckle, brushing away blonde curls tossed wayward by the strong sea breeze. "Stranger danger is a foreign concept for this one since she already knows everyone on the island. I'm Nicole." The woman extends a hand. "You must be Van. I couldn't get a sitter to attend the party last night, but I heard it was a fun evening."

"Nice to meet you," I say, smiling as Lily bounds into the water like she's part fish. "What's this talk about mermaids?"

"Oh." Nicole laughs again. It's a light sound bouncing over the rushing of the waves. "It's something islanders tell their kids when riptides are present." She pauses, considering. "Do you know what a rip current looks like? No offense, but since you're a...um..."

"Mainlander?" I offer with a chuckle.

Her smile is a bit bashful. "Yeah. Hopefully, people aren't giving you too hard of a time. We're trying to turn a leaf around here, but old habits die hard."

"Actually, it's been—"

"Hey, snugglebear. I'm ready to get into the water if you are." Geneva's fingers grip my bicep as she sends the fakest smile I've ever seen toward Nicole. "Sorry to steal him away, but it's technically our honeymoon staycation," she stage-whispers with a wink.

Snugglebear? And Geneva winks at people? What in the—

"Oh, of course." Nicole smiles at us both before wadding into the water after her daughter. "No better place for it."

Geneva drags me twenty feet down the beach before letting go. "You're welcome."

"For what?" I say through a laugh. "Saving me from polite conversation? I was two seconds from learning what a riptide looks like. Apparently, having that knowledge will keep me from a watery grave, but you'd probably prefer I remain clueless. It'd save you the trouble of divorce."

Geneva rolls her eyes at me. "Please. I wouldn't have let you near the shore if there was a riptide present. And that wasn't polite conversation. Nicole was flirting with you because you're new meat."

My brain wants to take a few seconds to process the protective first part of Geneva's statement, but the latter is *far more* interesting. There's no way that my reluctant wife is jealous, is there?

"New meat?"

She levels me with a flat look. "It's a small town. News travels fast, and then all the singles come out of the woodwork to shoot their shot. It's embarrassing to watch." Her gaze shifts over my shoulder, shooting daggers at Nicole even though she's innocently playing with her kids. "You should have seen the way Amanda threw herself at Finn before—"

My cheeks hurt. My grin has got to be obnoxious. Megawatt. Of seismic proportions. Put me on a red carpet and let me smile for the flashbulbs because Geneva *actually is* jealous.

"What?" Her arms cross over the gray long-sleeve rash guard covering everything but her black bikini bottoms. "Why are you smiling like that?"

"We're married." I lift my left hand, wiggling my silicone ring.

A matching one rests on Geneva's finger. I'm not going to lie. I feel some kind of way, having a ring on this particular finger, but I'll sort those feelings out later. Right now, I want to get to the bottom of Geneva's unexpected jealousy and then take my first swim in the ocean. Though I've never been in the sea before, I'm familiar with the lakes and rivers surrounding Nashville.

"Nicole was just chatting to be nice. In fact, she told me she was sorry she missed our *wedding* party last night."

Geneva says nothing, just stares at the cotton ball clouds dotting the horizon, a muscle in her jaw flexing.

"You know what," I say, stepping close. "If you're worried about someone stealing your man—"

"You're not my man," she snaps, her fiery gaze returning to me.

I continue, undeterred. "Then we should act like this *really is* our honeymoon."

My fingers slide over her ribs as I inch even closer. Geneva's defiant chin juts up, never breaking eye contact.

"People are watching." A ghost of a smile lifts my lips. "Maybe drop your crossed arms?"

She huffs but releases her grip until her hands are at her sides.

"You could touch me, you know. Maybe set an affectionate palm over my heart like you did yesterday?" It's a struggle to keep the flirty grin off my mouth.

Her head tilts slightly, the end of her long ponytail slipping in front of her shoulder. "I could knee you in the groin."

I laugh, shaking my head. There's nothing I enjoy more than sparring with this woman. Actually, I don't remember the last time I had this much fun just talking. Even running errands earlier had been near blissful, and we'd simply picked up kitty litter and pineapple.

"I don't think you'll do that."

"Oh, no?" It's Geneva's turn to smile.

I take my time drifting forward, moving until my lips are a hair's breadth from the shell of her ear. It allows me to see her pulse thrumming on the side of her neck, how her lashes flutter with my close proximity, how her hands flex at her sides.

"No, darlin'. You won't."

"You—" She clears her throat. "You have to stop doing that."

"Doing what?" My lips hover beside her temple but don't make contact.

Geneva sucks in a sharp breath. "You know."

I lean back to catch her gaze and memorize everything about this moment—the high-pitched chirps of the sandpipers shuffling nearby, the comforting warmth of the sun on my back, the way the ocean breeze plays with the dark brunette strands of her hair. But it's the softness in Geneva's expression that I'll see when I close my eyes tonight. It's so hopeful while simultaneously wary, making my chest contort.

One hand releases her side, and I slide my fingers down her forearm until my index finger hooks with hers. "I'm not doing half of what I'd like to."

My focus drifts to her lips—just for a second.

Geneva sways ever so slightly forward before her shoulders tense and her finger releases mine.

Internally, I sigh. *One step forward, two steps back.*

But that's okay. I've got nothing but time. Three months of it, in fact. I don't want to exist in a world where I kiss Geneva Bradford and she isn't one hundred and ten percent certain she wants me to.

"I also want to do this," I say with a smirk.

Using my now free hand, I sweep Geneva's legs from under her, completely ignoring her protests and half-hearted pounds to my back while I run into waist-deep water and toss her over the next wave.

"I can't believe you—" Her words cut off with a growl as she lurches toward me, slinging her arms around my neck in an attempt to dunk me.

A laugh tumbles out of me before she hooks my leg and we both end up under the next crashing wave.

"Truce!" I shout as soon as we both surface.

"Not on your life."

This time, she jumps on my back, and I end up laughing at how much effort it requires to fling her into the water. I succeed, though—eventually.

It continues like that, back and forth, until a lifeguard whistles at us.

"You got us in trouble," I tell her, chuckling as we walk to shore.

"Me? This was all you." She's not grimacing, though.

Geneva's not snarling or glaring or scoffing. She's *smiling*. And though I love the devious little grin she gives me when she thinks she has the upper hand, I love this wild, carefree version of her even more.

"Look." I point at a red line on my left bicep with an exaggerated lip pout. "You scratched me."

"Serves you right," she mutters, brushing back her disheveled ponytail. The hair elastic should get a medal for fortitude—it's barely hanging on.

"Let me help you." I stop her with a palm to her upper arm in knee-deep water. "You look like a drowned opossum."

Geneva opens her mouth to protest, but when I gently tug at the elastic just above her shoulder, her lips snap shut. We're too close again. I know it. She'll push back any second, but I focus on loosening the tangled strands of hair that wind around the elastic and not on the single freckle on her heaving collarbones. Once successful, I can't help myself. I fan the silken strands around her shoulders, taking a deep breath before stepping back.

"There." I hold the elastic in my upturned palm.

The rhythmic rush of water around us has nothing on the pounding of my erratic heart.

Geneva's fingertips tremble as she slowly picks it up. The hair elastic hovers in midair for a breath before her brows pinch, her hand fists the band, and she pushes past me toward our towels.

Anyone else would be discouraged, but I hum a Raven Sacaria song as I stroll toward our spot in the sand, practically beaming.

I hadn't been joking earlier.

If there's one thing I truly enjoy, it's a challenge.

TWELVE

Geneva

"**S**o, you're married—but not really?" Brynn asks me a week later, barely winded, though we're keeping a breakneck pace as we race past the cornfields lining the road beyond Wilks Beach.

I exercise daily—sometimes twice a day—and used running as upkeep during my pageant days, but I'm struggling to keep Brynn's pace. Of course, I wasn't a D1 track athlete. Mother wouldn't allow it. There was no time for team sports or school friends—only pageants and pageant-related activities.

"It's a legal technicality that should be swept under the rug, but Van's going through some things," I hedge, not wanting to disclose the delicacies of his emotional state—even to Brynn.

That feels…disloyal. Like it'd be violating the tremulous trust forming between us.

The only reason I'm telling Brynn the truth is because Van has Noah to confide in. They've been hanging out when they're both free. I know I could—in theory—talk to my brother as well, but we never have.

Of course, I've never really talked to Brynn either. But of the women I went to Vegas with, Brynn is most like me. Logical. Practical. I'm assuming she'll understand my viewpoint more than romance-obsessed Vivian or boyfriend-committed Summer and Cade.

Brynn is single, like me.

I know I'm not *technically* single, but close enough.

Normally, I'd have no issue working through my problems by myself, but I never accounted for how having Van in my space would rattle me.

He's always doing something. The only time he takes a break is when his mother calls to catch up. At first, I thought he'd spend the rest of the week relaxing at the beach, and we'd keep to our separate schedules, but he's taken on his half of the housing bargain like I'll evict him at the slightest infraction.

On Monday, he borrowed someone's power washer and cleaned the siding, the front walkway, and the backyard deck. Tuesday, while I'd been volunteering, he set up an outdoor area rug, table, and chairs on the deck, and strung globe lights around the perimeter of the yard.

Wednesday, he tackled the front door before I kicked him out of the house. He came back a few hours later after learning to surf with Nick, Summer's boyfriend, jubilant and a little sunburnt. I should have escaped to my room but ended up hovering in the kitchen as he recounted his many failed attempts to get on his board, trying not to laugh.

Early Thursday morning, I thought I heard him rummaging around the kitchen, probably trying to fix my slightly uneven cabinet doors, but he'd been in the middle of a bodyweight workout. His bare feet had been on the stair overhang while he did inverted pushups in only his scrub pants. I might have monitored his form for a few reps—in a purely professional way—before I crept back to my bedroom. Later that day, when I returned from volunteering, there was a hand-me-down table for two with mismatched wooden chairs in the kitchen.

This morning, I woke up exhausted, probably from the emotional stress of having someone else in my space or from the extra workouts I've been doing to avoid said handsome person. I'd planned on lying around, but Van asked if we could take another trip to the mainland to pick out curtains. Even though he keeps his belongings tucked behind the couch, Carol Cook had been lurking around the front windows.

We somehow ended up getting a trio of baby boxwoods for the empty landscape bed that lines the front of the house and, after a twenty-minute standoff, a welcome mat. I fought Van until he found one in the back of the pile, extending it to me with a dimpled smile. It says *Go Away* in pretty, swirly script, and I love it more than I ever expected.

"Feels like a lot of trouble for a stranger." Brynn's voice brings me back to the present.

"There's also Joanna. I'm mostly doing this for her." What used to be the truth feels ashen on my tongue, but it also could be because I've been heavily mouth breathing for the past half hour. I've probably gotten half of my protein goal by accidentally ingesting bugs. "Where's the turnaround point?"

"Just ahead," Brynn tells me, impossibly picking up speed. "What does this have to do with Joanna?"

In as few words as possible, I explain the situation—mostly because I'm winded. I'm also hotter than I could've imagined. Exercising in the direct late-afternoon sunlight isn't something I've done in years, and if the sweat pouring into my shoes is any indication, I'm woefully unprepared for the elements. I don't have AC in my gym, but three industrial fans and an iced watercooler keep my patrons from passing out. That, and all my classes are in the evenings, except the two I offer on Saturday mornings.

"I get it," Brynn says, her voice softening. "I'd do anything for my family too."

Silence stretches between us for a few heartbeats before Brynn continues.

"I only wish I'd paid more attention to Vivian's happiness. I thought she was content with it being just the two of us. I thought she liked our life. I hadn't meant to hold her back. It's just...bad things happen when I deviate from my routines. Or at least they have in the past, so I thought—" She shudders, her confident footfalls stumbling for the first time since we started. "But that doesn't matter. My mental blocks shouldn't have made her feel like I wasn't on her side when she's the *most important* person in my life."

I don't know what to say.

I don't have a person like that in my life. Joanna, I suppose. And Noah. But I don't have the relationship with them like the one that Brynn has with her twin. The two of them love each other unconditionally, know and accept each other's best qualities and seedy underbellies. Meanwhile, I've been hiding behind a tough exterior, terrified that if I let Joanna or Noah see the real me, they'll reject me like everyone else did.

"Halfway."

Brynn slaps a split rail fence before leading me across the road so we're facing non-existent traffic on the way back. Not many islanders leave on Friday evenings, opting to either compete at the library's weekly bingo game or enjoy a peaceful meal at Bayside Table. Of course, I'm supposed to have dinner at Joanna's in two hours, which is why I texted Brynn in the first place.

That, and to get out of the house while Van played guitar.

It's no surprise that he's incredibly talented—genius brain and all that—but his repertoire keeps grating on my nerves. Van sings ninety-eight percent country music, which wouldn't be a problem, except they're all love songs. I'm inundated daily with lyrics about how much the songwriter loves the woman in his life, how dedicated he is to their family.

Yeah right. What a bunch of lies.

None of that is real. I know because my favorite pastime before Van occupied my living room was to watch the entertainment news show *Celebrity Circuit.* On that show, I've seen singer after singer get divorced because they've had an affair, DM'ed some underage fan, or were caught on hotel security footage with a leggy concierge.

"If it helps," Brynn adds, "I did some research as soon as Carol came running into the shop, telling me you two were married. As far as mainlanders go, Van seems like a really good guy."

I already know this from my own report, but Brynn doesn't need to know about the depths of my distrust.

"I'm not worried about him dismembering me in my sleep. My concern is how hard this will be on Joanna when it all falls apart." And *it will* fall apart. "She...she wants to give me her grandmother's wedding ring at dinner tonight."

Brynn is silent for a beat. The only sound is the layered chirping of crickets, the pounding of our feet on the pavement, and the exhausted thudding of blood in my ears.

"That sounds very permanent for a temporary situation."

"Yeah."

I glance at the black silicone ring on my sweaty hand, a mirror image of Van's—though I'm sure he would've preferred white, or yellow, or cerulean. Little gray spots swim over my fingers like unfamiliar freckles. I snap my gaze up, blinking hard. I've already drained the water I brought with me, and Brynn isn't carrying any.

"Could we slow down just a little?" I hate myself for asking, for showing weakness, but I also don't want to pass out miles outside town.

"Sure." Brynn looks me over, a furrow knitting between her brows. "Do you want to walk?"

"No. I'm good."

My brain is on fire, and my life is falling apart, but I learned early not to let anything show.

"Smile, honey. Even if you're breaking inside. They only want to see you smile."

I'm not quite sure how I manage the rest of the run, but Brynn allows me to do so in silence. By the time I stumble through my back gate, everything hurts. I whisper words of affection to my sweet hens as I quickly tuck them in for the night. Maybe after I drink my weight in water from the kitchen sink, I'll take the ice bin out of the refrigerator and dump it into a cold bath.

Van is punching numbers into the microwave when I open the back door—two, eight, then start.

"What are you doing?" My tone suggests that I caught him mutilating kittens for funsies.

"Reheating some hot chocolate. Did you have a good run?" Van turns, his smile fading as his gaze rakes me from head to toe.

I must look as disheveled as I feel. Fine. That's great, even. The sooner Van figures out he doesn't actually like my prickly personality, the sooner we can shut this whole thing down, and things can return to normal.

Because I know to keep that cataclysmic emotion at bay—hope. Every time Van shows interest in what I'm saying, or fixes something, or smiles at me for doing absolutely nothing, it surges in my chest. Then I'm forced to shove it down like overcooked meatloaf at a church potluck.

Push him away, I remind myself.

"Why didn't you use the thirty-second auto-start button like a normal person?" I ask, making sure my words are extra spiky as I fill a cup at the sink.

"I feel bad for the other numbers. They almost never get used, so I try to come up with different combinations. Next time, I'll use thirty-four." I feel his presence behind me, like he'd crossed the room while speaking, but I ignore it.

Half of the water sloshes over my shaky hand as I bring it to my lips, but that's fine because it's nice and cool. I don't know why I feel more flushed than when I was running outside. After I drain this cup, I might just put my head beneath the tap.

"You don't have to be so considerate all the time. Just use the one-push button," I say, making two attempts to turn the water back on.

Stupid hand. Why won't you work?

"Make me."

Though Van's words are an undeniable challenge, there's none of his usual teasing mirth infused in them. Some other emotion mixes with his consonants and vowels, but my brain doesn't have the capacity to determine what. Motor control is taking *way* too much effort.

As if on cue, the plastic cup slips from my hand, dropping into the sink at the same time my knees buckle.

"*Gen.*"

My name is breathed into my ear at the same second Van's arm latches around my waist, pulling me flush against him to hold me upright.

Worry, my unhelpful brain finally supplies. That's the word to describe what's infused into Van's deep, melodic voice.

But why should Van be worried?

I'm fine.

I'm always fine. I have to be.

"You're burning up." His other hand moves from my neck to my cheek to my forehead. I unwillingly lean into it because it's *soooo* cool.

"I just went on a summer run. Of course I'm hot."

Or at least that's what I mean to say, but it comes out in a nearly incoherent slur.

"We need to cool you down."

Then I'm weightless. I'm in Van's arms again, but unlike at the beach, I don't fight him. I don't have the energy to do anything other than lean my head on his shoulder as he carries me upstairs.

"What's that?" I ask, seeing a beachscape painting in a wooden frame on the upstairs landing—three seagulls float on an imaginary breeze above frothy waves.

It's another question that isn't fully articulated, sounding like garbled nonsense.

"Don't worry." Van's hands grip me tighter. "I've got you."

And that's the last thing I remember before my vision goes from gray to black.

THIRTEEN

Van

"Wake up, darlin'." I keep the tension out of my tone as I jostle Geneva in my arms so I can take her pulse.

It's strong and fast, just as I expected. My mind flies through the differential diagnosis and quickly narrows it down to two. The most likely is influenza. Even though today is September first, the flu has been making an early showing this year with several pockets already in the northeast. The second, more dangerous option is heat stroke hyperthermia—a medical emergency. Reminding myself that the fire station, with all its EMS supplies is mere blocks away, I gently set Geneva on the tile floor of the bathroom so she's leaning against her tub.

"Gen." I run the tap cold before kneeling and framing her sweaty face with my palms. "I need you to fight with me."

Her eyes flutter open. "What if I didn't like seascape paintings?"

Unlike the last two times she spoke, her words are clear and biting.

"There she is." A smile lifts my lips as relief douses every cell in my body.

Her finger comes up to poke me in the cheek. "Don't dimple-smile at me. This is a serious matter. What if I don't like comfy patio furniture? Or geometric outdoor rugs? Why do you keep making my house nice?"

"You saying I'm making things nice undermines your argument, dearest," I tell her, quickly removing her shoes and socks.

She grumbles at the endearment. "You're the worst, you know that?"

"I am. I'm a complete monster." I pause, making sure I catch her gaze before continuing. "I need to get my supply bag from downstairs. Can I trust you not to pass out? Or do you want to lie down?"

I try not to 'dimple-smile' at the flat look and dismissive wrist flick Geneva gives me, but it's impossible.

A handful of seconds later, I'm back with the medical bag I keep in my truck when I'm not working and my phone—just in case I'm wrong. And I really, really hope I'm not wrong.

Geneva is right where I left her, an unamused expression on her gorgeous—albeit flushed—face.

Good. She can scowl at me all she'd like as long as she stays awake.

"Can I get in the tub now?"

The wistful way Geneva gazes at the water sends a strange emotion tumbling through my bloodstream. Logically, I know I should be completing my assessment first, but for a woman who asks for nothing, I don't want to say no.

In the emergency department, to treat heat stroke, we'd dunk her in an ice bath or run cooled saline through her veins to rapidly cool her core body temperature. A ticking clock pings at my temple, but I acquiesce.

"Only if you take this off." I tug at the hem of her sodden tank. "I know that sounds like a move, but the less clothes the better. Everything else you can keep on, but I want as much of your skin in contact with the water."

Surprisingly, Geneva lifts her arms. She does so while giving me the death glare of the century, but she complies. Then she makes a blissful sound that's slightly distracting as I help her into the cool water. I dig in my bag, tossing my stethoscope on the ground before I find the temporal artery thermometer I bought during my pediatric rotation.

"Just let me..."

I cradle the back of her head with one hand and run the device over her forehead with the other. I expect Geneva to grimace at having her temperature taken, but her dark eyelashes flutter closed, almost helplessly. When her brow smooths peacefully, I set the device aside. The result on the digital screen reads 101°F, meaning Geneva doesn't have heat stroke—thank goodness.

My mouth opens to tell her, but instead, I dampen a wash-cloth and gently clean her forehead, her cheeks. The sound she makes in her throat—soft, vulnerable—sends goosebumps shooting over my skin, almost breaking me. Based on what I know about Geneva's history, it's probably been years since someone looked after her like this.

"Gen." I don't think I've ever heard my voice more ragged, tortured.

She turns her face away, lashes squeezed shut like she's in pain. "Do I need to go to the hospital?"

"No. But can you tell me how you're feeling? Is anything hurting? Pain in your stomach? Shortness of breath?"

Her mouth opens and closes twice before she mutters, "I'm fine."

"Don't lie to me." I say it too gruffly but don't regret it. I need to know what I'm dealing with.

Her shoulders sag in unmistakable surrender. "Everything hurts. I woke up achy and sore, but I figured it was just from hitting the bag extra hard this week."

"Okay." That's consistent with flu, especially this strain that has more head and body aches and less upper respiratory symp-toms. "What about a headache?"

Geneva nods, but it's not her defiant chin bob. It's a small, de-feated movement that makes my chest squeeze. "My hair hurts."

I understand what she means. My sister's scalp used to ache every time she got the flu growing up. The memory of sitting on our lumpy couch, Disney movies playing while we slurped popsicles, jabs me like a searing poker, and I quickly force it away.

"Alright, this is what we're going to do. Let's take your hair down." My hands are already working the elastic from her damp ponytail as Geneva draws her knees to her chest. "Then let's get you dry and cool and give you some antipyretics."

"Some what?" Her brow is smooth again, lashes closed as she rests her cheek on her knee.

The corner of my mouth lifts. "Tylenol. Ibuprofen. Medicines that reduce fever and will also take away some of the pain. You've likely got the early strain of flu that's circling around. Now, lean back for me. I'm going to rinse out your hair."

Geneva doesn't move, just opens her eyes. My heart rate ticks up at her soft yet assessing expression, and I can't not touch her. With the elastic free, I run one thumb over her temple and down her cheek to the corner of her jaw.

"I know I've changed a lot, asked a lot of you," I say, threading my fingers through her sweat-damp hair. "But can you let me take care of you? Just this once."

She's silent for so long I'm certain she'll refuse. The clicking on of the AC, the slight drip of the faucet, and the blood rushing in my ears is my only company.

"I'm tired."

"I know, darlin'." It takes all my willpower not to kiss her temple. "We'll get you in bed soon. Lie back, okay?"

Geneva's surprisingly pliant as I rinse her hair in the cool water, but she kicks me out of the bathroom so she can dry herself and change into a lightweight sleep set. I busy myself by pulling the comforter off her bed, turning her ceiling fan on high, and closing her blinds. When she opens the bathroom door to find me sitting beside her bed in a kitchen chair, she grimaces.

"What are you doing with that?"

"Knitting a sweater."

"*Van.*" My name is a growl, and it makes me impossibly happy. "I'm not some dainty Victorian lady convalescing. You don't need to sit at my bedside."

"You said you'd let me take care of you this once."

Her arms cross. "I technically didn't say—"

"We need to cancel dinner with Joanna. Do you want me to call her?" I cross one ankle over my knee, leaning back like the hard wooden chair is the most comfortable thing I've ever sat in.

Geneva reaches for her phone on the bedside table as she crawls beneath the sheet. "I can do it."

I can't help performing a visual assessment while she speaks to Joanna. Already, Geneva looks better. The sweating has decreased, and her color has returned to normal. Geneva refuses Joanna's offer of soup and to activate the Wilks Beach emergency text chain.

"But could you let people know that the flu is here and to take care of themselves?" she asks Joanna. "I'd hate to get anyone sick."

Geneva listens for a long time before saying, "No. No. I've got my handsome doctor husband to take care of me, after all."

A smirk settles over my mouth as she ends the call. "You think I'm handsome."

"I had to sell it, or she'd come over and get herself sick. Speaking of which, shouldn't you be wearing a mask or something?"

My hand splays over my chest. "Does this mean you care?"

"Never mind." She taps on her phone. "I need to call Brynn and let her know to watch out for symptoms."

A few minutes later, her head drops back on the pillows after she hangs up. "Vivian will be over with a tater tot-based casserole in an hour and a half."

"Sounds scrumptious." A wide grin splits my face.

Geneva scrubs her hands over her cheeks with a groan. "Why will no one listen to me?"

"Probably because you're an unreasonable grump." I settle my hands behind my head, smirking. "If you'd allow people to be nice to you, this would all be easier."

"But I don't pay into the system." She's strangling her phone again. "I don't make meals, because no one wants to eat dressing-free spinach salads, plain Greek yogurt, and grilled fish fillets. Heck, I don't want to eat it half of the time."

It's hard to miss Geneva's regimented diet. When I sauteed veggies in butter, she pushed them away like I'd dunked them in battery acid. I'm all for healthy eating, but there should be enjoyment too—at least occasionally.

"While I'm here, I'll teach you to make a few sharable staples—lasagna, veggie chili, shepherd's pie. Then you won't feel bad when you occasionally need to lean on your neighbors."

With a sigh, Geneva flops her hands wide on the mattress, pushing her phone away before closing her eyes. Long minutes pass as her breathing evens out. I pick up her phone, click it to silent, and set it back on the bedside table.

I try not to stare. I really do, but I have a former beauty queen resting before me. The slivers of evening light slip between the inefficient blinds, highlighting her cheekbones, her dark hair, her soft brows. I reposition the chair as quietly as I can until my shoulders are blocking the light. Geneva turns toward me then, stacking her hands beneath her cheek like a cherub.

She's sleeping so serenely that it makes sudden, unexpected fury sprint through my body. Geneva should get to be this relaxed all the time. I want to find her father, her mother, anyone who harmed her, anyone who made Geneva feel like she needs to guard this fiercely against the world and...and what?

Challenge them to a duel? Knock out their front teeth?

I'm not a fighter. I've never hit another person in my life, except for the one time I lashed out at Taylor when I was five, and Mama made me kneel on grits. I'm more comfortable either preventing the fight or doing the repair job afterward. Putting bones back together and stitching up wounds makes sense to me. Destruction doesn't.

The light fades while Geneva dozes, and plans run through my mind. I might have only a few short months with Geneva, and it's highly likely that she'll never like me the way I already like her, but if I can leave Geneva's life better than I found it, I'd be happy.

"I'm going to help you like pink again."

It's a nearly inaudible murmur but it's also a promise.

FOURTEEN

Geneva

I wake at different intervals throughout the night. Two times, it's from Van taking my temperature and giving me more medicine. Another time, I nearly trip over his long, extended legs on the way to the bathroom since he insists on sleeping in that impossibly small kitchen chair. A third time, I discover that Van snores—just slightly. It should be annoying, but the soft sound reminds me of the ocean waves beyond my window.

When I finally rise for the day, it's after ten, and the chair is empty. The drop of disappointment in my stomach nearly makes me want to punch myself there. I shouldn't *want* to see his dimpled grin first thing.

Rising in slow degrees, I take my time drinking the cold glass of water at my bedside table before padding into the bathroom to brush my teeth.

"Hey, sleepyhead."

Van peeks into the bathroom as I'm spitting out toothpaste, startling me and sending the foam flying, dotting the mirror.

"Oops." Van laughs, using the hand towel to clean the glass.

"Stop. That's covered in germs." I yank the towel from him. "You shouldn't even be near me. You're going to get sick."

His shoulder rests against the door jamb, making my small bathroom feel even smaller. "I don't think you understand how irresistible you are. It's physically impossible for me not to want to be around you."

Now that I'm receiving his dimpled smile, I decide I don't want it anymore.

"Go away."

Van waits a beat, his grin growing larger by some unknown bending of the laws of physics. "I'm making breakfast. Scrambled egg whites, asparagus, mushrooms, and sundried tomatoes. No butter hath touched the pan. Cooking spray only. Oh, and a side of pineapple."

I want to say no on principle, even though that sounds heavenly and I'm famished. My molars grind together, but my stomach rumbles like the traitor it is.

A single blond brow raises in challenge.

"Fine." I should be saying *Thank you. That sounds lovely. Will you marry me? Oh, that's right, you already did*, like a civilized person, instead of grunting single words like a Neanderthal.

"I also let the girls out earlier—fed and watered them. The clover is starting to germinate, so that's exciting."

"Riveting," I say, fishing my brush out of the drawer.

I roughly run it through my usually straight hair, and it snags on a tangle behind my head. My eyes close as I wince, pain shooting through my scalp.

"Easy." Van moves forward until he's right behind me. "Everything is still sore, remember? You'll probably hurt today and tomorrow. In an hour, it'll be time to give you more medicine."

His fingers loosen the brush from my hands before Van works at the tangle with searing gentleness. My eyes water, but not because of pain.

"Stop."

At my cracked request, Van's eyes find mine in the mirror. "This hurts?"

I tuck my lower lip between my teeth, shaking my head no.

His focus drops to the tangle, working again. When he speaks, his voice is a low rumble—warm and unfairly comforting. "It's okay, accepting help every once in a while."

And what happens when that help leaves?

That's the question I want to ask, but it's trapped in my too-tight throat. Instead, I close my eyes and let Van work out the tangles in my hair, trying not to think about how this is the first time anyone has brushed my hair because they wanted to. All the other times, it was to be evaluated by a judge.

Van's hands give my shoulders a quick squeeze. "Breakfast time."

Then, because he's a good man, he leaves me alone to collect myself before I walk downstairs.

Breakfast is delicious, and after a quick check on Hank because she's needy in the morning, I retreat to the couch and pick up the remote without thinking. I tab over to *Celebrity Circuit* and push play, not considering that Van is washing dishes in the adjacent room or that I'm technically germing up his bed. It's not until I hear him humming the catchy introduction song that I realize what I've done.

"Shoot." I turn off the TV, and for some unknown reason—probably because I have the flu and am not thinking straight—I throw the remote into the stairwell like it's the hottest potato. Fortunately, it thuds on my carpeted stairs and doesn't shatter.

"What happened to the show?" Van arrives in the archway between the living room and the kitchen, sudsy pan and soapy sponge in his hands.

"I don't know what you're talking about." And then I proceed to tug at my sweater and reposition my hands from my lap to my shoulders to crossed like a person who's unfamiliar with how fingers work.

The grin on Van's face can only be described as delighted. "Are you ashamed of watching *Celebrity Circuit*? Of course you are," he answers before I can say anything. "You're Geneva, strongest woman alive. You subsist on sunlight and Hank snuggles alone. *Heaven forbid* you enjoy yourself every once in a while."

He rushes to put the dishes in the sink, turn off the water, and plop next to me. "Where's the remote?"

I point to the stairs with one hand while burying my face in the other.

A burst of bright laughter fills my small living room, almost making my head hurt again.

"Oh, Gen."

The words are so affectionate I almost look up. Almost. I focus on staying motionless until I feel his weight dip the couch beside me. Even then, I keep my eyes screwed shut. It's not until Tasha Frazier's voice announces the rundown of top stories over a B-roll of video recaps that I blink one eye open. Van isn't looking at me, though. He's watching the screen, genuinely enraptured.

"I knew Gregory James was going to bow out of his last concert dates. That man is having a thyroid crisis if I ever saw one. I even emailed his team to check his TSH since the goiter was visible from—"

Van cuts off when Tasha reports the singer's dangerous hyperthyroidism and recent hospitalization.

"See!" He's practically giddy. "Oh, they broke up," Van comments as the recap moves on to two starlets splitting after five years of marriage. "I really thought they had what it took to go the distance."

"Who even are you?" I ask, leaning away.

A laugh escapes him. "What? A man can't enjoy a little celebrity gossip? Do I need to do one-handed pushups to prove my manhood now?"

Then Van vaults from the couch and proceeds to pump himself away from the floor, left hand behind his back, bare toes gripping the hardwood, counting back from one hundred.

"Stop," I say, but it comes out more like a chuckle.

"Can't stop. I need the levels of testosterone in my body to recalibrate." He flashes me that infuriating smile. "Ninety-one. Ninety. Eighty-nine."

"Van, stop." It's not until the words tumble out of my mouth that I realize I'm laughing.

He doesn't cease, though, just continues counting like the goofball he is. My stomach hurts, and my head hurts, and all my muscles hurt from the unexpected joy rippling through me.

"I'm serious." The words barely squeak out of me, rimmed with mirth.

"Oh, I can tell." At least he has the decency to sound a tad winded.

I turn off the show. It's the only way I can think of getting his attention. As expected, Van drops to the floor, rolls on his side, and props himself up with one arm.

"Hey. I was watching that."

"No, you weren't. Now get back over here and sit down like a normal person."

I'm unprepared for how Van's tongue darts out to touch his upper lip, how his smile melts into something hot. "Yes, ma'am."

The wave of heat sweeping my skin is definitely from my fever—*nothing* else.

I expect Van to settle himself a respectful distance away, so when he sits down next to me, taking the remote from my hand and tucking me into the crook of his shoulder, I open my mouth to protest.

"*Or*," he says first, "you could not fight me, and we could be cozy, watching this show together."

"You'll get sick." My argument sounds weak, even to me.

Van's chin is close—way too close—when he looks down and brushes a strand of hair away from my face. I've never seen him with morning scruff before. Even when Noah came over super early, he'd been clean shaven. My fingers itch to trace the line of his jaw, to discover if Van's facial hair is as coarse as it looks.

"Then let me get sick, Geneva. It'll have been worth it."

I want to disagree but feel the resistance seeping out of my muscles. Even though I slept for over twelve hours, I'm unbelievably tired. And Van is warm, and smells incredible, and something about the subtle rise and fall of his chest is lulling. I don't say anything, but my silence is answer enough. Van pulls the gray throw off the back of the couch and tucks it around me one-handed.

"Just so you know," he says into my hair as the show resumes. "I plan on planting those boxwoods shirtless this afternoon to restock my testosterone stores. I'll even dig the holes with my bare hands."

I swat him in the chest, and Van chuckles, squeezing me lightly. But afterward, I don't move my hand. His heart beats slow and even as we learn about a former child star's fall from grace.

"Shame," he murmurs.

For the first time in a long time, I try not to think. I try not to calculate every possible outcome and how eighty-six percent of them will end with my heart carved up with more precision than high-end sashimi. Instead, I let myself relax into the moment with someone who I'm just starting to know, but who feels like a memory.

FIFTEEN

Van

I end up getting the flu. But even as I lie here with a 102.1°F fever, sweat dotting my forehead and exposed chest, I don't feel a drop of remorse. Because for the last four days, Geneva let me take care of her. Not only that, but she's speaking to me in full sentences. She's smiling, occasionally laughing—albeit with a good amount of coaxing, but hey...beggars can't be choosers.

By some stroke of good luck, Brynn never ended up getting sick. Geneva assures me that civilized society would've come to a screeching halt if Seabreeze Beans closed down. Locals were, however, taking the temporary closure of Geneva's gym in stride. They were also bringing meals every night and dropping off supplies we needed since becoming unofficially quarantined.

Since we're the only ones sick on the island, it makes sense for the two of us to wait out this virus in Geneva's cottage. I'd expected Geneva to be clawing at the walls at the prospect of being shut in, but she let me feed her and get her as comfortable as possible in whatever room I had a project in.

We hung the curtains downstairs. After a bit of arguing, I convinced her to have my new friend Nick—resident surfer and construction foreman—bring us blackout curtains for her bedroom and the small upstairs guest room that's stuffed with unpacked boxes. The upstairs guest bathroom I've been using finally has a towel bar, a newly installed medicine cabinet, and a shower head that doesn't squirt water all over the walls. I never did get those boxwoods planted, but Wendy has been coming over in the morning with a watering can and freshly baked muffins.

The one thing Geneva complained about was missing the Labor Day parade yesterday. Apparently, Wilks Beach is chock full of quirky town festivals, and their anything-but-a-decoration-themed Labor Day parade is one of her favorites. Participating townspeople cover their cars in elaborate float-like displays but are prohibited from using anything that could be considered a typical decoration. We squeezed in front of the single window in the guest bedroom, barely able to see the 'floats' as they passed on Sand Bend Road.

Geneva gave me a rundown on each entrant and commented on who she thought should win. Aldon's truck—the owner of WB Renovations—was covered with orange five-gallon buckets, resembling a giant sandcastle. Camille—a middle school art teacher—used her students' painting aprons to give her sedan a colorful second skin. Judith and Bonnie—two quiltmakers who work on their creations at the library—attached various quilts to broomsticks making the car look like a porcupine who'd tumbled through a fabric store. Geneva's favorite, though, was from the Wilks Beach Garden Society who used watering hoses, plastic plant pots, empty soil bags, and rakes to create a jungle theme.

A part of me wished that we could've attended the spectacle roadside, like everyone else, but I know in my core that if we'd been surrounded by others, Geneva wouldn't have been chatty while describing the floats or borderline gleeful when each design came into view. These last few days have been a behind-the-scenes look into who Geneva really is, and like the selfish jerk I am, I don't want to share her with anyone.

At least not yet.

Early this morning, Geneva's fever broke. I would have rejoiced, but mine popped into existence overnight. But honestly, I've never been happier to have full-body chills and aches, because Geneva is letting me rest on her incredibly comfortable king bed for the moment. After having my feet dangle off the couch, this is a luxury accommodation. That, and her sheets carry the delectable scent of her sandalwood perfume. I'd never known a woman to wear such an earthy scent, but it's heady on Geneva.

"I told you you should have worn a mask," she says from the ensuite bathroom.

I close my eyes, wincing. The water splashing in the sink is entirely too loud. How does a tiny faucet sound like Niagara Falls?

Geneva lets out that long-suffering sigh as her weight dips the bed, but then a cool washcloth swaths my forehead, and all thought leaves my fiery brain.

"That is the best sensation in the world."

She hums as her fingertips tilt my face toward her to use the cloth on my cheeks. My mind automatically corrects itself. *No, you touching me is the best sensation in the world.* Her fingers are cold from the sink water, and they make me want to weep as they sift through my sweaty hair. I feel my facial muscles slack, my lips part slightly.

"For someone who's supposed to be brilliant, you're pretty stupid." The words aren't cutting, though. They're soft and accompanied by tender passes of her fingers through my hair. "This fever is going to fry your genius brain."

"My brain can handle it," I say, not opening my eyes.

She snorts, and the corner of my mouth lifts.

"There you go, being all cocky aga—"

"*Confident.* I'm confident, Geneva."

There's a long pause where my semi-melted brain assumes that Geneva decided to give me a pass on this particular tête-à-tête. I am in the throes of the flu after all.

"Gen."

The word is barely a whisper, making my eyes fly open. But Geneva is already heading back to the bathroom, running the sink before returning to the bedside with the washcloth, a glass of water, and pills.

"It's time to take more medicine. And you should probably finish that glass since you essentially waterboarded me the last few days."

My mouth quirks again as I push up on an elbow. "Encouraging fluid intake and waterboarding are two very different things."

She rolls her eyes. "Tomato. Potato."

"Even with a raging fever I know those are different vegetables."

Geneva sets her hand on her hip, that upper-handed smirk of hers returning. "You said anything under 103°F isn't that serious, but now your fever is *raging*?"

"I said..." I push up farther and then stop because the motion causes the sparse sweat on my chest to accumulate and slide down the center of my breastbone. I look down in time to see it veer left over my ribs and plop onto the sheets.

When I glance up, Geneva is staring at the damp spot, jaw tight.

"I'm sorry. I'll clean that up. Actually, let me throw these in the washing machine so you'll have clean sheets tonight." I sit up, ignoring the military band that's beating drums in my head.

Her hand on my shoulder is so blessedly cold as it stops me from sliding off the bed—cold and firm. Before I can say anything, her other hand smoothes the washcloth over my face again. I'm slightly embarrassed by the sound that leaves my throat, but surely this is what bliss feels like.

"You're not sleeping on the couch when you're this sick, so there's no reason to wash the sheets yet."

I'm not sure I heard her correctly, but it's hard to focus on anything when Geneva is pressing the washcloth to the back of my neck. My head bows forward helplessly.

"Then where—"

"Noah has an air mattress that I can borrow. I probably should have offered it to you, but I didn't think…"

I'm about to ask Geneva what she was going to say, but her fingers are in my hair again while the washcloth moves over my jaw, and all thought leaves me. I'm just an empty—incredibly sweaty—shell of a man, and Geneva can do whatever she wants with me.

"I won't be as good at this as you. I'm not a doctor. I don't…take care of people."

My heavy eyelids blink open to catch a wrinkle of worry between her brows.

"You're doing fine, darlin'."

I also want to argue that she *does* take care of people. I've seen it in the short time we've been together—with the woman in Vegas, by defending Carol, by protecting Joanna's tender feelings. Heck, Geneva took immaculate care of me that first night we met, distracting me when it felt like my life was quicksand.

Attending the Raven Sacaria concert in Vegas had nearly done me in. I'd already been avoiding the grief threatening to swallow me for months, working every extra shift I could find. When a memory of Taylor popped in my mind, I pushed it away. If I was constantly in motion, I didn't have to think about what I'd lost. But singing along with the artist my sister loved so much, I just felt…so broken.

Then Geneva had rescued me by making fun of my favorite cocktail and challenging me to dares. It'd been the only time I'd felt remotely whole in months.

Being here, keeping my word to Taylor, and fixing up Geneva's house has been a good distraction, but with fever raging in my brain, the thoughts I usually subvert come flooding in. My chin drops, and my eyes close as I think about the future my sister and I will never have.

She'd just started dating a great guy, and call me foolish, but I'd been looking forward to giving Taylor away at her wedding. After that, I planned on being the best darn uncle anyone had ever seen, so knee deep in tea parties and finger paints that her kids would beg for me to watch them.

But...that future no longer exists.

That's the hardest part of my sister's death. When an otherwise healthy person dies young, you can't use any of the well-worn platitudes to make yourself feel better. There's no *at least they lived a long, fulfilling life.* All you feel is emptiness for what will never be.

"Van?" Geneva whispers, her hands framing my face.

If I open my eyes, tears will spill from them. I'm not embarrassed of crying, but I'm pretty sure it'd make Geneva uncomfortable, and I'm already sweating all over her bed and living in her house when she didn't *want* me here.

The sigh leaving me takes all my energy with it.

"I think it's time to get some sleep."

I nod into Geneva's hands but don't say anything, just shift until I'm lying again. I know it's weak of me to keep my eyes closed, to turn away as Geneva clicks off the bathroom light, but I don't feel like I have anything left. I'm vaguely aware of cool fingertips on my back, but consciousness is getting patchy. It could very well be rivulets of air from the ceiling fan. And I'm one hundred percent certain that the soft brush of lips I feel at my temple is nothing but a dream.

SIXTEEN

Geneva

I want to call 911 twenty-seven times over the next twelve hours. When I'd been feverish, I'd still been able to sit in whatever room Van was tinkering in and occasionally throw insults at him. Van is barely able to stand when I decide to put him in a cold bath, hoping that will help like it did with me. Fortunately, I'm strong enough to bear his weight, but now I'm concerned about my ability to get him safely out of the tub.

Once Van is reclined back with his eyes closed and a washcloth over his forehead, I tell him I'll be right back and sneak into the hallway with my phone.

"I think I messed up," I say when Noah picks up my call. My fingers tug at the collar of the oversized sweatshirt I'm wearing because I have my AC turned as low as it'll go.

"Excuse me? I know you're recovering from the flu, but are you delirious? You must be to admit that. Put Van on the phone."

"I *can't*." I glance around the open doorway, catching Van's strong jawline.

Still above water. Good.

"He's worse off than me."

"Here we go," Noah groans. "*Men are babies. Women can go through twice as much pain while simultaneously nursing a newborn, making dinner, and solving world peace.*"

"No." I pause. "Well, yes, that's all true, but that's not what I'm talking about."

Noah finally catches on to my anxious tone. "What happened?"

"Nothing? His fever hasn't gotten worse, but he's weak. I have to help him with everything."

My brother chuffs. "I *bet* he's helpless. That's exactly how I'd play it if I had someone pretty to take care of me."

"He's not like you," I growl. "He's not lying or playing games. He's sick." I didn't realize that I'd yelled the last part until I hear Van's voice from the bathroom.

"Gen, what's going on?"

I put the phone to my chest and peek around the door. The washcloth dangles in Van's long fingers as his Adam's apple bobs, concern etched onto his flushed forehead.

"Nothing, snookums," I say entirely too brightly.

When Van's blond brows pinch, I lift the phone into view. That seems to make sense to him, because he leans his head back, placing the washcloth over his eyes.

"Tell Joanna I say hi and that the soup was incredible."

"Will do!"

"I hate when you use your chipper pageant voice," Noah says when I put the phone back to my ear.

"I hate it too. Now pretend you're a helpful member of society and tell me how I'm going to get Van out of the tub. Is there some sort of special fireman carry for water situations?"

"I am a helpful member of society," Noah grumbles. "And I'm a much better man than I used to be. You, of all people, know that."

"*Noah, focus,*" I hiss as quietly as possible because Van thinks I'm talking to Joanna. "This isn't about you."

I ignore his mumbled, *"It's never about me,"* and memorize his instructions on how to safely lift Van if it comes to that.

"You can always call me back, and I can get him out. I'll wear PPE so I don't bring the flu back to the station."

"If I'm truly stuck, I will."

While Noah is mid-jab about how I must really like Van—since I never ask for help, and yet, here I am, calling him—I hang up on him.

"Joanna's good?" Van asks when I lean against the bathroom countertop.

He mistakes my noncommittal hum for something else, sitting up slightly and tugging off the washcloth.

"If you want to tell her the truth as soon as we're out of this..." His fingertips drum on the side of the tub. "This...situation, it'd be okay. Actually, if you'd rather I..." He stops again with a hard swallow. "If you want me to—"

"Let's rinse your hair." I perch on the edge of the tub, unable to take the pressure in my chest at the way Van looks like he's being slowly eviscerated. "That made me feel better."

It's weird that I get nearly as much joy out of cradling Van's head and running my fingers through his short silken strands as I did when he rinsed my hair days ago. Once he sits back up, I dry his face and hair with a towel before asking if he's ready to get out. Then I roll up the sleeves of my sweatshirt, bracing my legs like Noah told me to, and lean down to wrap one arm around Van's back.

"On three," I say into his damp shoulder.

"Gen, I can get up by myse—"

"One. Two. Three." I tug and then promptly slip on the floor mat that I'm not used to because it wasn't there a few days ago.

My feet fly back while my chin juts forward, knocking into Van's collarbone as I end up over the edge of the tub and atop of him in the cold water. Releasing his back, I push my palms against the side of the bathtub, but that only presses our bodies closer, our legs interlacing as my face ends up a mere inches from his.

"Um." A shuddered breath leaves my lips open. "Sorry, I was trying to..."

All I can think about as that sentence drops off is that I'm grateful that I'm wearing leggings in addition to my sweatshirt, because Van is in nothing but a pair of *very wet* sleep shorts. His body is a chiseled inferno beneath me. It's honestly surprising he hasn't heated the water by conduction.

"It's okay."

Except, Van's voice doesn't sound like it's okay. His body tenses beneath me—and not in a *what a delightful surprise you're throwing yourself at me again* kind of way. He seems genuinely uncomfortable.

"I promise I'm not usually this clumsy."

I try to shift my hands to push away, and in doing so, my left palm slips, tossing my ponytail over my shoulder and smacking Van in the face.

My eyes fly wide, and air becomes gelatinous in my lungs as time seems to freeze. We stare at each other for three thudding heartbeats before his lips twitch with a puff of breath. The slow grin spreading over his face is more beautiful than ten thousand sunrises, and a single thought hits me like a sucker punch.

I love when this man smiles.

When I mirror his grin, his gaze softens. But when Van's fingers brush my hip, I vault myself out of the water like an alligator going for the kill. Water sloshes everywhere—on the floor, on the new bathroom rug, even on the countertop.

"Sorry. So sorry," I stammer, hand to my chest to check if my heart is still working, because surely Van just electrocuted me with that slight touch.

What happens to your heart after being electrocuted? It stops? Or does it start up again? Van would know—he's an ER doctor and everything—but there's *no way* I'm asking him.

"We should get dry," I say instead. "Because you're wet, and I'm wet, and the bathroom is wet..."

Stop saying wet! my brain screams.

Van chuckling does not help matters. In fact, the sound sends effervescence bubbles coursing through my veins.

I rush to my closet to grab some more clothes, talking over my shoulder. "I'll get changed in the guest bathroom and meet you downstairs. I brought your bag up earlier. It's in the corner."

After what's probably ten minutes but feels like three years, Van lumbers down the stairs in a fresh t-shirt and shorts. My brain is so muddled after *Wetgate* that I didn't even think to offer help—which is borderline dangerous since I'd been concerned about his ability to get out of the tub mere minutes ago.

Taking my thumbnail out of my mouth, I bolt up. "Let me—"

"Easy." Van holds up a hand to stave me off. "I'm doing just fine. I'm actually feeling a lot better after cooling down in the water."

"Oh." I tuck my feet beneath me on the couch, clutching the throw blanket like it's a life raft in a tempest. "That's good."

Van sits nearby, but not as close as he did before, and every single cell in my body pouts. I pick up the remote to dissipate the nonsensical sensation.

"Want to watch *Celebrity Circuit*?"

"Sure." He stretches out, groaning a bit with each movement.

Once the recap is finished, I pause the show. "Once you're feeling better..."

Van rolls his head on the back of the couch until our gazes meet.

"Maybe we can pick up a rug for in here? My feet get cold in the winter."

"Yeah?"

The way Van's face lights up, you'd think I just asked him to take a billion dollars off my hands or handed him a dozen puppies...or kittens...or parrots? I should really find out what makes Van happy, because I'd like to do it more often.

"Yeah," I say before clearing my croaky throat.

Van watches me for a minute, probably using that x-ray doctor vision of his. "Why haven't you decorated? Noah says you've had this place for years."

Normally, this is where I'd clam up, shove my shoulders back, and shoot a snappy remark. That or say nothing. I've gotten really good at stony silence. My nail picks at a loose thread on my sweatpants like it *absolutely* needs my full attention.

"I didn't want to admit I liked being here. If I never settled in, it'd be easier to move if things didn't work out."

Saying the truth out loud feels like a literal gash on my side, but I resist the urge to check for blood.

"But you have a business here. You're part of the community." Van's voice is achingly soft, but I don't look up.

"That'd be easy to sell," I say, shaking my head. "Carol would be all too happy to have the property back."

"Carol?"

I glance up. "Her late husband owned the auto shop, but it'd been unoccupied for years before I moved here."

What I don't mention is that the anger consuming me at being abandoned by my mother and friends after a lifetime of my father being barely present made me impossible to be around. I honestly don't know how Joanna tolerated me before I bought the property. One night, after lashing out when I shouldn't have, I stumbled upon the empty auto shop.

There'd been an abused punching bag and tattered gloves in the corner by the old office. It looked like the previous owner used to work out after closing the shop for the day. Moonlight streamed through the garage windows as I took decades of frustration out with clumsy, untrained strikes. The feeling of calm that slipped into my bones after being able to finally release my pent-up frustration was addicting. I came back the next night and the night after that.

I was still guarded with others, but I stopped seeing the people of Wilks Beach as the enemy. Whenever I wasn't helping Joanna with her divorce, I researched how to become a boxing instructor. Then I priced out equipment and necessary structural changes, dipped into my savings from past sponsorship deals and prize money, and found out who owned the building.

Van processes the information about Carol being the previous owner of my gym, no doubt updating his mental map of Wilks Beach. After meeting someone or hearing a story from me, he's never forgotten a detail. His genius brain must layer all those minute facts together and lock them away.

"But maybe"—I'm back to staring at my pants again—"you showing up out of nowhere and forcing me to live in my own house isn't the worst thing. It's definitely close to the worst thing." Instead of forcing my lips into a line, I allow them to lift. "Second to worst, for sure. Right above mistaking maggots for rice."

For someone I had to human crutch-walk to the tub, Van's arms are ridiculously strong as they drag me across the couch until I'm tucked into the crook of his shoulder.

"Play our show, sassypants," he says, spreading the blanket over us both.

"Sassypants?" The smile on my face must be obnoxious, but Van is looking at the screen. "Coming out with the big guns. What are you going to call me next? A meanihead?"

Van sniffs. "Some of us are not as naturally good at insults as others."

I chuckle, resting my head on his steady chest and pushing play.

And as Tasha reveals surprise baby news—It's twins!—I mull over Van's word choice, deciding I don't completely hate it. Instead, I relax beside my accidental husband and enjoy *our* show.

SEVENTEEN

Van

The bubble had to burst. I knew that. I knew this day would come, but I'm unprepared at how much I want to revolt like a feral toddler at the prospect of leaving our little nest. Definitely not a love nest, but a friend nest? We're undoubtedly closer, but I'd love another week of keeping Geneva to myself.

"Tell me again about this," I say, extending my palm so a firefly can bounce briefly off my skin.

It blinks its light, flitting to join the others over the area of clover that should only be seedlings but has already grown into thick groundcover.

Geneva is practically resplendent in the patio chair across the table, the soda water and muddled pineapple spritzer I made for her dangling from elegant fingertips. For a brief moment, I wonder if she's noticed the change too.

Does Geneva realize that even though she's wearing heels, a satiny black sleeveless blouse, and chic black trousers in preparation for dinner at Joanna's later, she's reclining with her legs leisurely crossed at the ankle? Does she realize how much she's shared about her past over the last few days? Does she notice that neither of us has removed our rings? We spent the last ten days secluded in quarantine, hidden away from the scrutinizing eyes of this tight-knit community and never once slid them off. Does she realize that instead of scowling at my question, she gives me an indulgent smile?

Her brown irises look even warmer with little hints of gold flecking from the globe bulbs. I'd take a picture of her, but Geneva would roll her eyes at me before I could capture them accurately.

"The lore is that the island is magic. Not like in fairy tales, but small, more subtle things." Her gaze shifts to where the lightning bugs make two interconnected rings in the air. "Like this. Noah told you about the library gifting books, but things also grow incredibly well here. The gardeners of the island enjoy produce in half the time it takes to mature elsewhere."

That knowledge washes over me, and I try to set aside reason to accept that things are slightly different here on Wilks Beach. I suppose I have the island to thank for Prunella, Stella, and Hank's new feeding area.

But that makes me wonder about...

Unease tumbles in my chest as I scratch my ear. "What about wind?"

"What do you mean?"

"Does it"—tension tightens my spine, but I manage to get the word out—"speak?"

Her brows pinch like I'm insane, which honestly is laughable. We're talking about things that shouldn't even exist in a yard that seems to defy the laws of time while fireflies dance in concentric circles.

"I've never heard of that, but I can ask Carol."

"No, it's fine," I mumble, pushing down the lump of pain in my throat.

The fireflies dissipate when Geneva's phone pings with a text. "Joanna is ready for us."

"I think we've done a good job of mostly sticking to the truth about Vegas," I murmur as we wash the dinner dishes.

Or rather, I'm washing, the sleeves of my shirt rolled up. She's waiting with one hand on her hip and the other open-palmed to accept the next clean dish to dry. Geneva makes the pose simultaneously impatient and alluring, but I miss *my Geneva*. All of the softness she'd exhibited at home wisped away like tendrils of smoke the second we walked out of her backyard gate earlier. When it's just the two of us, Geneva is still snarky and whip-smart, but she's also unguarded. It should be physically impossible, but she's even more breathtakingly beautiful when she lets me in.

Geneva snorts. "It's not like I could say we got drunk, thought we were playing pretend, and accidentally ended up husband and wife."

A few days ago, I'd thought she wanted that—to come clean, to have me out of her life.

"I think focusing on Elvis as our officiant, what the chapel looked like, and how fun it was was a safer bet." I keep my voice low because though Joanna excused herself to find her grandmother's ring, she could be back at any second.

Geneva's dismissive huff makes me smile. I wait for one of her poisoned zingers, but she stares out the tiny window over the sink, lost in thought. When her fingertips whiten on the edge of the farmhouse sink, I bump her with my shoulder.

"Breathe, darlin'. You're doing fine."

Then Geneva sways toward me, her shoulder lightly resting on mine, and I drop a kiss on her temple. It feels like the most natural thing in the world, the absolute right course of action. But when Geneva's chin snaps up, her eyes wide, I realize that though I've thought about it dozens of times, I've never kissed her before.

Our eyes meet for a halting breath before Joanna's distraught voice distracts us both. "It's *gone*."

"What's gone?" Geneva asks, all but running across the room.

"The ring. My family's ring. I always keep it in the bottom drawer of my jewelry box, and it's not there." She releases a frantic breath. "It should be there."

I quickly dry my hands and move to where Joanna is leaning against the door jamb like it's the only thing holding her up. "Is there any chance that you moved it somewhere else? A sock drawer perhaps?"

"I—I don't think so, but maybe?" Joanna says, her eyes brimming with tears.

"Okay." I give her arm a little squeeze. "We'll find it. Let's all look together."

The three of us spend the next thirty minutes overturning every purse, hatbox, and storage bin in Joanna's walk-in closet.

"This doesn't make any sense," Joanna mutters to herself, digging to the bottom of a built-in drawer filled with outdated workout clothes.

It's a small space with the three of us in here, even though half of the closet is completely empty.

"Is there any chance it's in one of these drawers?" I point toward what must be the *His* portion of the closet. The only thing on these shelves is a fine layer of dust.

"Those were cleared out years ago," Geneva says, kneeling on the carpet, folding Joanna's neon leotards into neat stacks. "When Joanna kicked my father out."

"So you wouldn't mind if I looked through them?"

Her fingers nearly rip a leg warmer in half. "Not sure what good it would do. The only thing that man left behind were broken promises."

Joanna's gaze flits up to me, her fingers trembling slightly. "But maybe we should check? I never went through them."

Geneva's expression shutters, and she blinks at Joanna. "You didn't?"

"No. I figured..." She shuffles toward the drawers, but it's like watching a person walking against the force of a wind tunnel.

"Let me." Geneva sets a hand on Joanna's shoulder while sliding hers back.

It's a posture I've seen before—Geneva preparing to go into battle for someone else. But in this moment—heck, in all future moments—*I want* to be the one to protect Geneva. Even though she's fierce, even though she can handle everything herself, *I want* to be the one.

"I can do it."

I expect an irritated glare in response, but Geneva's expression actually softens. "It's okay."

Geneva hesitates in front of the drawer like she's expecting it to be full of jumping snakes. There might as well be tense movie music playing as she slowly slides the top drawer open. Joanna clutches at my forearm before I sling a reassuring arm around her shoulder. Unlike Geneva, Joanna is short, the crown of her head not even clearing my collarbones.

A tight exhale leaves Geneva's nose as she turns around holding an antique burgundy ring box out to Joanna.

"I should be ticked that he meddled with my things, but I'm just so relieved it's here," she says with a light chuckle. "Here you go, Van."

I let go of Joanna's shoulder and take the box, struggling to keep my emotions from playing on my face. Holding this weathered ring box—something that's been cherished for generations—my stomach bottoms out.

Suddenly, our fake marriage feels more cruel than kind.

To Joanna. To Geneva. To me.

My skin flushes hot, and I'm absolutely certain my ears are the color of beets. A rough swallow squeezes down my tight throat as I realize I don't want to give this to Geneva if it's not real. I can't take Joanna's family heirloom and pretend it means nothing. My lips part as I lift my gaze, but the ring box slips from my shaking hands, falling open on the carpet.

The three of us stare at the paper that tumbles out of the otherwise empty box.

Joanna stoops to pick it up, reading, "Good luck getting this back."

Geneva snatches the paper, scanning it quickly before crushing it in her palm. "That narcissistic, scheming piece of—" She cuts herself off. "I'll be back."

Her heels make three distinct clicks through the adjacent bathroom before I throw a forearm around her waist, lift her off the floor, and bring her back to where Joanna is hovering in the doorway to the closet. I know I'm risking bodily harm by manhandling Geneva, but I don't end up with an elbow to the jaw or a heel to the groin.

"Let's think about this for a minute before we storm off to do physical damage," I say into her hair, not releasing her quite yet.

A few seconds tick by before she nods. Only then do I let go and give her space.

Joanna's lips move as she silently reads the note, a tear falling and blotting the ink. "I was just so happy to be done. He dragged out the divorce for years. You remember." Her chin lifts to catch Geneva's gaze. "It was awful. Why would he want to take this?"

"I'm going to get it back," Geneva tells her, her hand settling over Joanna's shoulder. "Don't worry."

"He'll pretend he doesn't have it. Even if we bring this to him"—she lifts the crumpled note—"he'll claim he doesn't know what we're talking about. Going through the legal process to get this back will take forever."

"It doesn't matter. It's yours. He can't take what isn't his." Geneva's hands fist. "And if he doesn't listen, there are other ways to get it back."

"*Okay.*" I clap to get their attention. "As fun as seeing my new wife through a visitation window after getting arrested for assault sounds, I've got a better idea."

Gorgeous, defiant, skeptical Geneva crosses her arms, but there's no stopping my growing grin.

"Oh yeah? And what's that?"

I glance between the two women, hesitating a breath. "We'll steal it back."

EIGHTEEN

Geneva

"**I** knew that fever fried your brain," I say, staring at Van in disbelief. "Shouldn't you be concerned about protecting your most valuable asset?"

Van's grin turns suddenly wicked, but I continue before he can speak.

"Not *that*, you..."—a more biting insult is at the ready, but since Joanna is here, I settle on—"numbskull. Your medical license. If you get caught breaking and entering, you'll end up in jail just the same. Except, my assault charges won't hurt my career, but yours will."

"Not sure you should insult your husband by calling him a numbskull," Joanna says out of the corner of her mouth.

"Oh, don't worry." Van sends that dimpled smile her way before his flirty gaze crashes with mine. "I'm into it."

Electricity gathers at the base of my spine and runs backward until it's stinging my scalp. Joanna's bathroom is markedly larger than the small closet we spent the last half hour in, but the walls feel like they're simultaneously closing in and steaming as if the shower was left running.

Resisting the urge to fan my face, I say, "This is an insane idea, and we're not humoring it."

Silence hovers for a moment as Joanna's gaze grows distant, pensive.

"*Joanna*," I say, warning in my voice. "We're not doing this. Henry probably has cameras over every inch of the property. Plus, we don't even know where the ring is. We'd get caught searching for it—that is, if we even get in."

But Joanna is not listening. She's sliding her phone out of the back pocket of her jeans. "We don't know, but Stacy might."

"Who's Stacy?" Van asks, half-leaning/half-sitting on the bathroom countertop and crossing his arms.

The motion is casual, not closed-off. The mirror behind him reflects the fabric of his light-gray plaid shirt pulling tight across his back muscles. I get lost for a minute, wondering what it'd feel like to run my fingertips down the strong column of his spine.

"She was our maid while we were married. He didn't like the idea of using Melissa's cleaning service because she was a local. Melissa is William's mom and cleans most of the larger houses on the island,"

Joanna supplies when Van's forehead wrinkles. "He didn't like the idea of the person cleaning your home also talking to you at the grocery store—the snob. Stacy lives in Virginia Beach and still works for him today."

"How would you know that?" I ask.

"Because after Stacy found out what he'd done, she told me that she was going to quit, but I insisted that she stay with him. Because even though he might be a philandering, lying, backstabbing, piece-of-garbage human, he pays his staff well. And she has three kids to support."

"Okay," Van says, "but what would make her want to help us now, years later?"

Joanna is slightly sheepish as she turns her focus to him. "I funded her divorce. My ex didn't know about it, but Stacy didn't have the means. She and those babies weren't in a good situation, and I wasn't about to stand by and do nothing. That was a year before everything fell apart."

Van tenses as he absorbs this information. Then, with a slow nod, his gaze flows from Joanna to me. One eyebrow lifts in a silent question.

I let out a noisy breath. "Call her. Don't text her. Text conversations can be pulled up in court. I'll see if I can get some information on Henry's habits, his schedule, and see if this is even possible."

Giddy is the only way to describe Van's expression. He's a kid hopped up on too much cotton candy, soda, and chocolate chip cookies. "So we're doing this?"

"Maybe," I say with a cutting glare.

But my golden-retriever husband takes that as a yes, shifting his shoulders in a delighted little shimmy. It shouldn't be attractive. It should be annoying, not adorable.

"We're doing a heist," he whispers to Joanna. "I've always wanted to be involved in a heist. They're my favorite movies."

"This is not a movie," I reprimand. "This is *real life*. And we're not doing anything without lots of information and planning."

"I don't know." Van shrugs, and it's the most playful thing I've ever seen. "I watched lightning bugs fly in shapes earlier. For all I know, this is a very elaborate hallucination, and I'm in a coma."

I march across the bathroom and pinch his forearm—hard.

"Ow. What was that for?"

My body pushes between his legs until our noses are inches from each other, my gaze steely. "To prove to you that you're alive. And to remind you that *alive people* can ruin said lives by doing stupid things like breaking into houses. Even if this foolhardy idea goes beyond planning stages, you're not going to be a part of it."

Van's expression dropping is almost comical. I almost chuckle at the forlorn pout making his lips seem fuller than they already are. "Why can't I be the lookout or"—he brightens with a large inhale—"the getaway driver?"

"You drive slower than all the grandpas on the island combined."

The day we got the boxwoods—when I'd been coming down with the flu and hadn't known it—I'd let Van drive us to the mainland in his truck. He slowed for every roadside turtle, waved everyone on at four-way stops, and always kept the speedometer *five under* the limit. I nearly chewed my nail off in frustration.

Van just grins before leaning even closer. "There's nothing wrong with taking my time. Don't you know good things come to those who wait?"

Now I'm angry for two reasons: the fact that Van is willing to put his hard-earned future at risk and that he's making my pulse kick into overdrive. My fingers lift to grip his upper arms, but I can't decide if I should strangle him or cup his jaw and kiss him.

Van tenses his biceps, and the flush spreading over my collarbones and singeing down my forearms already knows the answer to this conundrum. When he'd set his lips on my temple earlier, I'd been shocked initially, but then everything in me wanted the action repeated. I wanted Van to tenderly kiss my forehead, my eyelids, to softly brush the corner of my jaw, because I've never felt more cherished.

But now, I don't want sweet affection or tender caresses. I want to kiss the confident smirk off his face. I want Van to be as lost in this insatiable attraction, this incessant wanting, as much as I am.

Joanna clears her throat behind me, startling both of us.

"If it's okay with the two of you, I'd like to get a hold of Stacy now."

I step back with a noisy inhale, snapping to my full height. I hadn't realized how much I'd softened into Van.

"Oh, okay. Can we help with anything else? Finish the dishes?"

"No, no." Joanna waves me off. "You two just head out. Or better yet, I heard there's acoustic guitar music now on Sundays at Bayside Table. You two should get dessert there. It's too lovely a night to pass up."

I catch a mischievous twinkle in her eye before she heads down the stairs.

A few moments later, after saying our thanks, we're efficiently dismissed with containers of leftovers. We're silent on the walk home, lost in our own thoughts. A guitarist strums in the distance, but they lack Van's talent, the way he makes everything effortless.

Instead of using the back door like I always do, I punch the code into my repaired front door, my gaze dropping to my *Go Away* welcome mat. Something thick and enigmatic swirls in my chest, but Van's question distracts me from wondering what.

"Are we headed to Bayside Table after this?"

The lock disengages, and I push through the front door, waiting for Van to follow me before I snatch the leftovers from his hands and put them on a vintage sideboard table next to the stairs. The containers clunk onto the sage surface, rattling a mason jar filled with black-eyed Susans—because of course they do.

Of course there's this historic piece that Van bought off a middle-aged local trying to get a restoration business off the ground. And of course it's perfect, nestled right here. And of course, he'd find time today once we were both finally fever free to find me wildflowers.

A shuddered breath slips into my lungs because I'm pretty sure I don't deserve any of this, but I'm apparently the villainess everyone thinks I am because I'm *not* going to do the right thing. I'm not going to push Van away anymore.

"Gen?"

I spin, splaying my hand in the center of Van's firm chest and shoving him toward the couch instead. "Sit down, Van."

Van stumbles back, the heat of his smile as I push him downward melting the remaining cells in my brain. "Yes, ma'am."

NINETEEN

Van

When Geneva's lips collide with mine, I'm pretty sure I black out for a moment, but then her fingers in my hair bring me right back to life. Fireworks ignite along my scalp and sizzle down my spine when Geneva crawls onto the couch, hovering just above me. Her pant-covered knees settle outside of my jeans as I reach up to unfasten her hair elastic. Silken dark strands curtain around us as she pulls back with a short, breathy inhale.

My heart freezes in my chest as our gazes meet, but my fingers settle loosely over her thighs, because I'm not letting her bolt away this time. I'm not letting her recede into her shelter of narrowed eyes and harsh words. I'm prepared to tighten my grip and keep Geneva from hopping off this couch and saying something nonsensical, like this was a mistake, when us kissing is a foregone conclusion.

Then her expression contorts in a way I don't expect. It's almost painful watching the wisp of uncertainty stain Geneva's brow as her eyes dart between mine. How can she not know this is what I've wanted since an Elvis impersonator pronounced us husband and wife? Ever since that missed opportunity—when we both laughed it off and said our goodbyes—I thought about kissing her more than I should have. And then, when the possibility to re-enter Geneva's life presented itself, I upended everything to be here.

"Yes." The word is a low rumble in my chest as I skirt one palm up her leg and along her ribs until I'm framing her jaw.

My focus follows my thumb brushing the line of her jaw, the hollow of her cheek before I return to her warm brown eyes. The way her brows furrow makes me shift my hand to the back of her head to bring her forehead to my lips. And when Geneva bends, when a ragged exhale shakes out of her, goosebumps shoot over my skin.

"I'm an unlovable porcupine," she says as I set a soft kiss over her temple.

"You're not."

"You're right. Porcupines are too cute. I'm more like a sea urchin—black hearted with dangerous spikes."

A soft chuckle leaves my mouth as I kiss her cheek. "Darlin', you have no idea how sweet you are."

When Geneva balls her fists on the tops of my shoulders, I lean back against the couch. My hands collect one of her curled ones and slowly unfurl each of her fingers, my gaze focused on my work.

"I recognize this isn't going to be something you'll accept with a single conversation. You're far too stubborn for that." My eyes dart to hers with a smirk. "But one of these days, I'm going to help you see that it's *your opinion* of yourself that's negative. Everyone else likes you."

When Geneva snorts, I let my smile bloom.

"They might fear you a little too, but that's because you've always got your guard up." I place a kiss in the center of her now opened palm. "You should let them see the version of you that I get to see."

She shakes her head in short, quick movements.

"Okay," I soothe, settling her palm over my heart. "Can you admit that I like you?"

Her face is a kaleidoscope of emotions, making my pulse uptick beneath her hand, because it's an absolute honor to know this version of Geneva. I understand the significance of her not being an impenetrable brick wall in this moment. She's giving me her trust by allowing me to witness her insecurity, by letting me see the sticky, unkempt parts of her soul.

When Geneva presses her lips into a firm line, I know we've reached an impasse. A deep breath fills my lungs as I relinquish a small nod.

"Can you admit that I've been dreaming of your lips since the night we met?"

Geneva's spine straightens, the corner of her mouth slipping up slightly. *This* is something she can accept. That I'd be attracted to her. That I'd want to kiss her. Just not that my chest aches watching the sweet way she snuggles with Hank, or when her eyes brighten when she laughs, or seeing how fiercely kind she is with Joanna.

"Good things come to those who wait?" she asks with an eyebrow quirk.

I don't tell her that it feels like I've waited my whole life for this, knowing she'll shut down. Instead, I lift my chin slightly and settle my flirtiest smile across my lips.

"So I've heard."

Geneva hums, closing the distance between us at a teasing pace. When her nose brushes mine, we both draw a sharp inhale through parted lips. My palm slides from over her hand on my chest to her neck, my thumb settling on her frantic pulse point.

At least in this, I'm not alone.

When her lips come over mine again, my hands tighten reflexively. I grip the satiny fabric over her waist at the same time my other hand palms the back of her head, immediately deepening the kiss. Geneva meets me touch for touch, fisting my shirt and clutching my shoulder—the soft sound in her throat in direct opposition to her grip strength.

Then her nails scratch down the back of my neck to grab the collar of my shirt and tug me closer, and I can't restrain the groan vibrating through me. Everything is explosive in a matter of seconds. Our chests press firm, our breaths tattered puffs through exploring lips. Hungry kisses trail over my jaw before she nips my earlobe, and tiny beams of light shoot across my closed eyes.

Forget what I said earlier, *this* might be the fever dream—the elaborate hallucination—because if this is reality, I am one ridiculously lucky man. Because Geneva is everything I want—fiery, complex, inexplicably beautiful. But there's also this deep sense of peace that I feel whenever we're bantering. Those two things shouldn't coincide, but the sensation of wholeness I feel in her presence is nearly incomprehensible, making me doubt reality.

It's foolish, especially since I have Geneva in my arms, but I untangle one hand from her gorgeous hair to pinch myself in the ribs.

Geneva sets a hot kiss over my collarbone before glancing down. "Did you just...pinch yourself?"

I hold my breath, hoping she'll get distracted by the swell of my chest, of how my shirt gapes a little with the action, and not how my fingers are frozen at my ribs. But Geneva continues to hover, waiting.

"Van?" She sits down hard, pinning me with a stare. "Did you?"

All the blood in my body concentrates in my ears. They're on fire, but hopefully with the dim light from the kitchen, Geneva can't see the shade of crimson.

"I was just checking."

Her jaw tightens. "Checking what?"

A sigh gusts out of me. "That this is really happening because..."

...it's uneven...because I like you so much more than you like me, and after kissing you, I don't know what I'll do if...when...

I've already lost so much. Having Taylor stolen from me has been like losing a limb. I keep waking up, expecting to find new voice notes from her on my phone, to be able to call her when something funny or annoying or amazing happens, to be able to hear her too-loud laugh again. I don't think I can handle losing Geneva too.

Pain ripples through my muscles at the thought. I move to drop my chin to my chest, but Geneva catches my jaw in her palm. Her eyes dance between mine for three excruciating heartbeats before she leans forward to press a soft kiss on my lips.

Every cell in my body hovers, weightless, when Geneva exhales, rocking her forehead into mine. When her lips dip again to press against mine with aching tenderness, I surrender. I'll have to take whatever agony is coming my way later because right now my self-protective instincts are as solid as a Jenga tower in an earthquake.

All I want is more—now, tomorrow, forever. All I can think about is her.

"*Gen.*"

I feel her smiling lips against mine. "Only you call me that."

But then Geneva is kissing me again, and I set my answer aside, following her down a series of slowly deepening kisses and not thinking about how tonight might be my undoing.

TWENTY

Geneva

Though I'm more excited than I expected to see my regulars at my boxing class the following night, I try to keep my face impassive. Because if I walk up to Vivian and her boyfriend, Finn, and say hi like I want to, they'd probably think I'm still sick and insist I go home.

Instead, I nod at Finn and give Vivian a small smile as they wrap their hands. Finn helps Vivian with her gloves even though she's been coming every Monday for weeks. It took me a few classes to figure out that she lets him because she *enjoys* being cared for. It'd been a baffling realization. One I couldn't quite comprehend until Van brushed the tangles out of my hair. I've been so staunchly independent for so long that I hadn't considered how nice it is having someone be there for you.

When Brynn walks through the open garage doors, Vivian practically squeals, bouncing on her toes before rushing to her sister's side. "You changed your mind!"

Brynn tugs at the hem of her athletic tee. "I thought I'd try something new."

Vivian nearly decapitates Brynn, she's hugging her so hard. I think I hear her whisper, "I'm so proud of you," but I could be mistaken. Then my brother strolls through the front door, and Brynn seizes up like a cat being held above water. I'm certain the only thing keeping her inside my gym is Vivian's firm grip around her shoulders.

To be fair, Noah's gait halts momentarily as well. But he does that every time he sees Brynn, like it's an involuntary tic. Normally, Noah would set a flirty smile on his lips and try to engage Brynn in conversation, but he must be having a tough day, because he drops his keys atop the open shelving for attendees' belongings and bypasses everyone without a word on the way to the bathroom.

"Maybe I should—"

"Oh, no." Vivian cuts Brynn off. "You're staying."

Brynn gives her sister a look, and then they do that weird twin thing when they talk without talking. It's a mix of micro facial expressions and body language that I'd first seen while we were in Vegas. They'd both silently debated what our next activity would be on our second night without saying a word.

A huff comes out of Brynn's mouth, but she follows her sister toward the hand wraps. When Noah comes out of the bathroom, Finn intercepts him.

"You're with me tonight."

Since Vivian started attending class, she usually partners with Finn.

"I figured that," Noah grumbles.

My stomach twists for my brother. I only know the broad strokes about their past relationship since we don't really talk about deep topics. Everyone in town knows Noah and Brynn were high school sweethearts who made it onto their respective athletic teams—track and baseball—at the same university out of state. It wasn't until Noah had been called up to play for the Virginia Beach Waves that things got rocky.

Him skipping the minors and being fast-tracked to the bigs before he even graduated wasn't something anyone saw coming. Brynn and Noah did long distance for a year as he quickly became the team's starting first baseman and one of the most coveted players in the MLB.

But then everything disintegrated in one epic flame-out. Noah lost his position on the team, his opportunity to return to the university, and Brynn in one fell swoop. The only detail I know that the rest of the town doesn't is that my scumbag of a father had a hand in it—something Joanna let slip when she'd been in the throes of their divorce. Noah has done the work since: gotten sober, gone to therapy, re-careered, but Brynn can't forgive whatever happened years ago.

Being the type of person who doesn't forgive easily, I can't blame Brynn, but I find myself feeling for Noah too. I'll admit that he's a great guy who deserves a second chance.

I pause to pat my brother on the shoulder on my way to turn the music up, making his forehead scrunch. My shoulders bounce in a *Take it or leave it* gesture, which has Noah attempting to put me in a headlock. As always, I'm quicker than him—sliding beneath his arm and nearly slamming into...

Van.

An unsteady inhale stumbles into my lungs as I straighten. "Hey."

He looks impossibly sexy in his blue scrubs, his hair a bit wild, like he drove home from volunteering at the free care clinic with his truck windows down. His gray eyes practically sparkle as they settle on me, and there's the ghost of a five o'clock shadow on his strong jaw that makes my fingers twitch at my sides.

"Hey." It bends the laws of physics, but Van's already large smile triples.

"What—" I clear my chalky throat. "What are you doing here?"

"Thought I'd try the best workout in town." He lifts the small duffel bag in his hand. "Just got to change first."

My lips twitch. Prior to getting sick, I'd fantasized about having Van in my class so I could mentally and physically exhaust him into understanding that we're completely incompatible. Now I just want to see what he's made of. He's always so annoyingly confident. It'll be fun to take him down a few pegs.

Van's brows raise in a flirty challenge, like he knows exactly what I'm thinking.

I keep my expression even as I pick up the remote for my music.

"Get on your bags," I command, my gaze darting around the room, daring anyone to lollygag. Then I return my focus to Van, allowing a slow, devious smile to split my face. "And if you're sore tomorrow, you can blame the newbie."

I see Van laughing, but Skillet's "Monster" blaring from the speakers drowns out the sound.

Forty minutes later, Van is still smiling, and I'm...completely ticked. Seething isn't a strong enough adjective. More like enraged. Incensed. If a fuming wolverine and a volatile honey badger had a baby, I'd be it after being dropped in the ocean and electrocuted for optimal aggression. Because not only is Van taking every physical challenge I throw at him like they're pieces of candy, he's doing it while *dimple-grinning* at me.

Sure, Van is drenched with sweat, breathing hard, and the strain of his muscles has gotten distracting more than once, but he's not even fazed. I'd run Finn through this when he'd arrived months ago, and though he'd completed each task, he sure as heck hadn't been smiling like a lunatic the whole time.

"Knock it off," I grit through my teeth when Van comes up from a weighted burpee to throw air kisses at me.

"I don't know what you mean," he says, flawlessly continuing the rep.

When a growl escapes me, Van smiles at the ground.

I need him to be lacking in this, in *something*. Even earlier, when the class had been boxing, I had no notes for him. There needs to be some way I can regain the power balance. I need to have the upper hand in this because last night...last night decimated me.

Not only was the kiss we shared mind-blowing, but his re-assurances wiggled their way through microscopic chinks in my well-forged armor. I wanted everything to be true. I wanted to be the version of myself that Van saw. He might've needed to pinch himself and check reality because witnessing the island's magic messed with his mind, but I'd been structurally rearranged by the *kiss itself*.

Then I awoke disoriented this morning, stumbling downstairs, looking for him and not even remembering he started his volunteer position today. The bereft hollowness ribboning between my ribs when I found Van missing had been disconcerting. Then I'd numbly moved through my day, thinking foolish things.

I wonder what Van had for breakfast. Did his drive to the mainland go okay? Is he replaying the kiss on repeat like I am?

"I get that this is some kind of weird courtship dance for the two of you, but the rest of us need to function tomorrow," Noah says, not even trying to come up from his weighted burpee. He ditches the dumbbells and sprawls out on the floor.

"Shut it, Noah."

From across the room where the other half of the class is doing ab-wheel rollouts on their toes, Brynn snorts mid-plank. Vivian seems to have taken a page from Noah's book. She's lying on the mat, head turned to the side, giving me the saddest puppy dog eyes I've ever seen. I want to mouth an apology to her, but since pre-fever Geneva would never, I settle on a commiserating head tilt. Vivian understands, though, her lips tilting in an exhausted grin.

"Had I known this class was ninety-percent yelling at Noah, I would have come years ago," Brynn mutters toward the floor, her arms shaking. "So cathartic."

"And punching things," Vivian adds, stacking her wrapped hands beneath her head and making herself comfortable. "You forgot how nice it is to punch things."

"And to beat Noah in a race." Brynn's grin is just this side of wicked.

"That was supposed to be a warm-up run," Vivian corrects. "You two weren't supposed to take off like cheetahs."

"It's not my fault he can't keep up."

My lips tip up, listening to their sisterly banter, but I catch myself before the rest of my class can see. Actually, I need to put an end to this altogether. Pre-fever me would never allow this much talking.

"There's way too much chit chat," I bark. "Should I make things harder?"

When a collective groan almost overpowers the music, I nod, satisfied.

"Three more reps, then you're done." I cross the room to switch to my Evanescence-heavy cool-down playlist.

Most group exercise classes skimp on proper cool-down and stretching, but I take everyone through fifteen minutes of guided movements, allowing for time for foam rolling if preferred.

I'm cleaning the dumbbells with disinfectant wipes when Vivian and Brynn walk over.

"Thanks for the unadulterated torture, as usual," Vivian quips, her tone light.

A ghost of a smile lifts my mouth as I continue down the rack.

There's a momentary pause before Brynn clears her throat. The unsteady sound from someone who just crushed one of my hardest workouts draws my attention.

"I was wondering if you'd like to come watch a movie with us on Saturday. We're inviting Summer and Cade too. Vivian will make her coveted espresso brownies, and we'll pop popcorn."

Receiving a simple invitation shouldn't make my heart race, but all my old doubts rush to the surface. The more time these women spend with me, the easier it'll be for them to pick out my faults. Then, if they're anything like the 'friends' I've had in the past, they'll use them against me. After that, Wilks Beach won't be my haven anymore. It'll become a battleground.

My mouth opens, but Van speaks first. "Girls' night in? Sounds like fun."

I turn, finding not only him but Finn behind me.

"It does sound fun." I give Brynn a small nod. "But we have that thing? Right, poodleface?"

I should know better than to expect Van to help me out. The way his eyes glint tells me I'm already dead in open water.

"Oh, that thing?" His lips lift in a roguish smirk. "Don't worry, darlin'. We've got the rest of the night for that." Then Van pats my hip and kisses my temple before walking away to refill his water bottle.

Vivian and Finn share a knowing grin while Brynn's eyes double in size.

"I guess I'll be there," I say, trying to hide how completely flustered I am.

Striding to collect used wraps for the laundry gives me just enough time to collect myself before both Noah and Brynn practically charge me.

"I thought this was fake," Brynn says at the same time Noah asks, "Did something change between you two?"

"You know?" they ask each other simultaneously.

Then Brynn crosses her arms. "Leave. I'm talking to my friend."

"She's been my sister longer than she's been your friend," Noah scoffs, mirroring her stance.

"Quiet," I hiss, my gaze darting around the emptying gym. "We're not talking about this here."

When neither of them moves, I sigh. "It's...complicated."

I still don't know what last night's kiss means for our tenuous relationship. Technically, we're married, but that was our first kiss. Was it also the best kiss of my life? Undoubtedly. But that doesn't mean that anything significant is going to change with this arrangement. Van is here to satisfy a commitment he made to his late sister. Expecting him to upend his entire life—his career—to move to our tiny island long-term is a foolhardy dream.

"Gen, what else can I help you with for close-up?" Van calls from where he's putting medicine balls back in their labeled places.

This shakes Noah and Brynn out of their standoff as the six of us finish picking up and cleaning. I'm used to doing this by myself after my most packed class, so I'm shocked when it only takes us a few minutes. We're saying goodbyes, and I'm about to lock up when Van remembers he left his gym bag near the bathroom.

"Just wait one second, then I'll drive us home."

I almost scoff that my house is mere blocks from here, but Vivian and Finn are nearby, saying their goodbyes before she walks home with Brynn. A happily married wife would accept a ride home from her husband. Noah gives me a pointed *This isn't over* glare before jogging in the opposite direction toward the condo tower.

Once everyone is gone, I lean against the door jamb, letting the soothing sounds of cricket song and the distant waves steady my pulse. My chin tilts back to watch the evening stars peek between the scattering of clouds hazing the sky. A content exhale leaves my lips as the Cheshire moon gives me a smile.

But then, Van's voice calls from inside. "Could you come here for a minute?"

TWENTY-ONE

Van

❦

The second Geneva steps beside me, I lift her, setting her atop the waist-high storage shelving. "I couldn't wait until we got home."

Then I take her lips in a bruising kiss.

Relief courses through me when Geneva's startled sound shifts into a muted groan. Her nails instantly slip into my hair then scratch down my back, pressing us closer.

"I've been thinking about this all day." My words are hoarse over her mouth before I deepen the kiss.

Just like last night, Geneva matches me touch for touch, just as ravenous as I am. My mind shouts words of gratitude into the universe when her fingers slide over my jaw before she pours herself into the kiss.

"And this..." My fingers tease over the inch of skin left bare between her tank and her leggings. "This sliver darn near made me lose my mind."

Geneva doesn't shiver as much as she flinches at my touch.

The smile brightening my face feels like pure sunshine. "Are you ticklish?"

"No," she says, tone serious. Her hands brace my shoulders as if she's ready to push me away if I try again.

I set my grinning lips at the crook of her neck, pleased when she becomes as pliant as a piece of seagrass. "You are. Interesting."

Geneva tilts her head away, giving me access as I work my way up to the sweet spot beneath her ear.

"What other secrets are you hiding?"

"Wouldn't you like to know?" Her tone is defiant, but her lashes fan on her cheeks, her jaw relaxed.

Seeing Geneva like this sends little crackles of electricity teeming through my bloodstream. It's a rush, having someone who's always perfectly poised near boneless in my arms. I want to help her be this relaxed all the time, not when it's just the two of us.

"I would, actually. I want to know everything about you." Before Geneva can argue, I slip my hand beneath her ponytail and bring her mouth to mine.

We spend a long, long while kissing in the darkness of her closed gym before I finally lean back.

"Have you eaten?" I ask between ragged breaths.

"Yes."

"Something other than Greek yogurt?"

Geneva glares at me, but her narrowing eyes only make my lips twitch upward.

"I'm all for healthy eating." I lift my sweat-sodden shirt, gratuitously flashing my abs. "But it's okay to vary your diet every once in a while. Let me make you a stir fry when we get home."

This is where Geneva should snap at me, but her gaze is trained on my stomach, the corner of her lip tucked between her teeth. On second thought, who needs a summer vegetable stir fry when I can devour Geneva's lips for the rest of the night.

"Okay." It's the flicker of uncertainty in Geneva's voice that has me dropping my shirt to brush a tender kiss over her forehead.

I'm going to take such good care of you.

My fingers give her legs a light squeeze. "Let's go home."

The rest of the evening is essentially a dream sequence. Geneva teases with me while I cook us dinner. We eat beneath the stars, the fireflies dancing in the distance. After we each shower, Geneva knocks on the door to the guest room, asking if I'd like to watch 'our show.' She only insults me six times while I make myself a hot chocolate to enjoy on the couch. Then when I tuck her beneath my arm, Geneva tilts her chin up and kisses my chocolatey lips.

"Hmm," she murmurs, her gaze making an unhurried sweep of my face.

"Not bad?" I ask, setting aside my mug.

Her nose wrinkles, but it's playful, not a Geneva-caliber sneer. "Still too sweet."

"Give it time, darlin'." My fingers frame her jaw, my heartbeat a slow, thick pulse in my chest. "You'll come around."

We don't pay much attention to the rest of the show.

"Get in, Tex. You're needed," Carol Cook says the following Saturday as I'm patting down a layer of topsoil over the freshly planted baby boxwoods.

I glance over my shoulder toward where she's idling in her white Pontiac and can't help but smile. Carol is wearing a bright-red blouse with sunglasses the size of ski goggles, the sea breeze sneaking through the passenger window blowing wisps of white hair away from her face. If it weren't a gorgeous eighty-degree day, I'd swear Carol was trying her hand at Mrs. Claus cosplay.

I stand, dusting my hands off on my shorts. "Needed for what?"

"Doctor stuff."

The corner of my mouth twitches. "That's specific."

I assume she's death-glaring me through her glasses, but all I can see is her pinched red-lipsticked mouth. After a few seconds of silence, I put my hands up in surrender. "Let me just wash up."

After grabbing my keys to get my medical bag out of my truck, I slide into Carol's tidy car. The powerful scent of wintergreen mints tickles my nose as I put on my seatbelt. Then I have to bite the inside of my cheek to keep from chuckling when she performs a crawling seventeen-point turn at the beach access dead end. A walker loops the end of the neighborhood street and is back on Sand Bend Road before we are.

"Care to tell me what's going on?" I ask once she turns left toward the condo tower.

She mumbles something about overgrown idiots, her hands squeezing at ten and two. "I'd rather hear about your marriage. You haven't been out much. Too busy trying for kids?"

I nearly choke on my spit at Carol's frankness but set a small grin on my lips. "I'm not one to kiss and tell."

Carol blows a raspberry in response.

"We were at music trivia on Tuesday," I tell her, hoping to distract Carol from digging further. She seems like the kind of person to demand to know a woman's ovulation schedule.

Though Geneva usually stays at home after teaching her evening classes, I convinced her to head out with me on Tuesday. She'd admitted, after winning a twenty-dollar Bayside Table gift card, that spending the late-evening hours listening to seventies rock and chatting beneath the stars had been "agreeable." I'd teased her about that particular adjective until I'd been able to press her against the side of the house in hopes of changing her opinion.

Begrudgingly—and breathlessly—she did.

Since Geneva going to karaoke is about as likely as finding ice cream in a hot oven, I didn't even offer. Though, honestly, it'd been nice to have her to myself the rest of the week. Even though we're supposed to be blissfully in love, she's skittish about me even holding her hand in public. It's such a stark contrast to when we're alone, because the second she gets home from class, Geneva kisses me to within an inch of my life.

Carol hums. Or at least I think it's a hum. Maybe more of a harrumph.

"When are you going to get a real job?"

My eyebrows shoot to my hairline. "Excuse me?"

Most people consider being a physician a reputable profession.

I don't miss the delighted quirk at the edge of her lips as she turns into the parking garage at the base of the condo tower. "You're volunteering, not working. You need to apply for a position at the hospital on the mainland. Unless you're going to throw your degree away and repair fishing nets for a living."

There is *so much* to unpack there. "Working in the fishing industry isn't—"

"Yes. Fine. All jobs are valid and necessary. Blah. Blah. Blah." She pulls her car across three tenant-only parking spots. "Answer the question."

Acid bubbles in my throat, because I'm going to have to lie again. With Geneva and I acting like a real couple, the little white lies about the status of our relationship have been easier to tolerate. I could tell people about the repairs we've been doing or the new recipe we tried from a bodybuilder's website without it being false. No one needs to know that I'm sleeping in Geneva's guest room or that our marriage has an expiration date.

"Oh, good. You're here."

I'm saved from answering by a local I've yet to meet outside the passenger side window. Based on his rushed demeanor and furrowed, sweaty brow, this isn't the casual house call I'd assumed it'd be based on Carol's lackadaisical driving. I bolt from the car, taking my bag with me.

"What's happening?"

"It's just a little cut," Carol calls from the car. "I only asked you to help because Dr. Prescott is on the mainland."

"Isn't Dr. Prescott an orthodontist?" I ask the man jogging next to me.

I remember meeting the barrel-chested man at our wedding party. He and his wife, Lidia, had even asked where we'd been registered. I'd had to lie through my teeth, saying that since we were consolidating two existing households, we didn't need a new air fryer or blender.

"Yeah," he says as we weave through the garage and a series of doors that lead into the interior courtyard of the complex. "But he's always done this kind of stuff before."

"What kind of—"

My words cut off when I find a man in a blood-stained blue camo tank top and green camo shorts holding a kitchen towel to his forearm. Another person rushes over with a handful of Band-Aids while a blonde woman hovers nearby, nervously chewing the side of her glittery thumbnail. Broken ceramic pots, soil, and dislodged petunias litter the patio around him. Another woman arrives with an array of colorful beach towels as I steer the bleeding man to sit in a nearby patio chair beyond the spray of magenta petals.

"I'm Van. I'm a doctor. Carol brought me," I tell him while pulling a pair of gloves on. "Can I take a look at your arm?"

When he uncovers an impressive gash, the blonde woman wails. "I wasn't trying to hurt you, baby. You just make me so mad sometimes. Why you gotta do that?"

"I'm sorry, honey angel. I know I'm not the easiest to love."

Before I can let him know that he's lucky this isn't deeper, because I don't have dissolvable sutures in my bag, the woman hops on his lap, her platform sandals nearly kicking me. I shift to the side as the two of them kiss like he's just come home from space and narrowly escaped death.

"Um..." Applying pressure to his forearm, I glance at the encircling crowd.

Carol pushes her way through the throng of people, using her cane against shins as necessary.

"Karen. Todd. Knock it off. Let the doctor work before you make even more of a mess." Her gaze flicks to the soil spewed over the stamped concrete patio with a disapproving sniff before she turns on the people behind her. "Why are you all just standing there? Pick this up. Many hands. Light work."

Karen finally agrees to move off Todd's lap but hugs his face to her stomach the entire time I work, which—considering that I don't carry anesthetics—is probably a decent distraction. Under Carol's direction, the rest of the looky-loos pick up the patio before the complex's maintenance manager hoses down the concrete.

It's a nice common area with mounted propane grills in one corner, tables and chairs throughout, and a pergola with gauzy curtains and plush couches at the far end. The potted plants that edge the space are far too large to be thrown, so Karen must have chucked the petunias from one of the balconies opening into the courtyard.

The way everyone works together, and how the other residents offer me water or food on behalf of the troublesome couple, who apparently have a tendency to "do things like this," makes something warm settle in my stomach. It's like being given a freshly baked cookie while hearing your favorite song on the radio. There's a comfort to Wilks Beach that I could happily settle into—if I were lucky enough to be asked to stay.

By the time I've given wound care instructions and packed everything up, the sun is bending around the building, casting the common area in a cool shadow. I wipe sweat off my forehead with the back of my hand. If I head home now, I'll just catch Geneva before she leaves for her girls' night at Vivian and Brynn's.

She's been surly about the event all week, but it's easy to see her crankiness for what it is—nerves. I want to be able to reassure her one last time, and...who am I kidding? I want to kiss her too.

I haven't gotten the opportunity today. Geneva slept in this morning, and while I'd been surfing with Nick, she'd taught her mid-day classes and then left from the gym. I wanted to text and ask where she was, when she'd be home, but I busied myself with leftover house chores instead, trying not to get distracted.

I completely underestimated how much I'd crave the soft touch of her lips on mine after kissing her. A part of my mind cautions against how swept up in Geneva I already am, but another part can't seem to focus on anything but the memory of the way she murmurs sweet sounds when I thread my fingers through her hair.

Grabbing my bag, I walk toward the exit. Carol disappeared long ago, so I don't expect her white Pontiac will be waiting for me in the garage. I can't even let Geneva know where I am, because my phone is sitting on the coffee table.

I'm two steps from exiting the complex when I hear broken English behind me. One word is crystal clear, though—doctor. Turning to find a man holding a flushed toddler, I nod and change directions.

TWENTY-TWO
Geneva

I stare at Van's phone as I sit on the couch, willing it to...I don't know, magically tell me where he is. Knowing Van, he probably was chatting with someone and was invited inside for lemonade and cookies—or something equally wholesome. Which...fine. It's good that he's not just sitting around waiting for me to get back from my last-minute meeting with Sean, my private investigator. I neglected to tell Van about the meeting because I didn't want to get his hopes up about this heist idea if it wasn't plausible.

Also, I wanted to digest the information in the file by myself first. Alone. Not surprisingly, my father is back to his old ways, currently dating three women—all of which are completely in the dark. I'd nearly caused permanent creases in the paperwork because my hands wanted to fist the words. Something positive that came from reading about his philandering ways was that Henry keeps a predictable schedule, making finding blocks of time when he won't be at home easy.

Now we just need to overlap one of those times with when Stacy would be using her personalized security code to enter the house to clean. Unfortunately, Henry tends to work from home on the day she usually comes over, so we'll have to find a plausible excuse for her to come over one evening instead. I'll need to touch base with Joanna to see if she's discovered any information from Stacy about the whereabouts of the ring.

The plan had been to share the report with Van before I needed to leave for the movie night with Vivian and Brynn. I'd wanted to see his face light up at me humoring his very-much-illegal idea.

And a part of me also wanted...

I run my hand over the bodice of the burgundy sundress I'd seen in a boutique window while I'd been on the mainland. I'd told myself the only reason I bought it was because it fit like a glove, but now I realize I wanted to see Van's reaction to this as well. I wanted his dimpled smile and his gray eyes twinkling at me for wearing something other than black.

And I wanted to see him...just because. After weeks of seeing Van every day, it felt like I was missing an essential part of myself today.

"Foolish," I whisper, squeezing my lashes closed. "You're being so foolish."

Dropping the report on the coffee table, I shoot to my feet. My fingers tug down the dress's side zipper as I stomp upstairs. After stuffing the dress in the corner of my closet, I slip into one of my standbys and tell myself the fabric doesn't feel itchy. I tug at the snug hem, draw in a large breath, and force my shoulders back.

I don't even remember the walk to Vivian and Brynn's, only that once I've entered the upstairs apartment after letting myself in like Vivian's text requested, I'm not met with the setup for a chill movie night. Raven Sacaria music blasts while beauty products and styling wands overload their kitchen table.

Vivian wears the same midnight-blue sequin dress she wore in Vegas, but Brynn is standing in high-waisted, bow-belted black shorts and a shiny gold halter top. It's Brynn's outfit that makes my eyebrows quirk. Even for the two nights we spent in Vegas, she wore a slightly dressed-up version of athletic clothes. My gaze flows to the floor, finding trendy black sneakers with gold accents on her feet.

"We're going out!" Vivian shouts, bouncing a little as she dusts body glitter over her sister's exposed shoulders. "See, I told you we didn't need to text her about the last-minute change in plans. Geneva always dresses nice." She holds the brush up to me. "Glitter?"

The corner of my mouth twitches. "No, thanks. And who's to say I wouldn't have come over in workout clothes?"

"But you didn't." Vivian winks at me, moving toward the Jack-and-Jill bathroom to wash her hands.

"You okay?" I murmur, noting Brynn's rigid posture. At first, I thought it was so Vivian could apply the light dusting without getting it on Brynn's clothes, but now I wonder if she's even breathing.

Brynn gives a curt nod and then keeps nodding. "Yes. I am. I will be." A deep breath flows in and out of her lungs. "This was my idea. I'm trying to be more flexible...more spontaneous. It's just that...now that we're about to—" She cuts off her sentence with a rough head shake. "It'll be fine that we're going dancing instead of watching movies. Nothing is going to happen."

The last few words are gritted through tight teeth.

I rest a hand on her forearm. "I'll watch out for us tonight."

"It's not—" She sighs, glancing at the ceiling before fidgeting with the hem of her top. "I worry about large things going wrong. Like, because we're not here, the roof will collapse, or a pipe will burst and flood the whole place."

My brow furrows, vaguely remembering Brynn saying something like this before. That her keeping to routines is a superstition she's held tighter than a lucky rabbit's foot.

"Nothing is going to happen," I say, giving her forearm a squeeze.

Brynn meets my gaze, taking another deliberate breath before nodding. Then her eyes widen as if she's just remembered something. She leans past me to see that Vivian is in the closed bathroom. "You never did tell me what's going on between you and Van."

"Not really much to say," I hedge.

I'd been evasive when Noah asked me earlier this week as well. My week with Van looked very similar to when we were quarantined…but with kissing. I've spent a good part of this week actively trying *not* to think about what that means. Are we automatically in a relationship now? I hope not. There's only so much of my prickly personality Van will tolerate before he comes to his senses. If we were in a real relationship and he decided I wasn't enough…

I rub a knuckle between my brows to dissipate the painful thought.

Maybe we're just roommates who kiss?

And roommates *who also* happen to be legally married.

That's got to be a thing, right? People have all sorts of weird situationships nowadays. There's probably even an acronym for what we're doing. I'm just not aware of it.

Brynn looks like she's about to ask a follow-up question, but the bathroom door opens.

"Who wants rosé?" Vivan asks. "Finn found us an *evening coordinator*"—she gives finger quotes with a slight eye roll—"like he did in Vegas. Gabriel will drive us and take care of everything since Finn is out of town visiting his sister."

And Gabriel will watch over Vivian—and the rest of us—like a hawk all night. For this town's initial misgivings about Finn, he definitely takes care of those he loves. And honestly, it's nice not having to worry about whether my drink has been messed with or have to shut down pickup attempts. In Vegas, Mateo kept the creepers away so we could enjoy the night life in its purest iteration, all-girl dance circles and telling other women how pretty they look in crowded bathrooms.

"That might be a good idea," Brynn says, pulling a pink bottle out the fridge.

Vivian hops up on the counter, flashing us the bike shorts under her dress before leaning left to pluck three wine glasses from an open shelf.

"I thought Summer and Cade were also coming."

"Cade has a family thing tonight." Vivian pours one very full glass and extends it to me. "And Summer is meeting us there after her dinner plans with her friend, Kayla."

I take a sip of the crisp wine. Hints of strawberries and citrus burst on my tongue. With Gabriel managing everything, I won't have to stay as razor-focused as I usually do. Normally, I'd also be concerned about my female 'friends' waiting for me to slip up and take advantage. Grab some unflattering pictures. Wrangle sordid details out of me. Basically, get dirt that they could use to get ahead. But Brynn and Vivian aren't trying to compete with me. I don't fully understand it, but they seem to enjoy my company.

I swish a larger sip of wine around my tongue before slowly swallowing it. Brynn is trying something that's clearly out of her comfort zone tonight. Over the summer, I watched Vivian grow from the town's most shy member to someone who's confidently herself. Maybe I can take my own step and let my guard down around these two.

Just a little.

Maybe.

My ears ring, and I can barely feel my toes, but I can't wipe the smile off my face. I had no idea how much I needed a night like this. Vivian is unapologetically doing the sprinkler while Brynn nails the running man. Summer plugs her nose and mimics sinking underwater, and I try not to laugh. Six other women round out our circle in the middle of the packed dance floor as lights flash and the thick bassline rivals the beating of our own hearts.

Gabriel isn't far off, purses hanging from his thick forearms. He's a nice guy—married, three cute kids, former Navy Seal, and current "evening coordinator." Though, I'm sure if I looked him up, his official title would be something in the vein of personal security. None of us have touched our purses since we've arrived, because in true billionaire fashion, Finn has taken care of *everything*.

A woman I don't know enters the middle of the open circle, throwing a pretend fishing reel toward me. I wave her off, but she's persistent, miming like I'm a stubborn swordfish caught on her line. Vivian's fingers playfully push my back. Normally, this would cause me to freeze up, but her giggled encouragement reminds me she doesn't mean any harm.

It's been a slow progression of moments like this all night. Me voicing my opinion in the car on the way here instead of staying silent. Me not holding back when I want to smile or chuckle. Me engaging Summer in conversation when she joined us instead of remaining detached.

The chorus of *wooos* that go up from our little crowd as I relent would rival any sports bar during the Super Bowl. The woman bows out, giving me the center spot. I'm not unaccustomed to being in the spotlight, and I can execute choreography with the best of them, but that's not what this is about. This night is about freedom and silliness and having a little fun with friends.

It's about finally letting go.

For once, I don't overthink it. I bend at the waist, make my elbows into perfect ninety-degree angles, and robot like my life depends on it.

Because I think on some level, it might.

We dance for hours. Brynn's espresso martinis help her keep up with her night-owl sister, but as we round 1 a.m., even I'm beginning to lose luster. Summer has already slipped away, needing to drive her car back to Wilks Beach. I'm just about to rein Vivian in when a Raven Sacaria song comes on. Since there'll be no leaving until the songstress finishes her power ballad, I find a spot next to Gabriel as Vivian tugs her sister back to the dance floor.

"After this song, I think we should head out," I tell him.

He nods, keeping his gaze on both women. "Sounds good."

When Vivian almost lurches to the side after trying to complete a spin, I wince. "You've got water bottles in your car, right?"

Gabriel chuckles. "Yes, I do."

I smile at the twin sisters laughing, arms looped around each other. Then I put all my weight on my right leg to ease my aching feet, and my heel snaps. My ankle screams with pain a second before Gabriel's arm snakes around my waist, keeping me from tumbling over.

"You okay?" His eyes do a quick, efficient assessment.

"Yeah," I manage through a pained grunt. "My heel broke."

I lift the offending shoe a few inches from the ground, grimacing as I try to rotate my ankle. Gabriel's gaze tracks to my foot, the action bringing our faces closer. He's about to say something, but an angry voice interrupts.

"Hey, buddy. How about you take your hands off my wife before I end you?"

TWENTY-THREE

Van

Hey, look at that. Turns out *I am* a fighter, because I'm going to bludgeon this man for having his arm around Geneva's waist, his face entirely too close to hers. It doesn't matter that he looks more like the incredible Hulk than a human. This man might have the bulk, but I have years of medical knowledge, detailing the most unexpected pain points in the human body.

"You know this guy?" the man asks Geneva, his lips dipping dangerously close to her ear.

Her mouth opens, but no words come out. Her gaze darts wildly, flitting from my eyes to my mussed hair before stalling on my collarbones. In my haste to get to her, I hadn't thought to change, so I'm wearing my threadbare shirt, my lounging scrub pants, and sneakers.

When the man's arm tightens protectively around Geneva's waist, blinding white fire sears through my brain.

"Gen, step back."

My words are a warning as my hands fist of their own accord. Some higher-processing part of my brain is calculating how to get Geneva away from this behemoth, but a baser part of me is looking forward to doing enough damage to send this man to the local ER.

"She can't." The man has the decency to straighten.

I should feel better now that their faces aren't inches apart, but fury still courses through my veins. I've never been this angry in my life. Burning energy fizzes and cracks through my bones, consuming me.

A harsh, hollow laugh escapes me. "I know my wife. There's nothing she can't do."

"It's my ankle," she says, her voice uncharacteristically breathy.

Since I'm locked in a staring contest with the man who's *still touching my wife*, I don't look down immediately. But when I do, I feel like the biggest jerk of all time. Geneva is balancing on one precarious heel, the other one clearly broken. I surge forward, and the man unravels himself, stepping away.

"Sorry, man," I say, sliding my hands over Geneva's waist to keep her steady. "I got the wrong idea."

A half smile tilts his lips. "I get it. I'm protective of mine too." He wiggles his wedding ring at me, making me feel like even more of a scumbag. "Ma'am, I'll collect your friends. Will your husband be taking you home?"

I lean back to catch Geneva's gaze, but she's not looking at me. She's staring off into the dance club, jaw rigid. "Yes."

Vivian comes over, happy to see me and clearly tipsy, but Brynn gives me a strange look as we all say our goodbyes.

"Why are you here?" Geneva asks once we're alone again.

She's Geneva from months ago—with her icy tone and steely posture. A part of me breaks apart hearing her question, but she hasn't asked me to let go, hasn't asked me to leave. Of course, that could be because she's currently one-footed.

I thought about the answer to this inevitable question the entire hour-long drive here. I knew she'd ask. I knew that I could very well muck everything up by telling the truth. But even though the darkness of this club might mask my blush, I don't want to hide this.

"I missed you."

Her expression shutters, and Geneva finally makes eye contact with me.

"And I got worried when you weren't home by midnight, so I walked over to Vivian and Brynn's, thinking I'd offer to walk you home. And when no one came to the door and you didn't answer your phone, I called Finn. He told me you all were here, and I just got in my truck. I know," I say as her mouth opens like she wants to argue with me. "I *know* how that sounds. It sounds possessive and crazy and a bunch of other negative adjectives I can't think of right now. It's just..."

I brush away a strand that's loosened itself from her ponytail, my gaze following the trail of goosebumps that erupt as I tuck it behind her ear.

"I knew you could keep yourself safe, but I didn't want you to have to. Finn failed to mention that you had a bodyguard driver." I scratch my ear. "Or rather I hung up on him before getting that detail. I just—"

A noisy exhale leaves my mouth. "You kind of make me lose my mind."

Geneva watches me, her breathing deceptively even. I'm not sure if she's going to scream at me, hit me, or hobble away—disgusted with me. Maybe all three? Or a one-two combo like the strike patterns she calls out in class.

"Did you read the report on the coffee table?"

My brows quirk, but I'll take whatever Geneva will give me, even if it's off-topic conversation.

"I did. Looks like we'll have to find an evening for Stacy to clean instead of her usual Tuesday midday."

Her nod is clipped. "I thought the same thing."

I can't help the slow smile lifting my lips. "So we're doing this thing?"

"*I'm* doing this thing." Geneva rolls her eyes at me but with a fraction of her usual sass. "You and your revocable medical license will be nowhere in sight."

"At least let me run coms."

"No."

Since her refusal lacks bite, I give her waist a little squeeze. "Gear, then. I'll outfit you with a grappling hook, night-vision goggles, and a utility belt. I guess you won't need heist clothes because everything you own is already black."

The hurt way Geneva's eyes dart away from mine before she chews on her lip punches the air from my lungs. My hand finds her jaw, my thumb soothing over her cheek.

"I'm sor—"

"I bought a dress today."

Geneva meets my gaze, insecure and challenging at the same time. How does she manage to be incredibly strong and breathtakingly vulnerable all at once?

"Did you?" I keep my tone open, like I'm verbally holding her hand, urging her along.

She presses her lips together, nodding.

"It's..." Geneva stops and swallows. "It's burgundy."

"*Darlin'.*" Her nickname has never sounded more reverent, more earnest. "Really?"

Those expressive eyes find mine again. "And it's a sundress," she whispers.

I can't help my appreciative groan as I tug her closer. Don't get me wrong. I'm a man with functioning eyeballs, so I love these snug dresses, but the idea of Geneva in something with a flirty, flowy skirt is nearly enough to make my knees buckle.

"You're showing me when we get home." I barely keep from nipping her earlobe with my teeth.

She shakes her head, lifting her palms to press against my stomach—lightly pushing me away. "Not after that machismo showdown."

"I thought women liked displays like that. When men beat their chests and growl words like *mine*."

Though Geneva's eyes flash at my last word, she continues her slow head shake.

My eyebrows raise as a smirk settles over my mouth. "You didn't like being called 'my wife'?"

Her fingers twitch before she can stop herself, and my abs tighten in response.

I tilt my head to the side, my smile darkening. "You di—"

My sentence breaks off in a laugh when Geneva pushes and turns to stomp away—right before we both remember that her right heel is broken.

"Ow," she says, lurching to the side before I catch her.

I'd been so distracted by finding her in another man's arms that I hadn't noticed how her ankle is purpling.

"Oh, Gen." I crouch to gently palpate the area, letting her brace my shoulders for balance. "I've got an ACE wrap in the truck, but let's get some ice from the bar first."

Before she can protest, I slip a hand under her knees, swooping her off her feet.

"You're annoying," she tells me, poking my chest.

"The worst," I agree, kissing her temple as I steer us through the dwindling crowd.

The bartender yells for last call, so it's perfect timing to grab some ice and get out of there. Once Geneva is comfortably in the passenger seat, I cover her legs with an extra t-shirt and perform a full exam using the penlight from my medical bag. Predictably, Geneva doesn't squirm or complain, just fists the seatbelt and grits her teeth as I rotate her foot. I wrap her ankle gently before propping it up on the truck bench and covering it with ice. Before I put my bag in the back, I give her a dose of ibuprofen.

"You'll need to keep off of it for a few days, but it only looks like a mild sprain. Can you teach while seated on Monday?"

"I guess," she says with the petulance of a cranky teenager.

I gently palm the back of her head and bring her forehead to my lips. "I've got you in the meantime."

"Don't I get a treat or something for being a good patient?" she asks as I lean back.

My eyebrows inch up, prepared to tease her, but then Geneva fists the collar of my shirt and crushes her mouth to mine. I brace one hand on the side of the truck, so I don't collapse onto her, and then fervently return her kiss.

We're only ten minutes into the drive home when Geneva huffs. "I really *did* want a treat."

The corner of my mouth twitches. "I know of a 24-hour wing place. It won't be as good as Hotties, but—"

"*Yes,*" she cuts me off, digging her phone from her small purse. "Need me to navigate?"

My smile blooms. "That would be helpful."

As a computerized voice instructs me on which turns to take, I let my palm fall onto Geneva's outstretched calf, pleased when she doesn't pull away. A country song hums in the background—one that Geneva would usually berate me for—as I brush my thumb back and forth over her smooth skin. She shifts in her seat, relaxing against the passenger door with a pleased sigh. I'm certain she's unaware of her serene expression, of how much she's softened from my touch alone.

And all I can think about as we ramble through the quiet streets of Virginia Beach is this is what happiness must be—taking your wife to get wings at two in the morning. But then, my mind jumps forward too fast, thinking of Geneva with a swollen belly and the other middle-of-the-night cravings that I'd be more than happy to drive to the mainland to satiate.

I drag a deliberate breath into my lungs, hold it, and exhale slowly. There's no guarantee that she'll want to be with me after our agreed three-month time limit. Geneva is one of the strongest women I've ever met, but she also spooks easily. Bringing up anything about our relationship before then will only send her running in the other direction. Geneva not being able to accept that I *like her* is proof enough of that.

If I push forward too fast, I'll ruin this.

Instead, I focus on now—on staying in the moment. One of my favorite songwriters is singing his best love ballad on the radio. The mid-September air sneaks through the slightly cracked windows, bringing a cool breeze and the crisp scent of leaves circulating through the cab. Stars wink in the distance beyond the wan street-lights.

I release another breath, but this one is full of contentment.

"I think I'll try a spicier sauce this time," I say, my lips already twitching as I anticipate Geneva's response.

When she simply snorts, my grin fully blooms, feeling a whole lot like sunlight radiating from the center of my chest.

TWENTY-FOUR

Geneva

"I'll order a car to drive me," I tell Van the following Tuesday, reaching for the crutch Noah brought over as soon as the news swept town.

In the Wilks Beach gossip version, I injured my ankle while high-kicking a man in the throat in order to save Vivian from an unsavory encounter in a darkened alley. A few of the town's matriarchs came by to offer thanks by way of healing salves and fresh baked sweets before I set the story straight. Judith Abernathy insisted I keep the salve and asked if I'd like a boxing-themed quilt since the weather is finally starting to turn. I politely refused, but after Van propped my foot up on the coffee table with a frozen bag of lima beans, they spoke outside for *way* too long.

This sprained ankle is really messing with me. I could accept when I had the flu and barely had the energy to stand that I needed to rest. And then, no one from town saw me in that vulnerable state except Van. But having to teach my class on Monday sitting down—even if it was on a countertop—was demoralizing. I can't check people's form and help them get the most out of their workouts when I'm twenty feet away.

"I can easily drive you," Van tells me as he finishes the last of the breakfast dishes like the jerk he is.

To be clear, I'm not mad at him because he's washing the dishes. I'm mad because that's *my job*. He cooks nutritiously dense frittatas that are surprisingly tasty, and I wash the dishes. It keeps things fair. But the kitchen chair where he usually sits and jokes with me is currently occupied by my stupid swollen ankle.

I'd really hoped to be done with this purply nonsense by today so I could drive myself to volunteer, but no. I can barely put weight on my right foot, which means that pushing the gas—or more importantly, the brake pedal—is out of the question.

I shove myself up from the chair, using the crutch for balance. "You shouldn't even be here today. It's bad enough you took yesterday off. What about all the patients who didn't get seen because you called out? You should be thinking about them. Not me."

There's no doubt that Van is an excellent doctor, but I'm sure that carrying patients from point A to point B is not standard care. Ever since we got home late Saturday night, he's been treating me like his personal transport. I want to say it's annoying, obtrusive, and borderline insulting, but it's *incredible*. Van picks me up like I'm not five foot ten and packed full of hard-earned muscle, easily toting me from room to room.

"It's not a problem. I'm new to the staff, so I'm just helping with overflow anyway," Van says, resting his hip on the counter while drying his hands on a dish towel.

He's *temporary* staff, I remind myself. Van is only volunteering at the free care clinic located in the farm area of Pungo because in two more months, he'll be back at his full-time job in Nashville.

Acid bubbles at the back of my throat, but it's probably from the sriracha sauce I put on my eggs.

I take two hobbled steps away from him. "I said no. Don't you know what 'no' means?"

Blame it on my throbbing ankle or that I couldn't get comfortable for the third night in a row and slept horribly, but I'm extra snappy today. It could also be from the windstorm that slapped against the house all night long. Even now, ominous clouds churn outside the kitchen windows. At least the weather matches my foul mood.

"It can't be that bad, Gen." His lips tip up, just the hint of his dimple peeking through.

"What are you talking about?"

His smile only grows at my curt question, and I try to mediate my heart's foolish response to the affectionate way he's gazing at me. Why isn't he annoyed that I'm crankier than a snapping turtle in a hailstorm?

"Wherever you've been slipping off to every Tuesday and Thursday. Whatever it is, I won't judge you. Just let me drive so I know you'll get there safely, then I'll head to a café and get emails done until you need me to pick you up."

Everything feels itchy. My skin is suddenly too tight, heat pricking down my neck. The impulse to bite, to lash out is right there, reliable as ever. *I've always taken care of myself before. I don't need you. I don't need anyone.*

Van crosses the short distance between us with slow, even strides. His eyes sweep my face before his fingertips graze my tight knuckles. I hadn't noticed that I'd been squeezing the crutch with both hands.

"Darlin'."

That's it. One little word. One impossible nickname that I should have never allowed in the first place, and my shoulders sag, and a ragged breath escapes my tight lungs.

"Why are you so nice to me?"

The words leave my lips without my permission. I want to call them back instantly, to stomp away and pretend they never happened, but I wait instead. Van exhales, his palm gently cupping my cheek.

"Are you going to believe me if I tell you the truth?"

I bite the edge of my lip. "Probably not."

Van huffs a small laugh as my doorbell rings. Then someone knocks...and then keeps knocking.

"Go away!" I bellow out of habit, and Van's responding grin steals the breath from my lungs.

"I'll get it." He tucks those words against my temple before walking to the front door.

I expect it to be Carol, saying she wants to hash something out with me but really wanting to snoop as much as humanly possible, so when Joanna comes sailing through my repaired front door, I blink. She almost never comes to my house, mostly because there's nothing here. To be fair, she doesn't go to Noah's one-bedroom bachelor condo either. Instead, we do monthly dinners at her house.

Though...now that I think about it, we haven't done that since Van showed up on my doorstep.

"I have news," she says after giving Van a quick hug and exchanging pleasantries. "Stacy found the ring."

"Oh, good." My tone is light, but my brain is fighting to remember the last time my surrogate mother looked this luminescent. She's practically beaming in her denim shorts and flowy blouse, ever-present bangles tinkling on her wrist. The breeze seems to have tossed her curls into a playful windswept halo instead destroying her effortless style.

"It took her a while because she had to be discreet in her search. Stacy also said that there's only cameras on the front and backyard doors, not the side entry to the garage," Joanna tells us with a triumphant smile.

Sean's report also detailed the external cameras, but I've got another question before I give her an edited version of that file's information. The last thing Joanna needs to know is that Henry is still up to his old ways.

"What about inside?"

"None." Joanna fingers the petals of a tangerine flower on the vintage sideboard table.

Van keeps finding flowers somewhere to fill that mason jar. I should tell him thank you. I should be writing him opuses of gratitude for everything he's improved in my life, not fighting him every second of every day. But there's always this slight twinkle in his mesmerizing gray eyes when I push back that tells me he enjoys our teasing repartee as much as I do.

"Good," I say before filling Joanna in on the details from Sean's report. "Though, I'd like to wait until my ankle is better before trying to retrieve the ring."

"Oh, of course." She frowns at my throbbing ankle. "Are you managing okay?"

"She's the most disgruntled patient I've ever had." Van grins from his position leaning against the closed front door.

I give him a death glare. "Lucky for you, I'll be out of your hair soon."

"You're driving her, right? To volunteer at OWRC?" Joanna asks Van.

"OWRC?" Van says, not taking his eyes off me.

"Oceanside Women's Resource Center. It's a women's shelter on the mainland."

If I hadn't already been locked into a stare-down with Van, I might have missed it. I might have missed the flicker making his eyes look almost blue. I certainly wouldn't have seen his chest rise in a slow inhale or how he rubs his knuckles over his heart.

"How—" I clear my throat as I snap my gaze to Joanna. "How do you know about that?"

"Oh, honey." She pats my arm like I'm a small child. "Everyone knows about that."

"They do?" I try to keep the pitch of my voice level—I really do—but it comes out all squeaky.

Joanna chuckles. "Wilks Beach is a wonderland of surf, sand, and everybody knowing everybody's business. When you first moved here and kept so much to yourself, people were worried you were one of *those* mainlanders, especially after everything that scumbag did to Noah and me. To all of us."

After the fallout of finding out about my father's double life, I threw walls up so high they grazed the moon. Whenever I was in town, I was all barbed spikes and poisoned glares. Of course the locals wanted to make sure I wasn't going to hurt Joanna or anyone else.

"I don't remember who kept tabs on you." She squints at the new lighting fixture. "Bex? Jonas? But once they found out you were volunteering to help women escaping terrible circumstances, we knew you were trustworthy."

"I—" My brows pinch. "I, um..."

I can't really be upset with the people of Wilks Beach doing their due diligence when I've done it several times since being blindsided.

A slight blush pinks Joanna's cheeks. "I told everyone not to mention it because I figured you wanted your privacy."

"It's just something from my pageant days I didn't want to give up," I tell her, almost shocking myself with my honesty when I'd usually fall into silence. "I started volunteering because I needed something that looked good for the judges, but I enjoy helping other women to see the strength in themselves."

It's something that fills my heart.

Joanna hugs me carefully, making sure not to bump my ankle. "Good people volunteer because they want to help, not because they want others to know about their good deeds."

"They also help retrieve family heirlooms even if they could get arrested," Van pipes up from over Joanna's shoulder.

I narrow my eyes at him as she leans back, framing my upper arms. "On that note, I don't like the idea of you doing this by yourself."

"I won't be alone. Stacy will be in the house at the same time as cover."

Joanna wrinkles her freckled nose. "I still don't like it."

"Don't worry, Joanna." Van sends her a wink when she glances his way. "I've got a plan."

TWENTY-FIVE

Geneva

Being the stinker that he is, Van says nothing about his plan for the whole time he drives me to volunteer or after he picks me up. He just keeps telling me that 'I'll find out later' with a mischievous smile that makes me want to poke him in the ribs.

Fortunately, I helped residents with interview skills today, so I was able to sit with my foot elevated as I guided them to come up with answers to questions about gaps in employment and how to frame domestic work in corporate terms. Telling the interviewers they performed financial planning and budget oversight for family budgeting or educational support and operations management for keeping children's school schedules goes a long way. Each of them essentially ran a small business centered around human development and operational efficiency, and they should be treated with the respect that comes with that.

With the wind being so bad today, I had to close the garage doors to the gym in order to teach my Tuesday evening class. The pain in my ankle is ten times worse from having to sit on the counter with my legs dangling. All I want is to go home, splay on the couch, and watch *Celebrity Circuit*.

After dropping me off, I'd thought Van might attend class and help me with cleaning up, but Carson and Jonas—two firefighters who work with Noah—take care of it instead. By the time Van returns to pick me up in his white truck, Carson is lifting me off the countertop. I don't miss the tick of Van's jaw when Carson insists on carrying me outside. Normally, I'd scold both of them for acting like testosterone turkeys, but I'm beyond exhausted.

Maybe I should add a bubble bath to my list of things to do once this day is over? Yes. Cancel everything else. My new plan is to dissolve into a bubble bath of bliss.

I'm fantasizing about slipping into warm sudsy heaven as Van helps me into the truck bed and sets a bag of frozen peas on my elevated ankle.

"How was class?" he asks, his palm resting on my legging-covered calf after the engine roars to life.

I nearly groan when his thumb begins a gentle massage. "Fine."

He nods, his gaze over the dark road, that muscle in his jaw jumping again. I'm too tired for words tonight, but I lean my head against the passenger seat and reach my fingers out until they settle over his.

Van flips his hand instantly, intertwining our fingers. His shoulders loosen as he begins humming the country song on the radio, and I close my eyes, oddly content for how much pain I'm in. As soon as we're home, I'll ask Van to get me some medicine too. When Van starts to softly sing, his velvety voice filling the small cab, my entire body relaxes with a happy sigh.

"Darlin'." It takes me several seconds to realize that Van has probably used my nickname more than once.

I draw in a deep breath, wiping drool from the side of my mouth. Had I fallen asleep on the two-minute drive home?

My eyelashes flutter as I blink to focus. "Yeah?"

That's when I notice his pink ears in the wan porchlight drifting through the windshield, how he's biting the edge of his bottom lip. "This was supposed to be a pleasant surprise, but I can see you're dead tired. If you'll just give me a few minutes to shoo everyone out, I'll bring you inside."

"Everyone?" I rub my eyes with a fist, destroying my mascara.

He squeezes my fingers still intertwined with his. "I wanted you to see how much you're loved. It was supposed to be fun."

I tense. I can't help it. Love was always wrapped in a condition. Dad would spend more time with us if I won pageants more often. Mom would love me if I was perfect.

But Joanna has seen me at my absolute worst and still wants me to have her grandmother's ring. Noah keeps showing up and pestering me, making sure I don't recede into myself. Vivian and

Brynn haven't stopped inviting me to activities, even though I've said no more times than yes.

And Van...

Van is suddenly too far away. I scoot closer, wincing as my foot collides with his thigh. Van murmurs something incoherent as he lifts my leg onto his lap so he can run his fingers over my temples, tucking away strands of hair blown free from the wind.

All day, there's been this restless hum just beneath the surface. I assumed it was agitation from being injured, but now I see it for what it is—fear. I want to be good for Van too. Because Van is golden laughs and sweet gestures, and I'm...me.

"But I'm a grouch."

The corner of his mouth tilts in an almost sad way as his fingers trace down my arm, leaving goosebumps in their wake.

"So what? Everyone here knows that."

"But...but—"

The pad of his thumb presses over my lips. "We like you as you are—gruff and cranky and so darned considerate you don't even recognize it. Be a grouch, Gen. No one is trying to change you."

My heart thuds in my chest, heavy but hopeful at the same time. I'm often confident in my actions, in my decisions, but this is something that's always evaded me. I've always been a bit rough around the edges. During my pageant days, I had to file that into softened curves and warm smiles. I overcorrected after moving to Wilks Beach. But now...maybe it's time to be the version of myself I only allow in the safety of a quaint wing shop. Maybe I can let both sides of my personality entwine in balance. Maybe I *can* have a pink house with a *Go Away* mat beneath my front door.

"I want to do whatever you've planned," I tell him, the incessant buzzing fading away.

"Really?"

The way Van lights up, the way his dimple pops as his smile creases the corner of his eyes nearly annihilates the fatigue dragging on my limbs. In the cozy warmth of his truck bed, I realize that I've also been waiting for this. For Van to be unabashedly who he is—pure, brilliant light. Van is undoubtedly the best thing that's ever happened to me, even considering the windfall of blessings I've received since arriving in Wilks Beach.

Let him be him, and let me be me.

"Yes." My own lips soften into a grin.

"You're sure?"

I roll my eyes. "On second thought—"

"Nope. Too late. You said yes." His palms frame my face for a quick kiss before he carefully gets out of the cab without jostling my ankle.

"I need pain meds," I shout as Van practically sprints in front of the truck to the passenger side.

"You got it," he says, tugging my door open and giving me double finger guns.

He's so effervescent, and it's such a goofy, unexpected gesture, the giggle tumbling out of me has a life of its own. Immediately, I slap my hand over my mouth. We both pause, staring at each other as wind swirls into the truck.

"Geneva Cecila Bradford." Van's tone is positively wicked as he leans forward, arms bracing the truck door. The stance accentuates his strong chest to a distracting degree, especially since he's wearing a fitted white t-shirt today. "Did you just *giggle*?"

I shake my head, my palm still over my lips.

The slow way the corner of his mouth tips up sends heat shooting over my collarbones and down my arms. I feel deliciously caged and cherished and desired. It's a heady sensation, making my muscles tense sequentially in anticipation.

Before he can lean any farther, the front door to my house swings open, bright light pouring into the truck cab. Silhouetted in the warm glow, Vivian gives an energetic wave.

"To be continued," Van whispers against my temple before picking me up and carrying me into the house.

TWENTY-SIX

Geneva

Not more than ten minutes later, we're settled around my overflowing coffee table. An impressive charcuterie board takes up most of the left side with several printed pages of a house's floorplan interspaced between glasses of lemonade and cans of flavored seltzer water. Van has me closest to the food with fresh ice on my ankle. It's propped on his lap while Vivian, Finn, Brynn, and Noah sit in mismatched chairs around the far side of the table.

"These were on the developer's website for the neighborhood, and based on the photos on Zillow and Google Maps, I think Henry's house might have this same floorplan." Brynn points a highlighter to the center of a printed page.

"Stacy told Mom that he has the ring in the desk drawer of the study off the main entry." Noah leans forward to gesture to another page, accidentally brushing Brynn's forearm.

The two of them snap back in their seats—his hand flexing, her rubbing the skin he inadvertently grazed. I'm genuinely surprised they're sitting next to each other when they could have easily bookended Vivian's and Finn's chairs.

"And Joanna is not here because?" It feels weird leaving her out of this impromptu planning meeting when the idea of retrieving the ring brings her so much happiness.

"I asked her if she wanted to come, but she said something about plausible deniability about heist details since she's already coordinating with Stacy for scheduling," Noah tells me, leaning back in his chair to rub the front of his right shoulder.

The old injury was bothering him at class yesterday, so I gave him some modifications. When Noah stretches his arm back to work deeper into the joint, I don't miss the way Brynn's eyes trace the unintentional pop of his bicep before she looks pointedly at her tapping toes.

"And you all want to be a part of this?" I ask, still shocked that they want to help, that they're even here.

Vivian's grin is so bright it could power a small city. "Haven't you watched those movies? You need a team, and there's no one better than us." She points to Brynn first. "The Getaway Driver since she struggles to stay under the speed limit."

"They're always too low," Brynn grumbles, and the corner of my mouth twitches.

"The Distraction in case something goes wrong inside. Noah can ring the doorbell, cause a ruckus, and say he's got a bone to pick with his dad."

"Wouldn't be the first time," Noah says, resting his elbows on his knees.

"Disguises, obviously." She thumbs the center of her chest. "I think your workout clothes would be best for maneuverability, but I'll sew you a custom black face and head covering in case you're caught on an external camera. I can also braid your hair. You should tuck it beneath your shirt and the head covering so they have one less identifier."

"The Backer who will get us an unmarked car to drive to and from the scene." Vivian's hand splays affectionately over Finn's forearm before looking at me. "You're The Infiltrator—the one entering the building and securing *the goods*."

I can't help the chuckle that escapes me at her bubbly explanation.

"Oh, and he's The Planner. The one that brought us all together." Her smile widens as she gestures toward Van with a flourish.

Finn tucks his shoe around the leg of Vivian's chair and scoots her close so he can drop a kiss over her chestnut curls. "Perfectly explained, gorgeous."

It's hard to believe that Vivian was the quietest person in Wilks Beach mere months ago.

"This is like something from a novel." Vivian beams at her boyfriend. "It's all very exciting."

"I'll also be running coms," Van adds. "I'd like you to have an earbud in while on the phone to let me know if something goes south. That way I can send Noah in if need be."

"I don't want you anywhere near this." My lips press into a tight line. "I thought we agreed on that."

Van takes my other foot between his large hands and begins massaging my arch. It's a struggle to keep my expression even, to not let my eyelashes flutter with bliss.

"I'm not letting you do this alone."

"Isn't that what they're for?" I sweep my arm toward the four people in my living room.

When Van simply shakes his head at me, that darned, confident smirk tracing his distracting lips, my hands fist at my sides. His strong fingers playfully pinch my Achilles, nearly drawing a gasp from my mouth. Warmth snakes up the back of my leg in curling tendrils as Van's mesmerizing gray eyes hold mine. It's not until Finn speaks up that I even remember everyone else is here, watching us.

"We should refresh our drinks in the kitchen," he says before encouraging everyone else out of the room.

"Be honest with me." Van's words are so low I almost miss them, but it's impossible to mistake his focused expression. All hints of flirtation are gone as he surveys my face. "Will you tell Vivian or Brynn or Noah if you're in trouble? Or will you push through, trying to protect everyone without ever thinking about yourself?"

I swallow, wondering how a craggy boulder got lodged in my throat.

"We knew from the beginning that I would be the one to take the fall if it came to that."

Van's exhale is long and slow. "But if we work together, that won't happen. If I'm the one on the phone, you'll tell me. Won't you?"

My mouth opens, closes, and opens again. The answer screams in my brain, but I can't get it past my teeth. We've only known each other a short time, but if I needed help, Van would be the one I'd ask for.

"You can be on the phone here."

He shakes his head. "I'd have to hang up to let Noah know he needs to go in, and you know I won't do that."

"You're making this sound like it's life and death." I roll my eyes to avert his piercing gaze. "I'm taking a small ring from my deadbeat dad's house. If the police show up, I'll explain that it wasn't his in the first place."

A deep breath fills my lungs before I continue. "Noah got his confrontation. He got his moment to tell Henry what a jerk he'd been. I never did. I got..." I don't say *left behind*. "I don't just want to do this. I *need* to do this."

"And I need to keep you safe," Van tells me, holding my gaze.

"Fine." I make a show of huffing, though something unlocks inside my bruised heart.

Van grins, his hands moving up my good leg and kneading my calf. "In the end, I think this could be a fun adventure for everyone. Even though it's technically breaking and entering...and theft."

"Justified theft," I counter.

He bounces a shoulder. "Sure. And if you let us be there for you, this can be a victorious story we'll tell for decades."

I like the idea of that way too much. I want to tell this story again and again with Van at my side, offering hilarious commentary. I want my pesky brother and my newfound friends to reminisce with us too.

"We talked about it," Vivian says, reentering the room. "And only you, Noah, Brynn, and Van need to be in the car. Finn and I will stay behind and make a celebratory dinner for us to enjoy afterward."

"I feel like we should have a team name or something." Finn rubs his beard scruff with one hand.

Everyone falls silent, thinking. I bite the inside of my cheek out of habit but then decide to let my instantaneous idea burst free.

"The Ring Leaders."

Vivian chuckles first, followed by Brynn. Soon, everyone is laughing along, holding their stomachs as we spill into another fit of mirth. It's wildly infectious. Each time one of us slows down, another person gets us started again. Van laughs so hard he ends up making these high-pitched squeaky sounds that should be unattractive but are adorably endearing.

When we finally settle down, my sides hurt nearly as much as the too-full ache in my chest. I gaze at my friends, my cheeks stinging from smiling. Then I turn my head, finding Van's gray eyes already on me, a look of absolute devotion tracing his handsome features.

Energy zips through every cell as our gazes meet, making breathing impossible. Van's chest shudders at the exact same time I struggle to fill my lungs with air. I don't even notice how strongly he's gripping my free ankle until he pulls his hand away to rub his ear, the slightest pink gracing his cheekbones. My heart trips and falls down three flights of stairs at that faint blush.

Brynn efficiently brings our focus back to finalizing the plan. After that, we enjoy the delicious spread and more conversation. At one point, someone suggests a heist-themed game of Pictionary and we use the back of the floorplans as the drawing board. Van and I team up with Brynn while Noah joins Vivian and Finn. I knew that my brother and Brynn were competitive—they're both former athletes—but you'd think a gold medal was up for grabs instead of bragging rights. Despite their thirst for glory, we all end up laughing as the game progresses. And when our team is triumphant, Noah only sulks a little bit.

Brynn hovers beside me while everyone else finishes cleaning up.

"You said there's nothing between you and Van, but the way you look at each other says otherwise." My gaze snaps from Van joking with Noah in the kitchen to Brynn raising her palms in front of her chest. "Not that it's a bad thing. All I'm saying is, Van seems to make you happy, and I'm here for you if you want to talk about anything." Her lips twist to the side, rueful. "I wasn't supportive enough when

Vivian was falling for Finn. I thought she'd get swept off her feet and abandon me, which…looking back on it, was a stupid fear."

My mouth opens, but only stilted air comes out. I can't respond because my mind keeps circling on one phrase—*falling for*.

The rest of the group comes back into the living room, and Brynn gives my shoulder an almost too hard pat, like she's my coach, and I'm about to go into the fight of my life. I numbly say goodbyes, acquiesce when Van offers to carry me upstairs, and stare at my reflection in my bathroom mirror for far too long as I brush my teeth. My molars have never been sparklier, my incisors pristine.

Am I falling for Van?

With my heart as battered as it is, am I even capable of that?

Fear, insecurity, and a looming sense of dread swirl in my stomach as I lie in my bed. As the windstorm thrashes against the house with its ghostly howl, I doubt there'll be any chance of sleep anytime soon.

TWENTY-SEVEN

Van

A t first, I think the thumping and cursing is part of the windstorm. After all, I've been hearing my name on gusts of air
since everyone left. My heart jackrabbited in my chest, thrashing like
a wild animal as I heard my sister's voice for the second time since
arriving at Wilks Beach. It's nonsensical, so I'm either hallucinating
or it's some weird magical trick, like the fireflies creating shapes in
Geneva's backyard.

Either way, the whispered *Evander* makes all the hairs on my arms
stand on end. Taylor only ever used my government name if I'd really
ticked her off. And I have no idea what she could be mad about. My
head shakes, tossing overgrown hair into my eyes and reminding me
I haven't had it cut since before I arrived.

"Taylor is gone, and none of this is real," I tell the empty kitchen.

The thumping continues until a crash has me racing to the staircase. Geneva's crutch tumbles down the last few stairs, clattering onto the hardwood floor.

"Hey." She gives me a rueful smile from halfway up the staircase, clutching the railing. "Apparently, this is harder than it looks."

I shake my head at Geneva but am beyond grateful for the distraction. Carrying her down the stairs, doing anything other than wondering why my sister's voice keeps repeating my name, is exactly what I need right now.

"Did you need something?" I ask, gathering her to my chest and heading downstairs.

"Not really, but I heard you were up."

A hum resonates in my throat. "Can't sleep either?"

She shakes her head as I set her in her kitchen chair and prop her ankle up on mine. The chairs are two different styles, and we've unspokenly chosen our favorites. Mine is a pressback chair with swirling designs etched into the oak, and Geneva's is a streamlined crossback chair stained glossy black.

"Cocoa?" I ask as the microwave beeps its completion.

Her head tilts to the side. "What number did you use this time?"

"214." I dump the packet into the steaming water and stir up the mixture. "Do you want some?"

"No, thank you. I'll have some pineapple, though."

I bend to grab Geneva's snack from the fridge, picking up her favorite seltzer water as well.

"No, thank you?" I ask, setting the two in front of her. "You feeling alright there, wifey? Normally you just bark orders."

She grimaces at the endearment before realizing I used it on purpose to get this reaction. Then her chin lifts, a daring flash in her eyes. "Don't pretend you don't like it."

My sip of cocoa goes down the wrong pipe. I slam my chest with a closed fist, coughing like I was just rescued from a riptide. Geneva hums, drumming her polished fingernails on the table before opening the container of pineapple. The way she sets a single piece on her tongue with a flirty wink is nothing short of—

"Evander!"

My gaze flies from Geneva to the window, half expecting to see my sister standing beyond the pane of glass. I don't, but that doesn't mean my heart isn't thrashing against my ribs. My hand shakes, making me slosh cocoa over the edge. With a curse, I set the mug aside, grabbing a paper towel to clean up the mess. After cleaning that, I wipe down the counters. I refold the kitchen towel, decide it's not good enough, and fold it again. Taylor was particular about keeping the house clean. It made it easier on Mama when she got home from whichever job she was working.

"Van, sit down."

"That's more like it," I joke, though my words sound uneven as I tidy Geneva's protein powders.

"Van," Geneva tries again.

It's the caring sweetness in her tone that makes me look over my shoulder. She leans forward, patting the chair her foot is currently occupying. Since my sister's voice sounds like a howling banshee instead of my memory of her, I cross the room. Geneva's gaze makes an efficient swoop of my face as I lift her ankle into my lap.

"What is it?"

I tap her shin a few times before I'm able to look into her warm brown eyes. "Do you hear that?"

"The wind?"

A painful pressure corkscrews down my spine. "Yes, but does it...sound like anything?"

Anyone?

Her brows crease as she tilts her ear to listen. "We get windstorms like this during hurricane season. It's pretty typical for September, but this is nothing but a tropical storm. We're not even in the projected hurricane track. Otherwise, people would be buying out Dotty's Market. You don't have to worry. I didn't even fill the tub for this one."

Rain pelts the window as Geneva finishes her sentence, drawing her attention. When she looks back at me, she bends at the waist again, settling her fingers over mine.

"It'll be okay. Everyone's first hurricane season feels worse than it is."

I shake my head, unable to articulate what's truly bothering me. So much grief has stacked itself up like unopened boxes that my chest feels like it's caving in. Each breath feels tighter than the last, like my lungs have shrunk. I've treated a few people for panic attacks in the ER, most of them thinking they're having a heart attack. I check my pulse at my throat, already knowing it's severely elevated. Its deafening beat is hammering in my ears.

"Van?"

"Evander!"

When the voices overlap, I squeeze my eyes shut.

"Please...please talk to me."

I force a chuckle, the sound of it dry and cracked. "Another courtesy word. Lucky me."

Geneva's fingers squeeze mine with a fierce grip.

"It—" I stop, debating whether or not I should even voice this out loud. "The wind sounds like my sister saying my name."

To her credit, Geneva doesn't flinch, doesn't call me crazy or wrinkle her brow. Instead, she nods. "Okay. The wind sounds like it's saying *Van*?"

"Evander," I correct. "Like I'm in trouble. Taylor never used my full name unless I'd done something I wasn't supposed to."

Geneva's shoulders raise with a slow inhale.

"It's just—" I tug at my ear. "It's unsettling."

"I can imagine."

My fingers go back to tapping at Geneva's shin, strumming a melody without strings as the exhausting battle wars within me.

The wind continues to thrash at the windows while Geneva pulls her leg from my grasp. Using the table as leverage, she balances on her good foot and moves her chair right beside mine. Her fingers slide into my hair as she leans her head on my tense shoulder.

"Will you tell me more about her?"

I inhale a shaky breath, knowing I need to. I'm drained from not grieving these last five months.

"She's the one who gave me my name."

When Geneva just waits, expression open, I continue. "The story goes that Mama had been looking through a baby name book and read the meaning of Evander—a good man. She'd laughed bitterly, saying there was no such thing, but Taylor latched on to the idea. Mama preferred Christopher, but Taylor wouldn't let it go. She'd been learning her letters in preschool and wrote Evander on every scrap of paper. Eventually, Mama agreed, saying the name would help ensure I turned out better than the man who disappointed us all."

Geneva's thumb rubs back and forth across the base of my skull. "She sounds like a fighter."

A genuine laugh tumbles from my mouth. "You and Taylor would have gotten along."

"Was she also a cranky dragon?"

I chuckle despite the crevasse opening in my chest. I've been trying not to focus on memories of Taylor for so long that speaking about her feels like relearning a language.

"No. Her disposition was more like mine, always trying to find the positive in any given situation. Or rather...I got my outlook from her."

I stare off into the sluicing rain, a slight smile curving my lips. "Her laugh was always a bit too loud—a touch too boisterous. She used to hoot every time she was excited. It drove Mama crazy, but

Taylor took life by the horns and squeezed joy out of every moment. And then she grabbed my hand and dragged me along. We didn't have much growing up, but she made everything fun. It wasn't until I did activities without Taylor that I realized that life wasn't inherently joyous. *She* made it that way."

Geneva intertwines our fingers when my voice cracks. I'm immediately grateful for the support. Otherwise, I'm pretty sure my sternum would break open.

"You can imagine my surprise when I found out that my friends didn't have M&M-eating contests after getting shots, or got to sit on the top of their apartment building to count the stars when they got straight As because their sister had stolen a skeleton key, or that she turned taking out the trash into a covert spy mission with code names and broken walkie-talkies."

"*That's* why you're so obsessed with this ring heist."

Another bark of laughter escapes me at the same time a single tear slides down my cheek. I glance at Geneva as she wordlessly catches it with her fingertips, her eyes the softest I've ever seen them. Her silent support catches me off guard. I've seen Geneva end a conversation the moment it veers toward the emotional. Her willingness to hold space for me gives me the courage to keep speaking.

"She also stood up for others, like you do. When I started showing signs of being advanced for my age and began getting bullied, Taylor defended me any way she could—words, fists, whatever was necessary. One time, she took kitchen scissors to a neighbor kid's bangs." A watery chuckle bubbles in my throat. "He looked ridiculous for weeks but never spoke to me again. Taylor took that natural protectiveness and used it in her job as a social worker, helping foster kids get the absolute best care they could. You two would have been unstoppable together."

"I'm sorry I didn't get to meet her," Geneva says, her words thin.

"Me too."

A peaceful quiet stretches between us as the storm pitters into errant drops and whispers of breeze. It's only now that I notice the wind has stopped murmuring my name. With Geneva's fingers playing with the hair at the nape of my neck, I rest my cheek to her crown. Exhaustion sags at my muscles, but it's like the kind you feel after a long workout, one you know you'll recover from.

When Geneva yawns, I ask, "Can I help you to bed?"

"No. Not yet," she says, stifling another yawn on the back of her hand. "Not if you're not ready."

"I think that's all I want to say tonight," I tell her, sitting up to catch her gaze. "But can we talk more if I need to later?"

Geneva's fingertips trace my cheekbones, my temples, before one thumb wisps over my eyebrow. "Whenever you need to."

I lean forward. I'm helpless not to, but the second our lips brush, I know this kiss is different than any we've shared before. As her hands cradle my face, I feel nurtured and adored and wanted in a way that's separate from our usual heated kisses. Geneva's fingers tremble as they slip down my neck and grip the back of my t-shirt to gently pull me closer. I'm two seconds from saying something I shouldn't, from murmuring what's been radiating from my heart since Saturday, since I could so easily see our future—our forever—together.

It was then that I realized how much I've been lying to myself. At the concert in Vegas, I rationalized the otherworldly shift I'd felt the first time I saw Geneva as a side effect of my overwrought emotional state. Even when I saw her later at the bar, I ignored that incessant pull, telling myself I was imagining things. When her surprised laughter felt like it was breathing life back into my weary soul, I shook my head at my foolishness. But a month later, when I came to Wilks Beach to simultaneously keep my word to Taylor and hold grief at bay, it felt like coming home.

Now, as Geneva kisses me tenderly, all I can think is...yes, now, here, *you*.

Always you.

"Stay with me tonight?" Geneva says on a breathy exhale, her brown eyes darting between mine. "Just to sleep. I want... I need to know you're okay."

I should make a quip about being confident and capable—doing so would return us to our usual teasing repartee—but instead, I rest our foreheads together.

"Okay."

After I carry her upstairs, I get comfortable on the opposite side of the bed and turn off the light, pleasantly surprised when Geneva rolls over and rests one hand on my chest.

"Good night, Van."

I smile. "Sweet dreams."

A soft snort fills the quiet bedroom. "You and sweet things."

"You have no idea, darlin'," I say, placing my palm over her hand. "You have no idea."

TWENTY-EIGHT

Van

"Well, well, well. What do we have here? It looks like a dead man."

It's barely light out when someone grabs the ankle I flopped on top of the covers and yanks. I have enough working brain cells to let go of Geneva before Noah pulls me halfway down the mattress.

"Noah! What are you doing?" Geneva bolts upright, pushing her hair out of her face.

Sometime in the middle of the night, she scooted closer to me, nuzzling her nose against the hollow of my throat. I wrapped my arms around her as her hair flopped over her eyes, tickling my chin.

"Just protecting your honor. No biggie. I'll be done in a minute."

I jerk my leg out of Noah's strong hold and hop to my feet just in time to avoid getting clobbered by him. "Nothing happened."

"Why are you even here this early?" Geneva asks, shoving blankets aside and wincing slightly as she puts weight on her ankle to stand.

"My new best friend and I were supposed to go for a morning run, but guess who wasn't downstairs or in his room when I let myself in?"

Oh. I'd completely forgotten. Since my internal clock wakes me up early every day, I hadn't thought to set an alarm on my phone. Slumbering in Geneva's sandalwood-scented sheets was, apparently, as effective as taking three sleeping pills.

"That's it." She grabs her crutch, hopping a few steps and outstretching her hand. "Give me back my key."

"No." Noah jukes and tries to get a hold of me again. "I need it for circumstances like this."

A quick spin to the left and I'm beyond his grip, putting myself between him and Geneva. I splay my palms in front of me. "I had a rough night and needed support. That's all."

"Support my—"

"Noah! You're being ridiculous."

This time, he does make contact, and I take his momentum toward the bathroom, keeping him as far from Geneva as possible. The last thing she needs is to get hurt again.

"If I wasn't injured, I'd knock you out myself," Geneva seethes as we scuffle. "I'm a grown woman. This is my house. And we're *married*."

"That's a technicality."

Using the techniques I learned from Ron—the behemoth of a security guard who works in the ER—I pin Noah's arms behind his back, pushing him against the bathroom door.

"I'm getting more action from you than I've had in months. Can we take it down a notch?"

Noah heaves out a sigh, his right cheek pressed flat. "Fine."

I wait a few breaths before letting go and stepping back, making sure Geneva is behind me.

It's not easy for Geneva to cross her arms while leaning on a crutch, but she manages it. I get secondhand shivers from the gelid gaze she sends her brother.

"We are going to have a conversation about this." Each word is hissed through gritted teeth.

Noah sags against the bathroom door, muttering, "I was just trying to be the good guy. I never get to be the good guy."

"You're literally a firefighter who saves lives," she practically shouts.

"That's different." He palms the back of his head, glancing sheepishly at me. "Sorry, man. I might have overreacted."

"Might have?!"

I place my palm between Geneva's shoulders to keep her from lurching forward and accidentally hurting her ankle. "Why don't we all have a cup of coffee?"

"There's not enough coffee in the world to make up for his shenanigans." Though her tone hits like a coarse brick to the face, her body softens into my touch.

Noah lifts a shoulder, his grin boyish. "If I shenan once, I'm gonna shenanigan."

"Out!"

With a huff, Noah tromps down the stairs. Geneva scrubs her fingertips over her forehead with a throaty growl.

"Hey." I keep my words and my touch soft as I run my palms up and down her arms. "It's a good thing to have someone so worried about you."

"*Unfoundedly* worried. We're both fully dressed." Her jaw tightens as she gestures to her striped long-sleeve sleep set and my scrub pants and shirt. "And so what if we had been...canoodling."

My brows shoot up. "Canoodling?"

"I'm not going to use medical terms, doctor," she tells me with a glare. "Even if we were...you know. We're married, and that's my business."

"It absolutely is," I agree, sliding my hands up to gently massage her shoulders.

Geneva tilts her head back, closing her eyes and taking a slow, steadying breath. "Okay, I think I'm ready to not murder my idiot brother now."

My lips quirk. "Dismemberment before breakfast is generally discouraged."

"But it's oh so fun." My wife's grin is completely unabashed, lighting her whole face.

It's impossible not to hold her when she smiles at me like that. The crutch clatters to the floor as I sweep Geneva in my arms. Instead of immediately striding downstairs, I nuzzle the sweet spot beneath her ear, my grin blooming when her breath catches.

"Thanks for last night."

She snorts. "Like you said, nothing happened."

I lift my head to catch her gaze, willing to risk it. Geneva may not have realized the significance of her being emotionally available while I worked through my grief, but I do. I don't want her to backtrack and pretend like last night wasn't monumental. I've seen the way she edges around serious conversations, how she redirects her brother or her friends. The way she asked about Taylor, the way she was there for me when I needed it most…

"I meant how you supported me."

"Oh." She ducks her chin for a beat before her eyes meet mine. "You're welcome."

We find Noah grumbling beside a steaming coffee pot, arms crossed. I get Geneva comfortable before placing my now-cold cup of cocoa in the microwave. Our gazes snag before I press 58 on the keypad. The eyeroll I receive makes fizzy energy skip to my toes like a stone over a pond.

"Stop making goo-goo eyes at each other. It's creeping me out." Noah pulls down two more mugs, aggressively setting them on the countertop. "Wasn't this supposed to be a ruse? A fake marriage?"

"Things changed."

I almost swallow my tongue at Geneva's resolute words. I've been wanting the undeniable spark between us to transform into something real but was afraid to ask if she wanted the same for fear of her shutting me out. But Geneva's firm posture and no-nonsense glare dares her brother to argue.

"I'm going to be the only single person left on the island," Noah says, more to himself than to us.

Before I can reassure him, his phone rings in the pocket of his joggers.

"Hey, Mom." Noah listens for a long while, nodding faintly before glancing at Geneva's ankle resting atop the seat of my chair. "Yeah, it's looking better, so I think next Friday will work. I'm actually in her kitchen right now."

Joanna talks while Noah's smile turns devious. "Oh, I know she's not a morning person, but that's the right of the younger brother. I've got to keep her on her toes."

"Give me the phone." Geneva outstretches her hand.

Noah slaps it to his chest. "No. It's mine."

"Are you two sure you weren't raised together?" I ask through a chuckle, putting my cocoa back for an additional 22 seconds since it isn't hot enough.

Joanna murmuring against Noah's shirt reminds him that he's still on a call. "Sorry, Mom. Let me put you on speaker."

Noah sets the phone on the kitchen table before filling a mug to the brim.

"Morning, everyone. I've got good news!" Joanna's chipper voice radiates from the speaker. "Stacy found us a window to get the ring back. Apparently, he's taking one of his love interests on a trip next Friday. They leave in the early evening. Stacy's oldest has a football game, but after that, she can use her key to enter the house. We talked about it, and it makes more sense for her to forget something and then need to retrieve it than to clean the house at night. And with that dirtbag on a plane, Stacy can just text him that she went over to get it, and he won't even know she was there until he lands. It's perfect."

Geneva raises her eyebrows, nodding. "I like that he'll be out of town. That makes it easier in case something goes wrong."

"My thoughts exactly," Joanna agrees. "Will your ankle be okay by then?"

"Yes. I'm sure of it."

"Great," she chirps, bringing a tender smile to Geneva's lips. "Sorry Noah is bugging you."

"Hey!" Noah says as I add, "He's actually here for me. We're about to leave for a run."

"Oh." The timbre of Joanna's voice changes, turning a bit wobbly. "That's so nice that you all are getting along. All a parent wants is for their children to be happy."

Geneva looks down at the table. Her murmured, "Not every parent," is barely audible, and Joanna misses it entirely.

"Okay, I'll let you go. Love you."

We all say our various goodbyes before ending the call.

A stagnant hush falls over the room once Joanna's cheery voice isn't echoing off the cabinets.

"That's fortuitous, with the timing," I say, trying to brighten the mood.

Noah lurches forward, nearly strangling Geneva with his fierce hug. "I want you to be happy too. And if this goofball does that, then I'm glad."

Surprisingly, Geneva doesn't shrug out of his grip but settles her hands over his arms, embracing him. "He's no more of a goofball than you are."

Warmth ribbons between my ribs at the same time a drop of sorrow splashes over everything. Seeing Geneva and Noah—sister and brother—hug reminds me of how affectionate Taylor always was with me. It's odd having genuine joy for Geneva and my newfound friend while my stomach simultaneously swirls with longing.

After avoiding it for so long, I'm realizing that grief isn't supposed to make sense. It's amorphous and tangible at the same time. Sharp and dull. Fond memories and gnawing regret.

Everything all at once.

The deep breath filling my lungs draws Geneva's attention. A divot forms between her brows before she outstretches her hand to me. Noah notices, grabbing my forearm and dragging me into the embrace.

"Aren't group hugs the best?" he asks. "I miss a good dogpile."

Geneva grumbles unintelligibly as a bark of laughter leaves my lips.

My gorgeous wife tolerates the hug for exactly two more seconds before shrugging us off. "Get out of here. Aren't you two supposed to be running off that puppy energy?"

When I return downstairs with Geneva's crutch after getting changed, I find her and Noah chatting about some drama from the fire station. Geneva is trying her best not to look interested though I know how much she secretly enjoys gossip.

I drop a kiss on her temple. "Do you need anything before we leave?"

"No." Her lips purse in annoyance, but it's all for show. "But when you get back, I have a job for you."

"A job, huh?" I ask, lifting a suggestive eyebrow.

Noah makes a gagging sound. "Good thing I haven't eaten breakfast."

"You're welcome to leave at any time." She gives him a saccharine smile. "And never come back."

Noah pushes off the counter, huffing. "And after defending your honor..."

"Honor that is very much intact," she quips.

"Okay, you two." I nudge Noah by the shoulders toward the exit. "Disembowel each other later."

"Looking forward to it," Geneva calls sweetly as I open the front door.

Noah quickly switches to talking about his favorite sub-ject—baseball—as soon as we break into a warm-up jog. I listen, only knowing the cursory rules, since we never had the money for afterschool activities, and being raised by two music-loving women, I never got into professional sports. You'd be more likely to find me at a Lainey Wilson concert than an MLB game.

As Noah spits out stats like they're vital signs, I try to follow along, but really my mind can't stop wondering what Geneva has planned for later.

TWENTY-NINE

Geneva

"Y ou're sure about this," Van asks, blinking. He looks about as stunned as when I'd knocked the wind out of him in Vegas.

I roll my eyes, leaning on my crutch though my ankle feels much better than it did yesterday. It might have something to do with the incredible night's sleep I received being wrapped in Van's strong arms. Even with the activity of crutch-walking into the store, it doesn't throb that bad. Outside, I politely—okay, firmly—refused Van's offer to carry me from the car. Though it's quickly become my favorite household activity, it felt weird on the mainland.

"Yes."

"If you really mean it, then I'm going to kiss you in public."

I tense. Though we've let Brynn and Noah know that this—whatever *this* is—isn't fake anymore, we've kept all large displays of affection securely tethered to the house.

My chin lifts. "You wouldn't dare."

The slow way Van shakes his head as he pushes into my space makes my pulse race. Warmth explodes over my collarbones, in the pit of my stomach, and slips down my legs. He stops with his lips mere inches from mine, his gaze mischievous.

"Wouldn't I?"

"Evander," I caution, trying to gain some control when my body is ready to go all limp-noodle on me. "Don't even think about it."

"I never liked the way my full name sounded before, but—" He breaks off with a curse, rubbing his mouth with the knuckles. "It's like a song from your lips."

A startled exhale escapes me, not knowing how to respond. I *always* have a comeback, a quip, but Van has taken my brain, put it in the microwave for 47 seconds, and rendered me useless.

I should hate it.

I *definitely* don't.

"Am I kissing you, darlin'?"

My eyes dart to the paint swatch display, the myriad of colors taunting me. This is the reason we're here after all—to tell him that I changed my mind about the exterior paint color.

"Why do you care so much about this? It's just paint," I say, crossing my arms as best I can while using the crutch.

As predicted, Van is delighted by my grumpy question. "You know why."

I *think* I might know, but I'm not quite ready to admit it to myself. I'm not quite ready for *a lot* of things—to fully flesh out what's between Van and me, to own up to the fact that he's my favorite person to talk to, to acknowledge that just being near him lowers my blood pressure. If I don't work through these thoughts, I don't have to focus on what I'll do when our agreed-upon time is up.

Denial is a strategy I mastered early. High heels don't hurt that bad. Shapewear isn't suffocating. My muscles aren't exhausted after an hour on the bag. My good friend, denial, has yet to steer me wrong, so I'm betting it won't this time either.

"A quick peck on the cheek. That's it."

When he leans close, his lips over the shell of my ear, liquid fire shoots through my veins. "As always..." My eyelashes flutter when his warm breath skirts over my cheekbone. "I'll take what I can get."

I don't notice when Van takes my crutch and leans it against the display, because I'm distracted by the featherlight brush of his lips over my skin. So when he grips my waist to lift me in a Disney princess twirl, I burst into laughter—that is, until my swinging feet nearly clip a toddler running down the aisle.

"Sorry," I tell the mom as she chases after him.

"Next, you'll be telling me that you want to go to puzzle night at the library," Van says, vibrating with excitement as he gently returns me to the ground.

Last night, Finn informed us that the community survey results were in and that the library would be hosting a community puzzling night and puzzle swap on Wednesday evenings.

"Actually..." I *had* been thinking that we should make a few more town appearances as a couple. For Joanna's sake. Not because I want to see how fast it takes Van's genius brain to decipher a thousand-piece puzzle.

His mouth breaks into that unabashed, wholesome smile. "You keep surprising me. Okay, we'll do puzzles tonight, and in the meantime, we can paint the house."

I assumed Van would be excited that I decided to choose something other than gray for my exterior paint, but more in a he-won-a-challenge kind of way. His genuine wholehearted support makes my chest ache.

"It's too wet after last night's storm. Plus, there's another tropical storm forecasted in a few days. We'll have to wait until it's reliably dry. Probably next week or the week after."

It shouldn't be attractive to see a grown man pout, but when that man's callused hands simultaneously squeeze the sliver of skin left open from your cropped tank, all the wires get jumbled. Almost as quickly as disappointment slipped over his defined cheekbones, Van brightens.

"Hotties, then?"

My sweet golden retriever, always finding the bright side.

"I'm down for wings, but it's a little early." I hesitate, biting my lip. "I had another errand I thought we could run first."

Van waits, patient as ever as I garner the courage to say the next part. I've never needed a second opinion on anything, but the more I thought about this, the more I *wanted* Van to give me his. And just like the paint color, I have a hunch that it'll make that dimpled smile light his face. It's addicting—that smile. Since my ability for self-preservation vanished the second his eyes twinkled, I'm running headfirst into this idea, even though I should probably be keeping these parts of myself under lock and key.

"I thought I'd add a few new items to my wardrobe, and since you love color so much, I suppose it wouldn't hurt if you weighed in," I tell him, infusing my words with extra sass.

Van's fingers tense on my waist as a muscle ticks in his jaw. I'd expected a reaction similar to when I told him about the house color—pure, vibrant joy—so the heat slipping into his gaze catches me off guard.

"You're getting kissed now." The rough texture of his voice makes goosebumps erupt on my bare arms.

"You can't—" My flustered sentence cuts off when he leans in. Breathing becomes impossible when his lips hover at the corner of my mouth, close but not touching.

"I can't what? Kiss you in public? Do you have any idea how hard it is not to kiss you every second I'm conscious? Resisting you is a full-time job."

Since keeping my eyelashes open is taking all my focus, my chiding response gets caught in my throat. "Evand—"

"Say it." Van shifts even closer, every slight point of contact between us suddenly incendiary. "Say your husband's name."

A shaky breath escapes me as my fingers curl helplessly around his sleeve. I should be able to focus on something other than Van's undeniable presence. I should be able to center myself on the overbright lights of the warehouse, the errant noises of other shoppers, and the oppressive scent of sawdust. But none of that exists anymore. It's just me and Van and the absence of time, since the seconds feel like they've been stretched into days.

"Excuse me," a voice interrupts. "Could you hand me the Maine Cottage paint swatch. I'm not as tall as I used to be."

Behind us, an older gentleman with wispy white hair outstretches his arm toward the top of the display. His red plaid patterned button-up is tucked into neatly pressed jeans, and a wry smile creases his mouth.

"Of course, sir." Van extends the crutch to me before moving a step away to grab the paint swatch. "Is there anything else I can help you with?"

"No. That's it." He shifts his gaze between us, his hands drumming on the handlebar of his cart. "Bet you're newlyweds. You've got that spark between you."

When Van's ears pink, a thick pulse of adoration beats in my chest.

"We are," I say when Van doesn't respond.

The man hums, his grin growing wider. "Nothing better. I've been with my Mary fifty-six years—most of them good. Every marriage has its rough spots, but nothing beats that new love zip."

Again, I expect Van to jump in, to use one of the made-up stories he tells the locals of Wilks Beach when they ask about our marriage. How we're perfect for each other because of our differences, or that the moment our eyes first met, he'd known things would be different with me.

"I'm enjoying it," I tell the man, warm honesty infusing my words.

"As you should." When his phone rings in his front chest pocket, the man chuckles. "Speaking of Mary. If you'll excuse me."

I watch the man lean an elbow on the cart to move down the aisle while chatting with his wife before glancing up at Van. His gray eyes are unreadable as they scan my face, but the tension in his shoulders is unmistakable.

"Did you mean that?" A deep inhale broadens his chest. "What you just said?"

My brows pinch. Isn't Van enjoying our time together? I know we haven't had a formal discussion about the status of our relationship, like mature adults, but he's always smiling whenever I enter a room or finding little ways to touch me. I assumed...

"Yeah. Aren't—"

But I don't get to finish my sentence because my husband kisses me fully and deeply in the middle of a hardware store.

Thirty

Van

A week and a half later, my fingers tap an anticipatory rhythm on the interior of the sedan's door. "I cannot overemphasize how excited I am. If I wasn't buckled into this getaway car, I'd be doing back handsprings."

"I know, right?" Noah says beside me in the backseat. "Wait, you can do a back handspring? You've got to teach me."

I chuckle. "I can't, actually, but I just feel like this energy would just carry me through it. You know?"

"I get it. I kind of wish the jerk wasn't on an airplane so I could jump into action."

Geneva turns around from the passenger seat, glaring. "Do I need to separate you two?"

"No, ma'am," I answer while Noah crosses his arms and says, "I'd like to see you try."

A long-suffering sigh comes from Brynn. "Can we focus? Good planning only goes so far. It's following through with your commitments that counts."

Her gaze shoots to Noah's in the rearview mirror, a clear admonishment. Noah's grin vanishes as he snaps his gaze toward the darkened street. Stacy's son's football game went into double overtime, and then she needed to drive a few players home before trucking across town, so it's much later than we'd expected. We already ate Vivian's delicious dinner, but she promised brownies and ice cream upon our return.

Brynn steals another sip of coffee before she turns onto the street leading toward Henry's neighborhood. Since she needs to open Seabreeze Beans at five-thirty tomorrow morning, she's the one most affected by the unintentional time shift.

As planned, Stacy is pulled over, waiting in her car. When she sees us, she goes first, using her code to get both cars in. Fortunately, for as austere as the neighborhood is, there's no guardhouse or gate attendant, just a simple keypad at the gate.

Finn's ability to find a perfectly nondescript car with untraceable plates is a little scary, but I guess billionaires can get whatever they want. He even outfitted the car with a rideshare sticker and mini bottles of water to waylay suspicion. Brynn's phone glows in the dash mount with navigation cued up to take her two fares downtown. She's wearing gray sweats, and Noah and I are in dress shirts and pants to corroborate our cover.

Earlier, when I'd exited my bedroom in a yellow checkered shirt, Geneva had nearly dragged me by my collar to change into something less colorful. She picked my gray button-down from the closet and handed it to me. I smirked, reaching up to slowly undo my shirt, but instead of daring me to continue with a snarky chin lift, Geneva fled the room. Her energy has been off all night, but I can't really blame her when we're about to break into her estranged father's house.

Stacy pulls into the semi-circle driveway and parks in front of the five-car garage while we wait two houses away. Since Henry is a fan of fast, flashy cars, the garage isn't tucked away, but proudly displayed in front. That's slightly problematic as there are cameras catching nearly all of the ostentatious front yard. However, the personal door is tucked around the side, so as long as Geneva sticks to the privacy trees at the property line, she'll be invisible.

The lights emphasizing the front entrance columns illuminate Stacy making a show of digging through her purse and manually locking her car. She'd already texted Henry after his departure time that she noticed her driver's license had slipped out of her wallet. She explained that she's retracing her steps in hopes of finding it so she doesn't have to waste hours at the DMV.

"Okay, she's in," Brynn says.

When Geneva hesitates, I slide my fingers over the seat to give her shoulders a squeeze. "You've got this."

Geneva nods, tucking one earbud in and accepting my call before sliding the custom head covering over her braided hair. It makes her look like a ninja from an old movie, but I bite the inside of my cheek to keep from smiling. Brynn shifts into drive, crawling forward until we're beside the property line. The stealth with which Geneva slides from the car and into the darkness of the cypress hedge shouldn't be impressive given her athleticism, but my jaw still drops open. Brynn leans over to softly close the door before turning around and reparking near the hedge.

"I just realized that you should have a codename," I tell Geneva through my earbud. "It seems foolish that we didn't already establish it. How about wifey? The wifester? Wifemperess supreme?"

I hear a little grunt over the line—probably a suppressed growl—that makes me grin like a madman.

"Oh, I've got it—wiferoni. No BWE. Best Wife Ever. Of course, there's always Wifezilla."

Noah chuckles softly before sliding down in his seat to slip out of the lamp light.

"Just because you're in my ear doesn't mean you have to talk," she whisper-chides.

"Don't I, though?"

The sound of a door opening in the background and Stacy's voice directing Geneva into the house sends another fissure of energy crackling down my bones. Taylor would love this. If she were still alive, she'd demand to be the one to take the ring back, to right this wrong. There was nothing she hated more than unjustness, and she battled a lot of it as a social worker.

A half-cough/half-sob rips from my throat as sorrow ribbons through my ribs. I hit my chest with my fist, exaggerating the cough to cover the moment of vulnerability. Normally, I wouldn't care. My heart has always been there right on my sleeve for everyone to see, but I've learned working as a doctor that there are times I need to tuck it away. You can't fall apart if it's your job to put everyone back together.

"Are you okay?" Geneva's tender voice is a soothing balm to my aching soul. She's not even in the car, but she knows me so well she saw right through my coughing fit.

"I'm fine," I say and then add, for Noah and Brynn's benefit, "Just accidentally swallowed my gum."

"Tell me when we get home."

It's not a request. Ever since I opened up about Taylor, Geneva has noticed when heartache slides into my voice. Every time, she led me to the couch and waited for me to talk about it, usually with her knees against my thigh and her reassuring fingers in my hair.

"Okay," I tell her, knowing I'll feel better afterward. I always do. I've never been in a relationship where I've felt simultaneously challenged and cherished.

Being with Geneva has also made me realize that I've never really wanted something *for myself*. My whole life I've strived to not be my father. I've focused on being a good man. That meant serving others as much as possible. When we discovered how fast I could learn, I chose a career that not only helped people but allowed me to provide for Mama and Taylor.

But I want Geneva for me—selfishly, *desperately.*

"I'm entering the study," Geneva says at the same time Noah swears under his breath.

"He shouldn't be here, but I think that's him." He points down the road at the luxury car slowing at the last stop sign before entering this curving uphill street.

"Henry might be back," I tell Geneva. "Get out of there."

But unlike before, there's no snappy response reminding me she's the one that gives commands. A beep sounds in my ear, and I glance down to see the call has disconnected. I redial, but it goes to voice-mail.

"Maybe it's another person with the same Lambo," Noah says, his voice doubtful.

Geneva's message floods my earbud, and without thinking, I react. Darkness engulfs me as I sprint up the hedge line before the oncoming car turns the final curve toward the house.

THIRTY-ONE

Geneva

I t's easy to find the ring box shoved in the back of Henry's second desk drawer, right where Stacy said it would be. Just to be safe, I take a picture of the mess of envelopes, pens, rubber bands, and an assortment of random receipts so I can put the box back exactly where I found it. I didn't prepare a decoy but instead have a note of my own for when I remove the ring.

With only the light from the hallway slipping into the room, I lift the box's lid. The ring is even more beautiful than Joanna described. An intricate, looping pattern that resembles interlocking infinity symbols circles the entire ring. Each loop is bordered with tiny, round-cut diamonds that add subtle sparkle. Set within the larger loops are slightly larger diamonds spaced evenly around the band, creating eye-catching focal points. It's ornate yet elegant and would effortlessly complement the rest of my gold jewelry.

My palm presses to my racing heart when I realize how much I want this vintage ring, how much I want all of this to be real. But that means I'd have to be honest about how terrifying that is. It's daunting to offer yourself up on a platter and hope that the person scrutinizing your soul deems you worthy.

Feeling suffocated, I rip off Vivian's face covering and tuck it into my waistband. My eyes close as I take several rounds of breath to steady myself. When Van's dimpled smile flashes into my mind, my scattered breathing evens out. Every time I reveal another barbed part of myself, Van holds it in his hands like I just gave him a treasure.

Determination floods my bloodstream as I make a decision.

I'm not letting Van go unless he asks me to. I'm going to fight—for him, for *us*.

So what if I have a truckload of emotional baggage because my dad had two families and my mom only wanted me around to win beauty pageants. You know what having crappy parents does? It makes you resilient. It shows you how strong you really are. And I'm tough enough to get out of my own way and *grow*. I'm capable of accepting my past and choosing something different for my future. I'm willing to strive to be a better person for Van, but more importantly, *for myself*.

My fingers are steady as I remove the ring and slip my note into the box. After zipping the ring into a secure pocket in my leggings, I use the photo on my phone to put the box back exactly where I found it. A victorious smile lifts the corner of my mouth until headlights flash through the front windows. Footsteps run down the hall as the whir of a garage door opening breaks the silence of the large house. I bolt to the study entrance and collide with someone much taller than Stacy.

Van almost looks like an angel with the warm light of the hallway haloing his blond hair, a flush to his cheeks, and his collared shirt pulled sideways. That familiar zing of electricity slips down my spine when our gazes collide, and instantly, I feel at home.

"Your phone disconnected," he says, out of breath.

My eyes widen as reality slaps me in the face. Van's here—in *my father's* house. Something must be terribly wrong.

"Shoot."

I'd been so focused on taking back the ring, I hadn't noticed. And before I entered the house, I'd changed my alerts to silent because I'd gotten a few texts from Camille about the Mom and Me boxing class we're working on together and didn't want to be distracted.

"Yes, and—"

Stacy rushes into the hallway from her spot in the kitchen. "Hide."

Van's arms cage me, and before I know what's happening, his body flattens me into a mixture of winter coats. It should be a nice sensation, being wrapped in Van's scent, but an uneasy tension makes my muscles twitch. The door snicks closed behind him at the exact second a voice I haven't heard in years booms through the hallway.

"Stacy? I saw your message. Are you still here?"

The unhurried footsteps move toward the closet until Stacy calls out from the direction of the kitchen. "In here, sir. So sorry to be here after hours. Did you happen to see my driver's license?"

Van's heaving chest is tight against my back, his arms still wrapped around my middle as we wait for the footsteps to recede. A wool coat itches my cheek, but I don't move a millimeter. My blood sloshes around in my skull.

It takes entirely too long for Henry to move. Is he right outside the closet door? Is he planning on hanging up a coat? When we finally hear the click of his dress shoes walking away, Van's chin dips against my neck.

"Hold on. I'm messaging with the hotel, canceling things. Your ID? No, I haven't seen it."

"Why is he here?" I whisper once it's clear Henry is in the kitchen, chatting with Stacy.

"I don't know," Van murmurs, his breath puffing at my ear. "We'll have to stay put until we can think of something."

The space is tight, especially with every inch of Van pressed against me. I usually enjoy being close to him, but everything is instantly too small. The coats pressing in—scratchy and heavy—feel more like an impenetrable wall. I try to take a deep breath, but my chest won't expand. It's stuck. *I'm* stuck. My palms sweat within my nitrile gloves, and the urge to rip them off is more oppressive than the need to get out of—

"Breathe, darlin'."

Memories overlap, almost as overwhelming as the panic swirling in my stomach. Van at the bar in Vegas, that ghost of a smile on his lips. Van leaning into the driver's seat, coaxing me to eat wings at a park. Van telling me it's okay to accept help while gently detangling my hair. Van in Joanna's kitchen, washing dishes like he belongs there. Van threatening another man in a nightclub, his hair and eyes wild.

"Geneva, *breathe*."

"Gen," I correct weakly, my forehead sagging on the closet rod. "Only my husband calls me Gen."

His startled exhale tickles my neck before his lips find my temple for a gentle brush. My eyes fall closed, the sensation of being cherished like starlight in my veins.

"I'm going to give you some space."

Van's arms leave my waist as he leans as far back against the door as he can. It takes several rounds of focused breathing, but the incessant whirl in my mind subsides. I've never gotten claustrophobic before, but I've also never been trapped like this.

"Maybe it's upstairs?" Stacy's overloud voice draws my attention. "Can you help me look?"

"Why would your ID be upstairs when you always leave your purse in the kitchen?"

I clench the coat sleeve in front of me as they pass the closet before starting up the grand central staircase.

"I had to pay for my son's football pictures that day and was waiting for the team mom to call for my credit card number," Stacy lies. "I had my wallet in my jeans pocket."

As Henry begins to mansplain that she should take more care with important documents, their voices recede. When it's obvious they're tucked away upstairs somewhere, Van cracks the door and glances out. I never thought I'd be happy to see the inside of my father's new house, but I practically squeak at the beam of light slipping into the closet.

"Let's make a break for it." He steps back.

In my haste to get far away from the death-trap closet, I trip over Van's shoe. My palms come down to brace my fall, but Van catches me around my waist just in time. I hover inches from the floor like Ethan Hunt in *Mission: Impossible* as the voices upstairs come to an abrupt halt.

"What was that?" Heavy footsteps move toward the upstairs landing.

I'm pretty sure my heart stops. The plan was to get out of this house undetected, but I mentally prepared for a run-in with dear old Dad. What I didn't anticipate was Van rushing in like some kind of hero—though, honestly, I should have. I'm two seconds from wiggling out of Van's sturdy hold, throwing my face covering over his head to protect his identity, and forcing him out the front door when Stacy screeches.

"What? What is it?"

"I think I just saw a rat crawl into your favorite pair of John Lobbs!"

The second Henry's footsteps race out of earshot, Van sets me on my feet.

"Sorry," I whisper, tucking a loose strand of hair behind my ear. "I'm not usually this clumsy."

The corner of his mouth quirks. "I know. Come on."

We tiptoe down the hall toward the garage doorway, shutting it carefully back on its hinges once we're through, then repeat the process on the external door as well. As soon as we're both in the darkness of the cypress trees, we sprint—hand in hand. An inappropriate laugh bubbles in my throat, but I manage to keep it trapped. Since Noah had shifted to the passenger seat, Van and I dive into the back.

"Drive," I tell Brynn.

"Don't have to tell me twice." She peels out as quickly as I usually do when leaving my driveway.

It's not until we've exited the expensive neighborhood and are back on the freeway that anyone speaks.

"I assume you didn't get caught, but did you get it?" Noah asks.

A guffaw finally escapes as I reach into my pocket, lifting the ring into the light that strobes from the passing streetlamps.

"Yes! What a rush." Brynn slams the heels of her hands on the steering wheel. "That was so close."

"I was two seconds from barging in and bringing the whole house down."

"Good thing I made you wait." Her eyes cut to Noah, but they're teasing not defensive.

"Yeah. Yeah."

My brother slumps against the window, but I don't miss the slight curve of his lips.

"I can't believe Van got to you in time," Brynn says. "I thought for sure I'd need to listen for sirens."

Reaching over, I intertwine our fingers on the backseat and meet Van's gaze. "He did. He found me just in time."

Van brings my knuckles to his lips before his dimpled smile brightens his face, and he lets loose an elated hoot. I chuckle and surprise myself by howling along with him. Noah and Brynn join in, and before long, we're all hollering and laughing like lunatics. The delighted look on Van's face makes up for all those panicked seconds in the closet, a hundred times over.

"You did it," he murmurs as Brynn and Noah excitedly talk over each other.

I squeeze his fingers before returning the ring to its secure pocket. "We did it."

We're still high on the excitement of our escapade when we pull into the short driveway of my cottage, and Vivian and Finn spill into the midnight darkness. Van was right about this, about us all sharing in the victory after working together. I'm beginning to think Van might be right about *a lot* of things—something about that genius brain of his.

Vivian hugs me the second I step out of the car, her forehead nearly colliding with my collarbones. "I'm so glad it worked. Your mom will be elated."

For once, I don't correct her. I usually do when someone in town refers to Noah as my brother or Joanna as my mother. But I'm beginning to finally believe that this is where I belong. This is where my family—my *chosen* family—loves me as fiercely as I love them.

"What did you leave in the ring's place?" Finn asks, wrapping an affectionate arm around Vivian's waist.

My chin lifts. "A note."

Noah grins as he asks, "What did it say?"

The smile curling my lips isn't just defiant—it's justifiably righteous.

"You never deserved us."

THIRTY-TWO

Geneva

Normally, I'd stay in the building and work on the business side of running The Garage Gym in the hour between Saturday morning classes, but today, I lock the doors and jog down the road to Joanna's house.

It'd been harder than I'd anticipated not telling Van last night that I want things to be different, especially since he was lit up like a sparkler after our successful heist. I seriously thought he wouldn't go to bed, like a kid on Christmas Eve. His endearing energy made a goofy grin split my face, but I didn't fight it like I used to. I just let myself be happy alongside him.

Today, the nerves over finally telling Joanna the truth have been niggling at me. I'd been unable to eat breakfast and was more distant in class than I'd been in weeks. I'd heard through the Wilks Beach rumor mill that being married has softened my teaching style. None of my boxers said it to my face, though. Doing so would only have the reverse effect, and they're smarter than that.

The sound of Betty Davis's thick, gritty bassline reverberating through the front door makes my shoulders settle slightly. Joanna usually listens to the unapologetically bold singer when she's in a good mood.

I take a moment to tilt my face toward the warm sunshine of this unseasonably warm day and settle my breathing. Then my gaze falls to the garden beds on either side of Joanna's doorstep, bursting with wildflowers. Purple asters, goldenrod, and Queen Anne's lace preen from their garden beds, almost tickling your ankles. Five years ago, they were filled with manicured blooms, tended by a gardener at my father's command.

At that time, I stood on this doorstep with a different kind of news, but what I need to tell Joanna today is nowhere near as heartbreaking as that. She might not take this news well today, but I know in the end, Joanna and I will be okay.

"Oh, hey, honey." Joanna answers the door with a blue bandana tied around her curls, cleaning gloves on her fingers. She leans farther out of the doorway, looking for Van. "Where's your hubby?"

"Surfing with Nick." Or at least that's what his note said when I woke up this morning. "Can I come in?"

Joanna brightens. "Of course."

In the kitchen, she pulls off her gloves and turns down the music. "Do you want some coffee?"

I debate saying yes, just to have something to do with my trembling hands, but then straighten my spine and gesture to the table. "No, thank you. Could we sit for a minute?"

Her blue eyes flicker with worry, but I give her a soft smile. It took accidentally marrying a stranger to show me that it's okay to be more open—with myself and with those I love.

I shock her by taking her hand when she settles it on the table. "I need to talk to you about Van..."

Joanna rotates her family ring between her fingers as I finish telling her the truth. I handed it to her after explaining all the details of last night's successful retrieval.

"So I'd love to have this ring, but I want it under the right circumstances." I pause, biting my lip. "When I'm ready."

She nods to herself before taking a deep breath and lifting her chin. "I'm sorry I put so much pressure on you to be happily married."

"You didn't," I say firmly. "You were just excited about news you thought was real, which is totally understandable. And besides..." Churning, uneasy energy swirls in my stomach, but I force myself to verbalize what has been flitting in the back of my mind for weeks. "I want things to work out between Van and me. I...I really like him."

The steady warmth in my chest feels more significant than the word 'like,' but saying I like Van when I never discuss or even tolerate emotions in conversations is monumental enough. The last thing I need is to accidentally send Joanna into premature grandbaby-planning mode.

Though...

My mind flips through an imaginary montage of Van as a father. He'd happily let his nails be painted or wear a tutu and a tiara for a stuffed animal tea party. He'd probably make the best pillow forts and encourage our kids to take pony rides on his strong back. If there was a craft project or school spirit day, he'd be all over it, which honestly, is a good thing because I'm pretty sure I'd be terrible at all those things.

I'd never thought about having kids, just like I'd never thought about getting married, because it didn't seem possible. No one wants a prickly cactus for a mother. But maybe, with Van there to soften out my rough edges, we could make the perfect parenting team.

A hopeful smile lifts my lips.

Normally, this would be where I'd slam all these feelings—these sticky, *gross* emotions—into a black spiked lockbox and throw them in a corner. But instead, I sit with the uncomfortable resonance and slowly inhale.

None of this might come to fruition, and if it doesn't, that's okay. Or rather, *I'll be* okay. I've already proven that I'm strong enough to handle whatever life throws at me. But it's also safe for me to dream a bit, to think positively about the future and then fight for it.

"I don't want you to take this the wrong way," Joanna starts, and my abs flex on instinct, "but Van really likes you too."

My forehead wrinkles. "Why would I take that the wrong way?"

She tilts her head from side to side, hesitating. "Because you have a tendency to push people away when they show you affection."

Oh.

Yep. I totally do that.

"I'm..." It feels as if Joanna just sucker punched me. "I'm working on that."

The soft smile lifting her lips is breathtaking, like the first light spilling over the ocean's edge at dawn. She leans down to pet Princess, who's wandered into the kitchen. Demon will probably hide under the couch until after I leave, which is fine with me. That cat lives up to his name.

"What now?" Joanna asks, unable to tamp down her growing grin.

This is the part I'm not quite sure about. My fingers subconsciously twist my silicone ring. I want to explore a real relationship with Van, but I don't really want to take this off. I don't want him to move out. I don't want anything to change, which is probably incredibly selfish of me.

I just... I like the little life we built together—even if it's not real.

I like hearing his velvety voice singing those obnoxious love songs downstairs while I get ready in the mornings. I like that we can talk about an upcoming boxing match and the latest celebrity gossip with equal enthusiasm. I like dinners with him on the patio with Stella, Prunella, and Hank quietly going to roost.

"I don't know." My shoulders bunch as my gaze drops to the table.

Joanna's hand settles over my fidgeting ones. "When you decide, let me know. Until then, your secret is safe with me."

The moment is soft and nurturing and everything I wished I'd had for *so many* years. I flip my fingers and squeeze hers, meeting Joanna's warm gaze. After a shared smile, a thought occurs to me. I want to show Joanna the same care and support she's always shown me.

"What about you?"

Her freckled forehead crinkles. "What about me?"

"You'd said that you'd been having a hard time lately."

"Oh...about that." Joanna's cheeks pink as she averts her eyes. "This all made me realize that I'd been worrying too much about everyone else's lives and not putting enough focus on my own. So"—she takes a huge breath and lets it out in a rush—"I've decided to start dating."

"You have?"

One of the things we bonded over when I moved to Wilks Beach was our mutual distrust of men. But things have definitely changed for me, so maybe...

Joanna picks at her cuticle, suddenly looking half her age.

"There was this boy—" Her sentence breaks off with a short laugh. "Well, he's a man now. We knew each other in high school. I always thought he was sweet, but he was so shy. I didn't think he was interested. Anyway, dozens of years and two divorces later, he's taking me out on his boat next weekend." She flaps her hands. "I don't think I've ever been this nervous for a date. I mean, I haven't worn mascara in years."

A smile curls my lips as I lean forward, excitement sparking down my forearms. "Can I help you get ready?"

Joanna looks up, her shoulders dropping from her ears. "I would love that."

I'm mentally curating Joanna's ideal eyeshadow palette when I leave ten minutes later, so I don't notice Cade rounding the neighbor's large hedge until her bubble-gum pink hair nearly flies into my mouth as we collide. Her arms are over her head as she...

Is she taking a picture of the sky?

"Sorry," I tell her when we separate. "I was in my head."

Cade laughs. "I'm *always* in my head. Hey, check this out." She shows me the image on her camera app. "Doesn't that cloud look like a rhinestone cowboy hat?"

"Uh..."

The picture on her phone looks like a regular white cloud to me. If I squint, it *might* be considered hat shaped.

Cade lifts her chin skyward, grinning ear to ear. "Oh, now it's a turtle."

I don't glance up, taking her word on it.

"I'm actually glad I ran into you, because I wanted to talk to you."

Surprise flashes in Cade's blue eyes, but she quickly schools her expression, slipping her hands into the pockets of her short purple overalls.

"What about?"

This is something that's been bugging me since that first planning night, but being new to real friendships, I wasn't sure how to handle it. In my old world, exclusion and limited access were as common as spray tans and forced smiles.

I'd known that Vivian had asked Summer and Nick to join the heist, because Nick pouted when Summer shot it down. When Summer explained she didn't want them lying to her police officer brother for the rest of their lives, Nick took it as a sign she planned on keeping him around. But I should have talked to Cade sooner, and it shouldn't have taken literally running into her to make me realize just how wrong excluding her was.

"I want to apologize because last night we—"

"Oh yeah, the heist!" Cade practically squeals. "How did it go?"

"You knew?"

"Yeah. Vivian asked if I was interested, but since I have *zero chill* and no covert capacity, I figured you'd be more successful without me. Also, that kind of chaos is William's worst nightmare." She pulls her lips to the side, thinking. "Secondary to explosive, Christmas-themed clutter. I love him, so sometimes I skip things for his mental health, and other times, he pushes himself past his comfort zone for me."

I blink, processing that information as Cade rolls right along.

"It sounded like two truckloads of fun, though." She grabs my wrist, pulling us toward the ocean. "Tell me everything."

"I have to head back to the gym to teach my second class."

"Not a problem." She flips us with surprising strength. "I'll be your escort."

The corner of my mouth kicks up when Cade wraps my hand around her left arm, patting it twice and accidentally leaving a few specks of green glitter behind.

"Sorry," she says as the stubborn glitter refuses to budge.

"It's fine," I tell her. And honestly, it is.

Because who doesn't need a quirky, glitter-covered friend in their lives? I used to think I didn't, but now I see how wrong I've been.

Cade squints at me. "Who are you, and what have you done with Geneva?"

An easy laugh escapes me.

Her eyes widen. "Okay, now I'm really concerned. You're not in your standard black. You're speaking instead of grunting. And I don't think I've seen your lips lift that much...like, ever."

I glance down at my wine-red tank. It's one of several new athletic tops I purchased in addition to a few sundresses when I went shopping with Van. A memory surges forward, heating me from the inside. Van's gaze darkened each time I stepped out of the dressing room, his hands gripping the arms of his chair as if that were the only thing keeping him from reaching for me.

"My leggings are still black," I say, dragging myself back to the present. "And I'll teach my next class with my usual strict, no-nonsense efficiency."

Cade tilts her head, assessing. "Yeah. I guess you're still Taylor Swift in her *Reputation* era, but the *Lover* transition is clearly on the horizon."

At my puzzled expression, she giggles and pulls me down Sand Bend Road. "Never mind. Tell me about the heist. Don't leave out any details."

A flare of caution sparks in my mind. The more people that know about what happened, the messier it might be when Henry realizes we took back what was rightfully Joanna's. But then I remember that this community—*my community*—always has each other's backs.

"I was almost caught," I say, diving right into the juiciest detail.

Cade's exaggerated gasp pulls another chuckle from me.

"Start from the beginning," she demands—and I do.

THIRTY-THREE

Van

"**H**ey, Mama. How you doing?" My accent slips a little deeper, as it always does when I call my mom.

"Good. Mark took me out for brunch, and then we walked Shelby Bottoms a bit."

"That sounds like a nice day," I say, stalling.

My fingers glide through the sand as I sit on the beach in my wet swim trunks. Several locals are spread out on towels, enjoying the last beach day before fall truly sets in. After last night's win, I woke up an hour earlier than normal with energy to burn. Nick was more than happy to meet me at the beach in front of his condo and let me borrow his foamie for a Saturday surf session. If I stayed in Wilks

Beach, I could see myself buying my own board and using it on my days off.

But...quite a few things need to line up before that can happen.

"How 'bout you?"

I let myself deviate from my plan, telling Mama about surfing—how even for someone who's athletic, it's harder than it looks. We laugh at me taking a header off the front of my board and the kids boogie boarding nearby paddling up to see if I was okay. It was sweet of them to check on me, but I've yet to find an unkind local in Wilks Beach. And yes, I'm rolling Carol into that mix. She's cantankerous but not cruel.

"Don't go smashing your head in while you're on break. You'll need those brains of yours to get back to work at Nashville Medical Center."

My chuckle dies in my throat, and I swallow hard. Lying to her every day has darn near killed me over these past few weeks, but I've managed to keep our conversations tethered to the people I've met around town, activities with new friends, and the repairs I've been helping Geneva with.

"Mama, we need to talk."

"About how you're in love with your roommate? I already know that."

"What?" I sputter, coughing. "What are you talking about?"

I'd planned on finally talking about Taylor. I wanted to discuss my sister—what I loved about her, what I missed about her—with someone who *knew* her. Speaking to Geneva has been a balm I hadn't known I needed, but talking about Taylor with Mama is something that's important to me too. Also, I think it might help Mama. I know every grief journey is different, and I spent a lot of time running from mine, but I realize now the only way to deal with these crushing emotions is to trudge through them, as much as that feels impossible some days.

"Oh, bub. Did you forget that I know you better than the back of my hand?"

No use denying something that's absolutely there—not when simply seeing Geneva is the best part of my day.

I run my fingers through my hair, taking a deep breath of briny air. "What else do you know?"

"That this break was an excuse to spend time with her."

I blink at the crashing waves before a laugh bursts from my mouth.

"Mamas know these things," she tells me without an ounce of smugness. "Just sometimes we keep it to ourselves. Like when you and Taylor used to sneak cookies, thinking I was clueless and couldn't do simple math. I was just letting you have your fun."

"So you were just letting me have my fun here?" I ask through a chuckle.

"Aren't you?" Her question isn't a challenge, more of an open opportunity.

"I am, Mama. I really am. More fun than I've had in a long time."

And it's more than spending time with Geneva. I hadn't realized how much I'd shut myself off from others by working overtime.

Even before Taylor's passing, I'd often pass up an opportunity to get together for a game of basketball or round of drinks in favor of picking up another shift. In my mind, it was a way to ensure I had enough money for my family, but I didn't realize how much *life* I'd been missing out on. Not having back-to-back shifts has allowed me to learn to surf, discover I really like DIY projects, and...to *breathe* for the first time ever.

She hums. "Are you coming back?"

This time, I hear a hint of hesitation over the phone line.

"I don't know," I hedge, because I honestly don't.

With Joanna's family ring retrieved, it became crystal clear to me that I want to stay. I want this fake marriage between us to be real. Geneva took it upstairs to clean last night. The plan is to return it to Joanna at family dinner on Sunday. Today, I'll need to find out if Geneva wants to give this—to give us—an honest shot.

I'd love to fully unburden myself and stop this acid from bubbling up in my throat, but telling Mama that we're accidentally married when Geneva might not want this to be real seems pointless. I've already kept the lie this long, what's another day? There'll be heck to pay when Mama finds out, but Geneva is undeniably worth it.

"I'm gonna want to meet her."

"You'll love her," I say without an ounce of doubt.

She gives me another hum, this one assessing.

The smile splitting my mouth feels brighter than the sun over the glistening water. "You will, Mama. I promise."

A sigh floats over the phone. "I wish Taylor could have seen you this giddy."

Guilt pinches at my side, stealing my next breath. There had been many times when I'd turned Taylor down in favor of working too. Now I'd give anything to go back and say yes, to have more time with my sister. But I had no idea that fate would sweep an ugly hand and take one of the best people I've ever known. And the worst part is, I fully understand how the human body just *fails* sometimes. I've seen it make miraculous recoveries, but there are conditions that can take a life in minutes—like Taylor's subarachnoid hemorrhage.

"I miss her, Mama." My words are barely audible over the rushing waves.

"I know. I do too."

The sea air tosses my still-damp hair, drying the tear slipping down my cheek. Mama and I are quiet for a long time, letting our sorrow and grief sit between us.

"We should talk about her more," Mama says.

The corner of my mouth twitches. "We should."

"Remember when she convinced you lemon juice was invisible ink?"

The memory surges forward. "I spent an hour scribbling secret messages all over the kitchen walls."

"And you heated one up with the hairdryer just as I was walking through the door after work..."

"...and nearly set the wall on fire. That was a mess," I groan, sitting up straight.

Mama laughs, the rich sound of it warming me from the inside. "You two. Always with some caper. I went to take a shower as you scrubbed the wall but ended up listening to both of you having a giggle fit instead."

"You did?" I didn't remember that.

"Uh-huh," she hums. "I loved how much you loved each other."

My heart contorts, but it's going to hurt anyway. At least this way, with Mama and me talking, we can get through this together.

A single memory burns bright in my mind, pulling my cheeks into a mischievous smile. This story Mama loves to tell. Anticipating my mom's laughter, I relax in the warm afternoon sunshine.

"What about the time fireworks went off in the pantry?"

THIRTY-FOUR

Geneva

I'm pretty sure I've lost my mind, but it's far too late to change the plans now—especially since the Wilks Beach emergency text chain was accidentally activated. Izzy, the events coordinator of Bayside Table, hands me another black balloon for the arch going over the stage, and I tack it in place from my position on a step ladder. Locals from the Wilks Beach Garden Society are creating table arrangements like their life depends on it while tonight's band rehearses the song I'm going to sing later.

Yup. I've gone insane.

But maybe in a good way?

While teaching my second class earlier today, I went full tilt just to keep everyone from thinking I've gone completely soft, but the whole time, I'd thought about what Cade had said. Her offhanded comment about her and her boyfriend making sacrifices for each other out of love made me realize that I want to do something to show Van how I feel.

I've seen grand gestures in movies—running through airports, unexpected flash mobs, lifted boomboxes. And though no one in this town has seen me do anything other than snarl while wearing dreary colors, I've spent more of my life onstage, singing, dancing, smiling until my face hurts, than I've spent inhabiting this grumpy persona. That's not a world I want to step back into, but I'm tapping into those skills tonight.

After class, I texted Izzy to ask if I could join the local band playing at Bayside Table for one song as a fun surprise for Van. When I called Noah to gather a few people and keep Van busy in the condo tower's game room with a couple rounds of pool so I could prepare, Cade found out and used the text chain to invite the whole town.

And it snowballed—or rather ballooned—from there.

Vivian called me, breathless, because she'd been working on an ombre sequin dress that could be perfect, except for one problem: it was black flowing into pink. I smiled to myself and said I'd be right over for a quick sizing.

Right now, Cade's mom, Camille, is sprawled in the grass, hand-painting a black *Geneva and Van* banner to accompany the balloon arch. I figured *Surprise! Your Wife Loves You!* might be a little confusing when the town thinks our marriage is real.

I've already overheard several puzzled questions.

"Didn't they just have a party?"

"It's a little over the top for a two-month wedding anniversary, don't you think?"

"I thought all Geneva could do is bark directions. Now she's singing?"

And honestly, I understand the confusion. At our impromptu newlywed party, I barely spoke. But my pushing-everyone-away defense mechanism is starting to fit like a shirt that shrunk in the dryer—and not in a cute crop-top kind of way.

I don't want to make a habit of hopping onstage, and I'm not certain I can fully carry the falsetto in this song, but I know one thing—this spectacle should keep the Wilks Beach rumor mill buzzing for weeks.

That, and Van will absolutely love it.

Which is why I ignore the angry hornets in my belly and tack up another balloon. Van's delighted smile will make all of this worth it.

I climb down from the step ladder and retrieve my black stilettos as Cliff and his friend, Leo, come by with a curt nod, telling me the last little surprise is in place. The plan is to hide until my song comes on. In the meantime, the balloon arch will stay up, but the banner—and the secret Cliff is helping with—won't come down until the end.

I check my phone for the time and see a message from Van.

Van

> I hope Brynn is feeling better. Can't wait to
> see you later. I missed you today.

When I got home from class earlier, he was still out surfing, so I quickly came up with a cover story about Brynn needing some girl time. I haven't seen my husband since the breathless kiss we shared in the hallway after celebrating our victory last night.

My grin has a light of its own. A normal person would text back 'me neither' and 'I missed you too'—both of which are *completely* true—but that's not how our relationship works.

Geneva

It's been less than twenty-four hours. Why are you so obsessed with me?

I laugh when Van answers right away.

Van

I can't help that you're magnetic.

My fingers type a comeback when another message pings.

Van

And I can't stop thinking about your lips and how much I want them on mine again.

I blink, pressing my phone to my sequined bodice as a flush burns up my neck.

That...escalated quickly.

My text message alert sounds as I try to slow my erratic breathing.

Van

I'm up next. I'll see you later, darlin'.

My shoulders slide back as the corner of my mouth lifts with devious delight. Van might have surprised me with that heated message, but he has no idea what's in store for him.

I haven't anxiously waited in the wings in years, and to be fair, I'm not really doing that now. I'm hiding in the storage closet off the side door to the bathrooms to keep from being spotted. A bucket of dirty mop water keeps rolling toward my shin as I listen to the Jimmy Buffet cover band start "Cheeseburger in Paradise."

Elegant, I know.

The song I've requested and the black balloon arch above the stage doesn't really vibe with the group of middle-aged dads in Hawaiian shirts currently occupying the stage, but they nailed the gritty sound of The Darkness in our impromptu rehearsal earlier.

I bounce nervously along to the boppy song as I wait. When the audience sings along about preferred condiment choices, I duck my head and edge along the crowd until I'm behind the edge of the balloon arch. Izzy waits with a microphone, and I snatch it and stride onto stage while Dale jumps right into the upbeat guitar riff intro of "I Believe in a Thing Called Love."

The crowd hushes in shocked silence as I start the lyrics without missing a beat. Even though most of them knew I was here to sing, I doubt anyone expected I would have this kind of stage presence after avoiding the limelight like corrosive acid for half a decade. The second I find Van and send a polished fingernail in his direction, the audience explodes.

The chorus flows from me as the band and I really find our rhythm, the hoots and hollers from the crowd nearly deafening. But all I can see is Van's dimpled smile beaming back at me. He's shaking his head slightly, like he's not sure this isn't some crazy fever dream.

I grin into the mic, strutting across the stage before the next verse. By the time we're ready to head into the bridge, I encourage the audience to clap along with big, exaggerated movements. Van bursts into laughter, his eyes the brightest I've ever seen them. Pure joy vibrates through my body along with the thrumming from Victor's bass. As the song comes to a close, I even play a little air guitar, hamming it up with Dale. Once the last chord hums as cymbals crash behind me, the sign falls open while Cliff and Leo fire t-shirt cannons full of black biodegradable confetti into the air.

I shout into the mic, "That's for you, Van!"

The response is earsplitting, forcing me to press one palm to the side of my head. But the ruckus makes me grin like a lunatic as the crowd pushes Van toward the stage. After handing Izzy the mic, I hop into his outstretched arms.

My whispered, 'Hi,' is swallowed by the crowd, but Van's responding grin is the sweetest thing I've ever seen.

"You're incredible," he breathes before he kisses me so hard I forget my own name.

The audience loses it again.

Van tucks me under his arm and steers us away toward the water's edge where we can talk as Lost Shakers moves on to "Margaritaville."

"That was— I can't— I'd seen videos, but—"

I silence his incoherent stammering with another kiss.

"I take it you liked the song," I say, a smirk settling over my lips.

Van shakes his head, his smile megawatt. "Like is too small a word."

Part of me wants to keep playing coy, but now I want Van to understand what that display of confetti and sequins was all about. I grab his hand, pulling us along the edge of the grassy area until we're at the end of the property. Even back here, with people playing lawn games, it's too crowded. The wave of shyness engulfing me is unexpected. I mean, I just strutted beneath stage lights while belting at the top of my lungs.

"Let's head to the beach," Van says, kissing my knuckles.

We stroll in unhurried silence until the lulling sound of the waves pulls a relieved sigh from my mouth.

"Gen," Van starts at the same time I say, "I wanted—"

We laugh at ourselves, kicking our shoes off at the end of the walkway before continuing into the cool sand. The beach is empty except for the light of the gibbous moon reflecting off the waves. Somewhere far off, a dog barks once, and then the night is still again, wrapping us in quiet.

"May I?" I ask once we're halfway to where the waves tumble upon the sand.

Van hums. "A polite request. Am I in trouble?"

"When aren't you in trouble?"

Another second passes, and I almost want to backtrack and leave this unsaid. But then I mentally remind myself how incredibly strong I am. If this doesn't go the way I hope it will, I'll find some way to survive.

Probably.

I stop, pulling Van to face me. When the apple top note of Van's cologne washes over me, I slide my shoulders back and lift my chin.

"I want you to stay."

Van doesn't say anything, just stares.

"Here. With me."

It's a near duplicate of when I elbowed him in the solar plexus, except he's not doubled over, struggling for breath. The ocean breeze pushes a curled strand of hair across my eyes, and I tuck it away, nerves eating at the bottom of my heart.

Why hasn't he said anything? Why isn't he beaming or whooping with joy?

"I— I—" I force a swallow down my tight throat and regroup. Might as well get everything out in one fell swoop. I already feel like I'm naked onstage.

"I don't want to start at square one. I don't want you to move out and pick me up for dates. I want you to tell me about your day the second you get home. I want you at my classes, infuriatingly good at every exercise. I want to continue doing house projects and taking care of the hens together. I want guitar music during my skincare routine. I want..." I pause, fiddling with my silicone ring.

"I don't want to take this off. But you should know that I returned Joanna's ring this morning and told her the truth about us. Maybe someday, when we're ready, you can ask for it back."

When Van simply watches me, I squeeze my eyes shut because saying all of this out loud suddenly sounds ridiculous.

Why would he agree to any of this? Why would he uproot his life for me?

The sensation of his callused fingertips on my temples makes breathing impossible.

"Anything else, darlin'?" Van's voice is darker, grittier than I've ever heard it.

I want to hide. I want to slink off into the night, but I open my eyes. "No."

He studies me, his gaze drifting slowly over my face. "Why don't I tell you what I want?"

I nod, the tension in my muscles enough to crush my bones.

"I want hot wings after the hardware store..."

A punchy breath leaves my lungs, and the relief rushing my body is so overwhelming that an unexpected tear tracks down my cheek.

"I want you to challenge me every day," he says, catching it with his thumb. "I want to buy a surfboard and get sunburnt more than I should."

I laugh, the sound watery as another tear escapes.

Van soothes that one away as well. "I want to work at the hospital on the mainland, but not as many hours as I did before. Something livable, something that allows me to pick wildflowers and put them in a vase in our living room and make dinner most nights when you get home from class. I want to tell Mama we're married. I want to shout that you're *my wife* from every rooftop in this town. I want this life with you, Geneva."

"Gen," I correct, and Van's dimpled smile winks back at me.

When I rise on tiptoe, Van meets me halfway. Our kiss is tender, nothing like the heat of the one by the stage, but by now, I've learned that these kisses mean more. The air between us hums, and from behind my closed eyes, I see a flurry of light. We break the kiss to find ourselves in a vortex of thousands of fireflies.

"This island," Van murmurs.

He continues to watch the circling insects, astonished, but with Van's face lit with tiny pulses of light, I finally voice what's long settled in my heart. "I'm falling for you."

My husband chuckles, his focus returning to me. "That's good, because I'm past falling. I'm shattered on the floor. The first time I heard your laugh in Vegas, it stole my breath long before your elbow did. And after getting to know you..." He shakes his head, grinning. "I never stood a chance."

"Oh," I say, my voice breathy.

Van presses close until his lips hover over mine. "Now, are you going to stop fighting me and let me love you?"

Dizzying warmth coils low in my stomach, sharp and sweet, as a slow smirk spreads across my lips.

"I'll love you, but I'll never stop fighting you."

When Van's lips crush over mine, the fireflies dissipate, and nothing in this world exists except the two of us.

THIRTY-FIVE

Van

The swift afternoon breeze tickles my cheek the following Tuesday as I finish up the siding. Geneva and I painted Sunday afternoon and all of yesterday until she left to teach her popular Monday night class. The house now fits with the peach, yellow, and seaside blue of her neighbors—not that Geneva would care about fitting in. I'm just glad she picked a color that makes *her happy*.

Sunday night, we went to dinner at Joanna's after breaking the news to Mama. At first, she was madder than a bull in a hornet's nest, but her voice caught on the video call as she welcomed Geneva to the family.

Geneva asked if Mama and Mark had time for us to visit sometime soon, saying she wanted to get to know her better. That made

Mama's eyes mist over, and she blamed allergies as she set the phone down to find some tissues.

After we disconnected, I kissed my wife breathless. I'm not sure how I got this lucky, but I'll never take a second for granted.

It turns out Mama couldn't wait to meet Geneva in person, because she asked if we could visit this coming weekend. Being in Nashville will give me the opportunity to not only show Geneva my favorite music spots but tie up some business as well. I'd like to say goodbye to colleagues and officially resign. Since my medical director is a romantic at heart, I know she'll understand. Closing out my apartment should be easy. I'd always worked so many hours that I never put any personality into it.

Not like Geneva's—not like *our* house.

A contented sigh leaves me as I rub my forehead with the back of my hand. Prunella and Stella peck at the clover beyond the tarp dotted with splats of pink paint while Hank inches closer to my boots, clucking softly.

"Girls, I think we're done." I survey the siding, hands on my hips.

It's a good thing, because another tropical storm is rolling in, the wind already picking up. Even though it's not supposed to hit us until tomorrow evening, this one shouldn't be too bad.

"I'm going to double-check the front and then clean up," I say, leaning down to pat Hank on the head.

I take the paint tray and brush with me as I round the side of the house, closing the gate so the girls don't get any wild ideas, like trying their wings at surfing again. When I turn around, one of my favorite locals is frowning at the house, one hand on the hip of her cable knit sweater, the other clutching her cane.

"Pink?" Carol asks when I come to stand beside her.

"It's Geneva's favorite."

"Since when?" Disdain drips from each word.

My shoulders bounce as I try to keep my smile contained. "Since she realized she can be *both* tough as nails and feminine, grouchy and caring. A beloved grump."

Carol sniffs, but her chin dips in what I'm considering approval. Of course, she could just be holding in a sneeze.

My mouth opens to ask Carol about her day when a voice lilts on the wind.

"Van."

I wince reflexively, nearly dropping the paint tray. Though Taylor isn't using my government name, the sound of her calling sends shivers down my spine. I assumed after finally chipping away at my mountain of grief, I'd be spared these unexpected encounters. A shaky inhale fills my tight lungs as I try to slow my heart rate. It takes several seconds to notice that Carol's assessing gaze is zeroed in on me.

"What?" I ask as it feels like she's lasering off years of medical knowledge.

"You can hear that?"

I'm about to deflect when I hear my sister's voice again.

"Van."

This time, I fumble the paint tray, spilling pink paint down my jeans.

Carol hums, her tone indiscernible. Then she tilts back her head and yells into the sky, "He's busy. We're having a conversation if you haven't noticed."

I must be hallucinating, because the wind dies down *immediately*—almost as if chastened. Goosebumps prick my skin as the hairs on the back of my neck stand on end.

"What—" I swallow. "What is going on?"

Carol waves a hand at me, irritated. "You think you'd get a break once they've gone, but some people just can't take a hint and leave you alone."

A man's laugh—deep and husky—echoes between the houses. It could almost be mistaken for the distant rumble of thunder if not for the cloudless sky.

Another splat of pink falls on the gravel, prompting me to set the tray down and shove my shaking hands in my pockets.

"They can't talk as much as they used to. Only a couple of words, a short sentence at most. Which is good because Charles used to yap like a squirrel on espresso."

Laughter surrounds us again, playful and rich. Carol rolls her eyes at the sky before her narrowed focus drops to me.

"I assume you can hear him too."

I nod, the movement unsteady.

"Guess you're supposed to be here after all," she says with a casual shrug, like the sky isn't laughing at us, like all of this isn't outside the confines of reason.

My mouth opens, closes, and opens again as questions whir through my brain. "Who's Charles?"

"My late husband." She tilts her head back. "And a pain in my behind."

The chuckle resonates again, but this time, a breeze blows between us, warm and soft, as it lightly ruffles Carol's white curls. Her face fully relaxes, the slightest hint of a smile gracing her lipsticked mouth. When Carol closes her eyes with a satiated sigh, I can't help my responding grin.

She harrumphs when she notices me smiling at her. "Who's talking to you?"

Pain sears though my chest like someone pushed a hot poker through my ribs.

"My sister," my voice cracks. "Taylor."

"It's a double-edged sword," she says, pulling her lips to the side. "It's nice to hear them again, but it's not the same as them being here. Their voices are strongest at the beach and only during hurricane season. Most of the time, I can't bring myself to walk down, to—"

Carol suddenly looks small and vulnerable, not the spitfire who runs this town. Her shoulders, already curved from the hyperkyphosis that comes with age, now slump with fatigue. The worn creases of her face loosen as her scowl fades, grief creeping in.

I step forward to offer her comfort, but Carol snaps back to her usual self, batting me away with her cane.

"Back up, Tex. I don't need your paint-splotched mess dirtying my clothes."

"Van," I correct for what feels like the ten thousandth time.

Carol tilts her head. "I like Tex better."

Then, without another word, she cane-stomps over to her friend's house, letting herself in.

I let out an openmouthed exhale, blinking. "I guess I'm going to the beach to talk to my late sister."

My feet are leaden as I tromp over the deck boards of the beach walkway. Since there are several locals walking near the shore, I sit at the base of the dune, wrapping my arms around my knees before realizing I'm covered in wet paint. A chuckle escapes me as I rub at the pink now smeared on my arms, and I swear I can almost hear Taylor laughing along.

"Um, hi?" I say after several long seconds.

I rub my eyebrow with a knuckle, not sure I'm doing this right. None of this makes logical sense, but neither did fireflies swirling above Geneva and me as we finally admitted our feelings for each other.

The responding, "Hi," brings moisture springing to my eyes.

All I wanted right after Taylor passed was to be able to talk to her again, to be able to tell her how much she meant to me, how much I loved her. I'd told my sister all the time, but not being able to have that final goodbye wrecked me.

But now, to have the ability to tell Taylor how much she meant to me...

Silent tears roll down my cheeks. "I miss you."

"Van."

Air swirls around me, affectionately wisping my cheeks, my hair, my brow.

A memory surges forward from when I was six and couldn't sleep. I was supposed to start a new school for advanced children, and nerves kept me up. Taylor pretended that her hand was an octopus and had it crawl onto my forehead to suck out all the bad thoughts, like it was pulling a mollusk from its shell. She made exaggerated slurping sounds that made me giggle. When 'the octopus' had its fill, it slinked to my pillow and snored softly. I never slept better than I did that night, so naturally, I asked Taylor to do it whenever my mind wouldn't quiet down.

I look into the clear blue sky. "Do you remember..."

Twenty minutes or two hours later—time seems to have suspended while I've told my sister all the things I wished I could have—Geneva sits next to me in her sleek pantsuit. She had interview training at OWRC today.

She rests her head on my shoulder, intertwining our fingers. "Hey."

"Hey." I drop a kiss on her temple. "How'd you know I was here?"

"Carol told me to check on you." Geneva kicks off her heels and wiggles her toes in the sand.

"Did she now?"

I shouldn't be surprised. I'd intrinsically known how soft and sweet Geneva was despite her gruff armor. Carol is probably the same.

"What's going on?" Geneva's beautiful brown eyes survey my face, concern staining them an even richer hue.

As much as I'd like to tell my wife everything, I'm wrung out from speaking to Taylor. Besides, I know that Geneva will be there for me tomorrow, the next day, two weeks from now...*forever*. Warmth seeps into my chest despite the cool wind now ruffling our hair.

"Bye."

I draw my attention away from Geneva to nod at the sky. Though the idea of talking to my late sister had been terrifying initially, hearing the whispers of her laughter on the breeze has been unexpectedly comforting. The knowledge that I can come here and be connected to her again feels like being wrapped in a blanket straight from the dryer, which is something that Taylor used to do for me in the winters when our apartment never quite got warm enough.

A soft grin lifts my lips before I glance down at Geneva. "Can we talk about it later?"

My wife nods, never taking her focused attention off me. Her fingertips gently trace the dried tears on my cheeks. "Promise?"

I chuckle. "When have I been known to hold my tongue?"

Geneva's devious little smirk makes my day. "I swear you could talk the paint off the walls."

My beaming smile is reflexive. I'll never get tired of this back and forth with her.

"That so?" I murmur, leaning in until our noses brush.

The halting inhale that slips between my wife's lips makes victory surge through my bloodstream.

"Besides providing you with endless conversation, I can think of something else this tongue is good for."

Her eyes flash with heat, but she tilts her chin defiantly. "There you go, being all cocky aga—"

"*Confident*," I correct, smiling against her lips.

Then my fingers thread through Geneva's loose hair as I decimate those final inches, kissing my wife on the beach of my new home.

Van

EPILOGUE

2 years later

Geneva flings back the gray-and-pink boxing-themed quilt Judith Abernathy gifted us years ago and sprints toward the bathroom. I jump up, arriving just in time to gather her long hair as she loses what's left of our wedding dinner into the toilet.

"I'm sorry," I tell her, rubbing light, soothing circles on her back until her stomach settles.

"It must have been the scallops." Geneva leans back against the bathtub with a controlled breath. "Clara said they weren't from her usual supplier."

"Maybe." I extend a glass of cool water before sitting beside her on the tile floor.

Other than potentially contaminated seafood, our vow-renewal/official wedding ceremony had gone off without a hitch last night. In typical fashion for our relationship, it happened last minute with minimal planning.

Yesterday morning, Geneva stumbled downstairs after we'd all had breakfast. Her hair had been in her heatless curl roller with pillow marks on her face as she beelined straight for the coffee pot. Mama and Mark had been visiting for the weekend, using our guest room like they usually do. Though with Mark retiring and the two of them moving to Wilks Beach next summer, we won't get as much use out of it anymore.

"Good morning, sleepyhead," Mark says through a growing grin. "Nice of you to join us."

Geneva makes a semi-human grunt as she pours herself an overly full mug. According to my wife, Mark—like Mama and me—is 'an insufferable morning person.'

I box her against the counter, placing a soft kiss on her crown. When her disgruntled frown instantly melts into a soft sigh, my heart beats outside my body. I trace the curve of her jaw with my thumb, my breath catching when her gaze meets mine.

"Marry me."

The words escape as if spoken by my soul—breathy and honest. Geneva's wry smile only makes me love her more.

"We're already married." She taps her silicone ring against her mug before sneaking another sip.

"Again. Marry me again—in front of Mama and Mark, in front of Joanna and Noah, in front of all our friends, our town. Marry me again, Gen. Tonight."

Her eyes grow wide as I take her mug and set it aside, the slightest flicker of vulnerability slipping over her brown irises. With my body separating her from my parents, it's like we're the only two people in our kitchen. Beyond the window, the hens cluck softly. Morning light bends around the flyaways that've escaped Geneva's curler, highlighting them. She's so beautiful like this—raw and unguarded—my chest aches.

"You already know I'm here to stay. Let's make it official."

I've never felt so sure about anything in my life, but it's impossible to control my racing pulse as I wait for her answer.

When the corner of Geneva's mouth slips up, it punches the breath from me. "Only if Elvis presides over the ceremony."

I whoop, picking Geneva up and swinging her around the kitchen. "We're getting hitched!"

After putting on my one and only suit to formally ask Joanna for her family's ring, planning exploded. Joanna activated the Wilks Beach emergency text chain, rallying everyone to help set up an impromptu wedding ceremony at Bayside Table. Geneva and Brynn sped to the mainland to buy a ring for me while Vivian whipped up a last-minute cocktail-length wedding dress from some vintage-inspired lace she'd been saving for a special occasion.

Then as the sun set last night, the Lost Shakers performed Elvis's "Can't Help Falling in Love" as Geneva walked down the aisle. The misty-eyed look of adoration Geneva gave me while being escorted by Noah quickly became one of my top five memories.

My wife pushes her hair back now, her heirloom ring glinting in the light from the vanity. I glance down at the beveled edge, matte brushed gold ring on my hand with a smile.

"No. Put those away. I'm too queasy, and it's too early for dimples."

Her grouchy tone has the opposite effect on my grin.

"I can't help it," I tell her, pointing to my face. "This is what a ludicrously happy man who's deeply in love with his wife looks like."

I catch the exact moment her lips lift before she presses them into a line, glaring at me for extra emphasis. I'm about to poke at my adorable storm cloud when her eyes fly wide, and she lurches for the toilet again.

Several minutes later, Geneva is sprawled out on the couch with a plate of dry toast.

"*Why*," she wines. "It's our honeymoon."

Yesterday afternoon, Mama and Mark moved their things to Joanna's for the remainder of their visit so we could have some privacy.

"Second honeymoon," I remind her, setting a mug of ginger tea on the coffee table.

She flits a hand in my direction, annoyed.

I ease onto the couch, careful not to jostle her. "Let's catch up on *Celebrity Circuit* until you feel better."

"Okay." She rubs at the front of her shoulder joint, groaning. "I'm so sore. I didn't think I worked chest that hard this week. Maybe I pulled something."

"I'm sorry, love," I say, pulling her feet into my lap because I'm incapable of *not* touching her.

I still like to use *darlin'*, but being able to identify Geneva as *my love* is something I use often—that, along with wife, wifey, and occasionally, wifemperess supreme.

Geneva murmurs a grateful thank you as I queue up our favorite show.

We're three-fourths through the show's intro, highlighting all the stories they'll cover in the episode. When they focus on surprise baby news, realization crashes over me. There's a chance that Geneva's nausea and chest soreness isn't due to tainted food and excessive exercise. Though we've talked about having kids, it was always in a future sense—just like we'd eventually get official wedding rings.

Since we checked off that second one yesterday, maybe...

I pause the show, finding my wife already looking at me, her face pale.

"Are you going to be sick again?"

Geneva shakes her head, her collarbones rising and falling erratically as her inhales get shorter and shorter.

"I can't— We can't— I mean, I'd like to be *someday*, but what if—" She bites her lip. "What if I'm not any good at this?"

"*Geneva.*" I gather her to my chest. "There's nothing you can't do. You are the strongest"—I kiss her temple—"most caring"—my lips brush her brow—"*incredible* woman I've ever met. And that's saying a lot, since I had the privilege of being raised by Mama and Taylor." I give her a gentle squeeze. "You can do this. *We* can do this. Together."

Her eyes are still a bit panicked as they dart all over my face. "I don't know."

"I do." My lips find hers in a soft kiss.

When I pull away, her chin dips in a firm nod, her shoulders straightening. It's a version of Geneva I know well—one ready to take on anything.

"Okay."

"Once I get a pregnancy test at Dotty's Market, it'll be all over town. Carol will probably be banging on our door before the two minutes to get the results are up," I tell her.

"That's what the *Go Away* doormat is for." She spreads her palm over her flat belly, her gaze softening. "If this isn't food poisoning, then Joanna can parade around town, telling everyone."

"And if the proud papa wants to shout it from the rooftops?"

The affectionate look in my wife's eyes is nothing short of breathtaking. It feels like all those times before, when energy rockets through my internal organs, fundamentally changing me for the better. The air around us charges, and I half expect fireflies to appear, though it's early morning, and we're in our cozy living room.

Her mouth quirks in that little smirk I love. "I'd expect nothing less."

The moment sits between us, thrumming as if it has its own heartbeat, before Geneva takes my fingers and places them beneath hers on her belly.

"We might be parents," she whispers.

"We might," I whisper back, my mind reeling at the thought that my once-accidental wife might be accidentally pregnant.

Her face contorts suddenly, her brow wrinkling. "But what if we're not?"

Starlight feels like it's bursting beneath my skin. "That's the best part." I kiss my wife, astonished that this is *my life, my reality*. "We have the rest of our lives together. There's more than enough time for everything we've ever dreamed of."

"And for some things we never thought were possible?" she asks, her gaze both tender and uncertain.

My forehead rests on hers. "Especially those."

"Okay." Geneva takes a deep breath as she leans back.

"So we're doing this thing?" I ask, unable to keep my smile restrained.

She nods, her own grin magnetic. "We are."

A holler that would make my sister proud bursts from my mouth. I bolt to the front door before nearly pulling the thing off its hinges.

"Evander, what are you doing?" Geneva laughs, the sound fueling my soul. "You're shirtless in scrub pants. You're not even wearing shoes."

I wink. "Got to give the town something to talk about, darlin'."

Then I run from my house toward the tiny market at the edge of town and, hopefully, the *continuation* of everything I've ever wanted.

Acknowledgements

Firstly, I want to thank **YOU**, my incredible reader! I hope this book made you smile, laugh, and do that squealy-kicking feet thing that always happens to me when my main characters *finally* kiss.

Thank you to my amazing beta readers Randi, Sara, Cassondra, and Moni. Thanks again to Jenn for her immaculate copy edit and for being the kindest person—you're undoubtedly the best. Thank you to Lauren, Emily, and Emily for launch help. And, as always, Enni captivated the essential essence of Geneva and Van with this perfect cover design.

Geneva, hopefully this book lived up to having to wait so long for it. And I hope you love her as much as I do. Thank you to my family and friends for letting me talk about people who don't exist as if they're real (because to me, they are). I'm grateful for every one of you.

About the Author

Laura Langa is an award-winning sweet romance and romcom author, receiving the HOLT Medallion Award and Booksellers' Best Award. Laura strives to write stories that make readers laugh while tugging at their heartstrings, and to create relatable characters you'd want to befriend. Laura loves trees and all things green, hates flossing but forces herself to do it every night, has a concerning addiction to sugar, and believes that salt air can often cure a bad mood.

www.LauraLanga.com
www.LauraLanga.com/newsletter
Instagram @LauraLangaWrites